THE NEW WINDMILL BOOK OF

CLASSIC SHORT STORIES

EDITED BY MIKE HAMLIN, CHRISTINE HALL AND JANE BROWNE

HEINEMANN
NEW WINDMILLS

Heinemann Educational
a division of
Heinemann Publishers (Oxford) Ltd
Halley Court, Jordan Hill, Oxford OX2 8EJ
OXFORD LONDON EDINBURGH
MADRID ATHENS BOLOGNA PARIS
MELBOURNE SYDNEY AUCKLAND SINGAPORE TOKYO
IBADAN NAIROBI HARARE GABORONE
PORTSMOUTH NH (USA)

First published in the New Windmill Series 1994

94 95 96 97 98 10 9 8 7 6 5 4 3 2

ISBN 0 435 12423 4

British Library Cataloguing in Publication Data
for this title is available from the British Library

Cover painting, Gartenrestaurant, 1912, by August Macke by kind permission of
Kunstmuseum Bern, Hermann and Margrit Rupf-Stiftung

The editors and publishers would like to thank the following
for permission to reproduce copyright material:

Curtis Brown for 'Snap-dragons' from *The Lagoon and other Stories*
copyright © 1951, 1991 by Janet Frame

Penguin Books for 'I Used To Live Here Once' by Jean Rhys from
Best West Indian Stories (ed Kenneth Ramchand)

Bessie Head for 'Looking for A Rain God' by Bessie Head published in
The Collector of Treasures by the Heinemann African Writers Series 1977

Random House UK Ltd for 'The Mahogany Table' from *One Thing Leading to Another*
by Sylvia Townsend Warner, selected and edited by Susanna Pinney,
published in Great Britain by The Women's Press Ltd, 1985,
34 Great Sutton Street, London EC1V 0DX

Virago Press for 'The Fly-paper' from *The Devastating Boys* by Elizabeth Taylor 1972
published by Virago Press 1984

The publishers have made every effort to contact copyright holders. We would
be pleased to rectify any omissions at the first opportunity.

Typeset by CentraCet Limited, Cambridge
Printed and bound in England by Clays Ltd, St Ives plc

UNDER 10 PAGES: ~~16~~ ⎱ TOTAL 19
OVER 20: 2   ⎰ USABLE 17

Contents

Introduction

Although people have written and told short stories for hundreds of years, it was not until the nineteenth century that the short story came to be seen as a genre in its own right. Critics and writers discussed short stories in ways that encouraged readers to think about them as something more than cut-down novels. The subject matter, form and general characteristics of the short story came under close consideration, and by the end of the century the short story as we know it today was a well developed and very popular form in Europe and North America.

Why did the short story develop as a popular form at this particular time? One important factor was the growing popularity of magazines and journals. The technology for printing was improving, and cheap magazines were widely read. Many of the Victorian novels we now think of as single volumes were originally published as serials in magazines. Most of the authors collected here began their writing careers with publications in journals. The reading public had a taste for fiction and the short story was the ideal form for writers who wanted to earn some immediate money and reach a wide audience. As more people were given the chance of receiving basic education, literacy rates improved and more people were able to enjoy magazines and books.

In the days before television or radio, reading aloud was a much more popular form of entertainment than it is today, and we know that short stories or instalments of serials were often read aloud within families or groups of friends. Because these short stories reached a wide audience they often dealt with themes and issues with a direct importance to people's lives. Like popular fiction today, particular types of story – such as romance, mystery, horror or detection – had an especially wide appeal.

The opening decades of the twentieth century saw a continued growth in the range and style of short stories. Exciting developments, sometimes mirroring advances in the early cinema, were being made in story form; fresh ideas were influencing content and wider audiences were being addressed. The classic short stories of James Joyce, D. H. Lawrence, Katherine Mansfield, Ernest Hemingway, F. Scott Fitzgerald and other writers represented here, were now revolutionising the genre. Short stories, during this time, began to acquire a new intellectual status as well as a popular vitality, and the international achievements of these writers remain with us to this day.

We have included stories from different cultures; seven are from Britain, five from the United States, two from Ireland, one each from South Africa, New Zealand and the Caribbean, and two are in translation from originals in French and Russian. Nine have been written by women, ten by men. We have grouped them according to theme to suggest ways of making comparisons between the stories, and to help you think about possible ways of interpreting them, but each of the stories stands alone, and you may well see links or contrasts between stories in different groupings.

We offer a brief introduction to each story because we think that some background information about the author will help you in your reading and thinking. Where particular words have either changed their meanings, or have dropped out of the language altogether we have suggested a modern equivalent at the bottom of the page. Above all though, we have chosen the short stories in this volume not just as examples of classic writing but because we think they will be appealing and interesting to readers today. We hope you enjoy them.

F. Scott Fitzgerald 1896–1940

Francis Scott Fitzgerald was born in the American midwest town of St Paul. Both mother and father were of Irish descent. The family had enough money to send their son to a series of private schools and finally to Princetown University. At Princetown he was a popular student and involved himself in dramatic productions, writing a large part of two successful musical comedies for the University Triangle Club.

However, successes with the theatrical set were not reflected in his academic studies and he eventually withdrew from Princetown before graduating. In reality, his marks had fallen so low that there was every chance of him being suspended anyway.

A short and fairly relaxed period in the army followed, with Fitzgerald serving as an aide-de-camp to a Major General in Alabama. It was during this time that he met his future wife Zelda. They became engaged but Zelda's father, a judge, refused permission to marry until Fitzgerald could support his daughter financially.

Fitzgerald moved to New York and worked for a time writing slogans for an advertising agency. He sold a short story or two, but he was largely ignored, so he borrowed some money and returned home to St Paul to write his first novel.

The book was *This Side of Paradise*. It was largely composed of autobiographical fragments and other bits and pieces collected over the years, but it was held together with tremendous energy and self confidence. It was well received, and the book was widely seen as the voice of a post-war American generation, in what was to be called the Jazz Age with its glittering evocation of flappers and speak-easies.

Suddenly the magazines were eager to print Fitzgerald's stories. He married Zelda and threw himself into his writing. Other works followed, including in 1925 *The Great Gatsby*, his best-known novel, celebrating the rise and fall of a bootlegger-dreamer.

During the next seven years he wrote many stories about Americans in Paris, on the Riviera and in Switzerland – the backgrounds of which he would use in his next novel, *Tender is the Night*. He worked hard, perhaps too hard, for during the thirties he entered a state of increasing physical illness and nervous exhaustion. Zelda had also suffered a series of severe breakdowns and they were both drinking heavily.

In the summer of 1937 Fitzgerald moved to Hollywood to begin a new career as a screenwriter with MGM. Debts were now paid off, insurance policies were put in place, and a remarkably productive period followed, with dozens of new short stories plus a final novel *The Last Tycoon* (1941). Scott Fitzgerald died of a heart attack in 1940 aged 44.

'Three Hours Between Planes' (1940) comes from this final burst of creativity towards the end of his life. Fitzgerald felt that his writing had now reached a new maturity, without the glitter and high spirits of his earlier work but with a much closer relationship to his own personal tragedy, 'the emotion is in the events themselves, which merely have to be stated in the barest language'.

Three Hours Between Planes

F. Scott Fitzgerald

It was a wild chance but Donald was in the mood, healthy and bored, with a sense of tiresome duty done. He was now rewarding himself. Maybe.

When the plane landed he stepped out into a midwestern summer night and headed for the isolated pueblo airport, conventionalized as an old red 'railway depot'. He did not know whether she was alive, or living in this town, or what was her present name. With mounting excitement he looked through the phone book for her father who might be dead too, somewhere in these twenty years.

No. Judge Harmon Holmes – Hillside 3194.

A woman's amused voice answered his inquiry for Miss Nancy Holmes.

'Nancy is Mrs Walter Gifford now. Who is this?'

But Donald hung up without answering. He had found out what he wanted to know and had only three hours. He did not remember any Walter Gifford and there was another suspended moment while he scanned the phone book. She might have married out of town.

No. Walter Gifford – Hillside 1191. Blood flowed back into his fingertips.

'Hello?'

'Hello. Is Mrs Gifford there – this is an old friend of hers.'

'This is Mrs Gifford.'

He remembered, or thought he remembered, the funny magic in the voice.

'This is Donald Plant. I haven't seen you since I was twelve years old.'

'Oh-h-h!' The note was utterly surprised, very polite, but he could distinguish in it neither joy nor certain recognition.

' – *Don*ald!' added the voice. This time there was something more in it than struggling memory.

'. . . when did you come back to town?' Then cordially, 'Where *are* you?'

'I'm out at the airport – for just a few hours.'

'Well, come up and see me.'

'Sure you're not just going to bed.'

'Heavens, no!' she exclaimed. 'I was sitting here – having a highball by myself. Just tell your taxi man . . .'

On his way Donald analyzed the conversation. His words 'at the airport' established that he had retained his position in the upper bourgeoisie. Nancy's aloneness might indicate that she had matured into an unattractive woman without friends. Her husband might be either away or in bed. And – because she was always ten years old in his dreams – the highball shocked him. But he adjusted himself with a smile – she was very close to thirty.

At the end of a curved drive he saw a dark-haired little beauty standing against the lighted door, a glass in her hand. Startled by her final materialization, Donald got out of the cab, saying:

'Mrs Gifford?'

She turned on the porch light and stared at him, wide-eyed and tentative. A smile broke through the puzzled expression.

'Donald – it *is* you – we all change so. Oh, this is re*mark*able!'

As they walked inside, their voices jingled the words 'all these years,' and Donald felt a sinking in his stomach. This derived in part from a vision of their last meeting – when she rode past him on a bicycle, cutting him dead – and in part from fear lest they have nothing to say. It was like a college reunion – but there the failure to find the past was disguised by the hurried boisterous occasion. Aghast, he realized that this might be a long and empty hour. He plunged in desperately.

'You always were a lovely person. But I'm a little shocked to find you as beautiful as you are.'

It worked. The immediate recognition of their changed state, the bold compliment, made them interesting strangers instead of fumbling childhood friends.

'Have a highball?' she asked. 'No? Please don't think I've become a secret drinker, but this was a blue night. I expected my husband but he wired he'd be two days longer. He's very nice, Donald, and very attractive. Rather your type and colouring.' She hesitated, ' – and I think he's interested in someone in New York – and I don't know.'

'After seeing you it sounds impossible,' he assured her. 'I was married for six years, and there was a time I tortured myself that way. Then one day I just put jealousy out of my life forever. After my wife died I was very glad of that. It left a very rich memory – nothing marred or spoiled or hard to think over.'

She looked at him attentively, then sympathetically as he spoke.

'I'm very sorry,' she said. And after a proper moment, 'You've changed a lot. Turn your head. I remember father saying, "That boy has a brain."'

'You probably argued against it.'

'I was impressed. Up to then I thought everybody had a brain. That's why it sticks in my mind.'

'What else sticks in your mind?' he asked smiling.

Suddenly Nancy got up and walked quickly a little away.

'Ah, now,' she reproached him. 'That isn't fair! I suppose I was a naughty girl.'

'You were not,' he said stoutly. 'And I *will* have a drink now.'

As she poured it, her face still turned from him, he continued:

'Do you think you were the only little girl who was ever kissed?'

'Do you like the subject?' she demanded. Her momentary irritation melted and she said: 'What the hell! We *did* have fun. Like in the song.'

'On the sleigh ride.'

'Yes – and somebody's picnic – Trudy James'. And at Frontenac that – those summers.'

It was the sleigh ride he remembered most and kissing her cool cheeks in the straw in one corner while she laughed up at the cold white stars. The couple next to them had their backs turned and he kissed her little neck and her ears and never her lips.

'And the Macks' party where they played post office and I couldn't go because I had the mumps,' he said.

'I don't remember that.'

'Oh, you were there. And you were kissed and I was crazy with jealousy like I never have been since.'

'Funny I don't remember. Maybe I wanted to forget.'

'But why?' he asked in amusement. 'We were two perfectly innocent kids. Nancy, whenever I talked to my wife about the past, I told her you were the girl I loved *al*most as much as I loved her. But I think I really loved you just as much. When we moved out of town I carried you like a cannon ball in my insides.'

'Were you *that* much – stirred up?'

'My God, yes! I – ' He suddenly realized that they were standing just two feet from each other, that he was talking as if he loved her in the present, that she was looking up at him with her lips half-parted and a clouded look in her eyes.

'Go on,' she said, 'I'm ashamed to say – I like it. I didn't know you were so upset *then*. I thought it was *me* who was upset.'

'You!' he exclaimed. 'Don't you remember throwing me over at the drugstore.' He laughed. 'You stuck out your tongue at me.'

'I don't remember at all. It seemed to me *you* did the throwing over.' Her hand fell lightly, almost consolingly on his arm. 'I've got a photograph book upstairs I haven't looked at for years. I'll dig it out.'

Donald sat for five minutes with two thoughts – first the hopeless impossibility of reconciling what different people remembered about the same event – and secondly that in a frightening way Nancy moved him as a woman as she had moved him as a child. Half an hour had developed an emotion that he had not known since the death of his wife – that he had never hoped to know again.

Side by side on a couch they opened the book between them. Nancy looked at him, smiling and very happy.

'Oh, this is *such* fun,' she said. 'Such fun that you're so nice, that you remember me so – beautifully. Let me tell you – I wish I'd known it then! After you'd gone I hated you.'

'What a pity,' he said gently.

'But not now,' she reassured him, and then impulsively, 'Kiss and make up – '

'. . . that isn't being a good wife,' she said after a minute. 'I really don't think I've kissed two men since I was married.'

He was excited – but most of all confused. Had he kissed Nancy? or a memory? or this lovely trembly stranger who looked away from him quickly and turned a page of the book?

'Wait!' he said. 'I don't think I could *see* a picture for a few seconds.'

'We won't do it again. I don't feel so very calm myself.'

Donald said one of those trivial things that cover so much ground.

'Wouldn't it be awful if we fell in love again.'

'Stop it!' She laughed, but very breathlessly. 'It's all over. It was a moment. A moment I'll have to forget.'

'Don't tell your husband.'

'Why not? Usually I tell him everything.'

'It'll hurt him. Don't ever tell a man such things.'

'All right I won't.'

'Kiss me once more,' he said inconsistently, but Nancy had turned a page and was pointing eagerly at a picture.

'Here's you,' she cried. 'Right away!'

He looked. It was a little boy in shorts standing on a pier with a sailboat in the background.

'I remember – ' she laughed triumphantly, ' – the very day it was taken. Kitty took it and I stole it from her.'

For a moment Donald failed to recognize himself in the photo – then, bending closer – he failed utterly to recognize himself.

'That's not me,' he said.

'Oh yes. It was at Frontenac – the summer we – we used to go to the cave.'

'What cave? I was only three days in Frontenac.' Again he strained his eyes at the slightly yellowed picture. 'And that isn't me. That's Donald *Bowers*. We did look rather alike.'

Now she was staring at him – leaning back, seeming to lift away from him.

'But you're Donald Bowers!' she exclaimed; her voice rose a little. 'No, you're not. You're Donald *Plant*.'

'I told you on the phone.'

She was on her feet – her face faintly horrified.

'Plant! Bowers! I must be crazy. Or it was that drink? I was mixed up a little when I first saw you. Look here! What have I told you?'

He tried for a monkish calm as he turned a page of the book.

'Nothing at all,' he said. Pictures that did not include him formed and re-formed before his eyes – Frontenac – a cave – Donald Bowers – 'You threw *me* over!'

Nancy spoke from the other side of the room.

'You'll never tell this story,' she said. 'Stories have a way of getting around.'

'There isn't any story,' he hesitated. But he thought: So she *was* a bad little girl.

And now suddenly he was filled with wild raging jealousy of little Donald Bowers – he who had banished jealousy from his life forever. In the five steps he took across the room he crushed out twenty years and the existence of Walter Gifford with his stride.

'Kiss me again, Nancy,' he said, sinking to one knee beside her chair, putting his hand upon her shoulder. But Nancy strained away.

'You said you had to catch a plane.'

'It's nothing. I can miss it. It's of no importance.'

'Please go,' she said in a cool voice. 'And please try to imagine how I feel.'

'But you act as if you don't remember me,' he cried, ' – as if you don't remember Donald *Plant*!'

'I do. I remember you too . . . But it was all so long ago.' Her voice grew hard again. 'The taxi number is Crestwood 8484.'

On his way to the airport Donald shook his head from side to side. He was completely himself now but he could not digest the experience. Only as the plane roared up into the dark sky and its passengers became a different entity from the corporate world below did he draw a parallel from the fact of its flight. For five blinding minutes he had lived like a madman in two worlds at once. He had been a boy of twelve and a man of thirty-two, indissolubly and helplessly commingled.

Donald had lost a good deal, too, in those hours between the planes – but since the second half of life is a long process of getting rid of things, that part of the experience probably didn't matter.

Anton Chekov 1860–1904

Anton Chekov was born in Russia in 1860 the grandson of a serf and the son of an unsuccessful tradesman who, when the boy was small, sold up and went to try his fortune in Moscow.

Chekov entered Moscow University as a medical student in 1879 and supported his studies by selling short stories to various magazines and newspapers. He qualified in medicine in 1884, but soon gave up any ideas of practising, and after the success of his first collection, *Motley Stories* (1886) which ran through fourteen editions in as many years, he devoted the rest of his life to writing.

At first Chekov was regarded as a cheerful, even humorous writer but increasingly his work reflected a sadness bordering on fatalism. Alongside this change of mood came a sharp reduction in output; from 129 stories in 1885 and 112 in 1886, to 66 in 1887 and only 12 in 1888. Typical titles from this second period include 'Gloomy People' and 'A Dreary Story', both published in 1889.

1889 also saw a turn for the worse in Chekov's health. He suffered from constant fever and nervous irritability, he had nightmares and felt an overpowering sense of frustration. In the spring of 1890 he undertook a long and risky trek across Siberia to visit the Russian convict settlements on the island of Sakhalin. He spent over three months there studying the life of the convicts, finally returning to Russia by sea.

On his return, he lived for five years in a small country house just outside Moscow. But his deteriorating health eventually drove him further south – to Yalta in the Crimea, where he built a villa and settled down. During this time Chekov wrote some of his best known plays: *Uncle Vanya*, *The Seagull*, *The Three Sisters* and *The Cherry Orchard*. These four important plays were all staged by the Moscow Art Theatre founded by Konstantin Stanislavsky. The productions pioneered a new kind of realism and an original use of stagecraft, they were great popular successes.

In 1901 Chekov married Olga Knipper, one of the principal actresses from the Moscow Art Theatre. Their short married life, spent mostly at their house in Yalta, was happy. In January 1904 Chekov was present at the first night of his *Cherry Orchard* in Moscow. Ill health forced him to return to the Crimea in April and on the 1st of July, he died in his wife's arms.

After his death, translations of his work began to appear in English and had a major influence on writers such as Arnold Bennett, Virginia Woolf, James Joyce and Katherine Mansfield.

'The Objet d'Art' was first published in Russian in 1886 and reflects the lighter, comic side of Chekov's work. The issue of the *Stock Exchange Gazette* referred to in the story contained an episode from Émile Zola's novel *L'Oeuvre*, which concerned a painter who transfers his affections from his wife to his paintings of the female nude.

The Objet d'Art

Anton Chekhov

Holding under his arm an object carefully wrapped up in No. 223 of the *Stock Exchange Gazette*, Sasha Smirnoff (an only son) pulled a long face and walked into Doctor Florinsky's consulting-room.

'Ah, my young friend!' the doctor greeted him. 'And how are we today? Everything well, I trust?'

Sasha blinked his eyes, pressed his hand to his heart and said in a voice trembling with emotion:

'Mum sends her regards, Doctor, and told me to thank you . . . I'm a mother's only son and you saved my life – cured me of a dangerous illness . . . and Mum and me simply don't know how to thank you.'

'Nonsense, lad,' interrupted the doctor, simpering with delight. 'Anyone else would have done the same in my place.'

'I'm a mother's only son . . . We're poor folk, Mum and me, and of course we can't pay you for your services . . . and we feel very bad about it, Doctor, but all the same, we – Mum and me, that is, her one and only – we do beg you most earnestly to accept as a token of our gratitude this . . . this object here, which . . . It's a very valuable antique bronze – an exceptional work of art.'

'No, really,' said the doctor, frowning, 'I couldn't possibly.'

'Yes, yes, you simply must accept it!' Sasha mumbled away as he unwrapped the parcel. 'If you refuse, we'll be offended, Mum and me . . . It's a very fine piece . . . an antique bronze . . . It came to us when Dad died and we've kept it as a precious memento . . . Dad used to buy up antique bronzes and sell them to collectors . . . Now Mum and me are running the business . . .'

Sasha finished unwrapping the object and placed it triumphantly on the table. It was a small, finely modelled old bronze candelabrum. On its pedestal two female figures were

standing in a state of nature and in poses that I am neither
bold nor hot-blooded enough to describe. The figures were
smiling coquettishly, and altogether seemed to suggest that
but for the need to go on supporting the candlestick, they
would leap off the pedestal and turn the room into a scene of
such wild debauch that the mere thought of it, gentle reader,
would bring a blush to your cheek.

After glancing at the present, the doctor slowly scratched
the back of his ear, cleared his throat and blew his nose
uncertainly.

'Yes, it's a beautiful object all right,' he mumbled, 'but,
well, how shall I put it?. . . You couldn't say it was exactly
tasteful . . . I mean, décolleté's one thing, but this is really
going too far . . .'

'How do you mean, going too far?'

'The Arch-Tempter himself couldn't have thought up anything more vile. Why, if I were to put a fandangle like that on
the table, I'd feel I was polluting the whole house!'

'What a strange view of art you have, Doctor!' said Sasha,
sounding hurt. 'Why, this is a work of inspiration! Look at all
that beauty and elegance – doesn't it fill you with awe and
bring a lump to your throat? You forget all about worldly
things when you contemplate beauty like that . . . Why, look
at the movement there, Doctor, look at all the air and
expression!'

'I appreciate that only too well, my friend,' interrupted the
doctor, 'but you're forgetting, I'm a family man – think of my
small children running about, think of the ladies.'

'Of course, if you're going to look at it through the eyes of
the masses,' said Sasha, 'then of course this highly artistic
creation does appear in a different light . . . But you must
raise yourself above the masses, Doctor, especially as Mum
and me'll be deeply offended if you refuse. I'm a mother's only
son – you saved my life . . . We're giving you our most
treasured possession . . . and my only regret is that we don't
have another one to make the pair . . .'

'Thank you, dear boy, I'm very grateful . . . Give Mum my
regards, but just put yourself in my place – think of the
children running about, think of the ladies . . . Oh, all right
then, let it stay! I can see I'm not going to convince you.'

'There's nothing to convince me of,' Sasha replied joyfully.
'You must stand the candelabrum here, next to this vase.

What a pity there isn't the pair! What a pity! Goodbye, then, Doctor!'

When Sasha had left, the doctor spent a long time gazing at the candelabrum, scratching the back of his ear and pondering.

'It's a superb thing, no two ways about that,' he thought, 'and it's a shame to let it go ... But there's no question of keeping it here ... Hmm, quite a problem! Who can I give it to or unload it on?'

After lengthy consideration he thought of his good friend Harkin the solicitor, to whom he was indebted for professional services.

'Yes, that's the answer,' the doctor decided. 'As a friend it's awkward for him to accept money from me, but if I make him a present of this object, that'll be very *comme il faut*. Yes, I'll take this diabolical creation round to him – after all, he's a bachelor, doesn't take life seriously ...'

Without further ado, the doctor put on his coat, picked up the candelabrum and set off for Harkin's.

'Greetings!' he said, finding the solicitor at home. 'I've come to thank you, old man, for all that help you gave me – I know you don't like taking money, but perhaps you'd be willing to accept this little trifle ... here you are, my dear chap – it's really rather special!'

When he saw the little trifle, the solicitor went into transports of delight.

'Oh, my word, yes!' he roared. 'How do they think such things up? Superb! Entrancing! Wherever did you get hold of such a gem?'

Having exhausted his expressions of delight, the solicitor glanced round nervously at the door and said:

'Only be a good chap and take it back, will you? I can't accept it ...'

'Why ever not?' said the doctor in alarm.

'Obvious reasons ... Think of my mother coming in, think of my clients ... And how could I look the servants in the face?'

'No, no, no, don't you dare refuse!' said the doctor, waving his arms at him. 'You're being a boor! This is a work of inspiration – look at the movement there ... the *expression* ... Any more fuss and I shall be offended!'

'If only it was daubed over or had some fig leaves stuck
on . . .'

But the doctor waved his arms at him even more vigorously,
nipped smartly out of the apartment and returned home,
highly pleased that he'd managed to get the present off his
hands . . .

When his friend had gone, Harkin studied the candelabrum
closely, kept touching it all over, and like the doctor, racked
his brains for a long time wondering what was to be done
with it.

'It's a fine piece of work,' he reflected, 'and it'd be a shame
to let it go, but keeping it here would be most improper. The
best thing would be to give it to someone . . . Yes, I know –
there's a benefit performance tonight for Shashkin, the comic
actor. I'll take the candelabrum round to him as a present –
after all, the old rascal loves that kind of thing . . .'

No sooner said than done. That evening the candelabrum,
painstakingly wrapped, was presented to the comic actor
Shashkin. The whole evening the actor's dressing-room was
besieged by male visitors coming to admire the present; all
evening the dressing-room was filled with the hubbub of
rapturous exclamations and laughter like the whinnying of a
horse. Whenever one of the actresses knocked on the door and
asked if she could come in, the actor's husky voice would
immediately reply:

'Not just now, darling, I'm changing.'

After the show the actor hunched his shoulders, threw up
his hands in perplexity and said:

'Where the hell can I put this obscenity? After all, I live in
a private apartment – think of the actresses who come to see
me! It's not like a photograph, you can't shove it into a desk
drawer!'

'Why not sell it, sir?' advised the wig-maker who was
helping him off with his costume. 'There's an old woman in
this area who buys up bronzes like that – Just ask for Mrs
Smirnoff – everyone knows her.'

The comic actor took his advice . . .

Two days later Doctor Florinsky was sitting in his consulting-room with one finger pressed to his forehead, and was
thinking about the acids of the bile. Suddenly the door flew
open and in rushed Sasha Smirnoff. He was smiling, beaming,

and his whole figure radiated happiness . . . In his hands he was holding something wrapped up in newspaper.

'Doctor!' he began, gasping for breath. 'I'm so delighted! You won't believe your luck – we've managed to find another candelabrum to make your pair! . . . Mum's thrilled to bits . . . I'm a mother's only son . . . you saved my life . . .'

And Sasha, all aquiver with gratitude, placed the candelabrum in front of the doctor. The doctor's mouth dropped, he tried to say something but nothing came out: he was speechless.

Sylvia Townsend Warner 1893–1978

Sylvia Townsend Warner was born at Harrow-on-the-Hill, Middlesex in 1893. Although her father was a school teacher at Harrow School, she received no formal education. Sylvia worked in a munitions factory during the First World War but then spent the next ten years as one of four editors working on the ten volume work, *Tudor Church Music*, published by Oxford University Press. Music was her first love at this time and although never a religious woman, she was an active member of the Tudor Church Music Educational Committee.

Her first novel, *Lolly Willowes*, which was published when she was thirty-three, is a witty tale of a spinster who turns into a gentle witch. It became the first ever 'Book of the Month' in America.

Sylvia visited New York in 1927 as a guest critic of the *Herald Tribune* newspaper and for many years her ironic, wry short stories were published by the *New Yorker* magazine.

Sylvia became involved in politics and worked for the Loyalists in Spain during the Civil War. She was, for a time, a member of the Communist Party and was active in the Association of Writers for Intellectual Liberty.

Unmarried, she lived in a succession of old, rambling houses in the south of England with a collection of cats and dogs. Other works included *Mr Fortune's Maggot* (1927), *The Corner That Held Them* (1948) and *A Stranger with a Bag* (1966); as well as a large number of short stories, Sylvia Townsend Warner published four volumes of poetry. She died peacefully, at the age of eighty-five in 1978.

'The Mahogany Table' was probably written in the 1960s. It concerns an elderly, single woman thinking back on her life as she drifts through the routine of her day, surrounded by her loved objects, all of which have particular memories for her. Although gentle in tone, the story is not without humour, which manages to acquire a darker edge through an unexpected ending.

The Mahogany Table

Sylvia Townsend Warner

The moment had come for Mrs Carrington to look at her wrist watch. 'Heavens! I must fly. We've got people coming in for drinks this evening, the morning's gone and I haven't as much as salted an almond. Why can't I be efficient like you? But of course, you're marvellous, quite marvellous. No, no! Don't get up. I can see myself out.'

The car went up the lane, its horn blaring. She had stayed her usual quarter of an hour and deposited her usual small cottage cheese. Letitia Foley carried it to the larder, and sat down again. Her glance traversed Mrs Carrington's wake: a dislodged cushion, a trail of white chalk mud, a tissue handkerchief, a paper clip. Paper clips rained from the poor woman as hairpins would have done in an epoch when hair was a crowning glory. Though there was no immediate call for a paper clip, paper clips came in handy at some time or other; meanwhile they accumulated in the Cloisonné box. All things in their season. When the mud had dried, she would deal with Pansy Carrington's wake. She sat and let the stiffening of attention ebb out of her limbs and imagined the reply she could have made to the parting assurances that she was marvellous.

'I am not marvellous at all. I am merely tidy, methodical, and an early riser. I get up at seven, I wash and dress and strip my bed to air it. I go down to the kitchen, which is clean because I left it in order overnight, and eat a sensible breakfast because a sensible breakfast is the best beginning for an active morning. I listen to the weather forecast and the news; if the post has brought me any letters I read them and decide how to answer them. I plan my meals for the day, and how best to use any left-overs. I make it a rule to keep no left-overs lying about. What with one thing and another it is now time to walk to the village to buy what I may need. I buy a packet of five cigarettes every morning; a regular walk means that I have to polish my shoes and keep myself in trim. By half-past eleven I have finished the housework and have the rest of the day before me to do as I please in. I never find time heavy on my hands; there is always something to do, polishing, or mending, ironing, spraying the window-plants, turning out a cupboard; there is always something interesting to do, and always time to do it in. *Ohne Hast, ohne Rast*, as the saying is. Sometimes I talk German to myself, to keep in practise.'

But such exemplary replies were never spoken. There was no call for them. Satisfied that she was marvellous, her visitors left it at that, talked about themselves, and went away.

There had been a time when a neutered cat called Dinah had twined through Miss Foley's systematic days. Dinah grew old and died, and was not replaced; for by then Letitia Foley too was growing old; and wondering what would happen to a cat who might outlive her would have been painful. A few years later she was forced to come to a similar prudent decision about her garden. It was a small well-flowered garden, in front of the house; if it had been at the back, she could have kept it as a private pleasure, an eccentricity of self-will; but from the day when a dandelion yielded so abruptly that she fell on her back and had to struggle to get up again, she recognized that weed as she might and be envied for her lilies and clove carnations, the garden was growing too much for her. No one had marked her fall; but she might not be so lucky another time. Brushed and polished and wearing gloves, she visited the local builder, and told him she wanted the garden levelled and put under concrete. 'You want a patio,' he said, all-knowingly. She said she wanted an estimate.

Dinah had died a quiet natural death; the garden was noisily slaughtered. But self-respect does not allow one to regret an act one has paid a great deal of money for, and by not thinking about the garden she contrived not to grieve for it. She missed not listening to the weather forecast. It had been a companionable voice; but now it was no more to the purpose than the news.

She brushed away the traces of Mrs Carrington's visit. For lunch she had planned a poached egg, but now substituted the small cottage cheese, and a healthy apple, and then satisfaction; for this was her afternoon for polishing the sitting-room furniture.

If the house was too large for a single woman, the furniture was undoubtedly too large for the house. She had known it all her life, and for much of her life had polished it. The pair of tallboys had come into the family with her Swedish great-grandmother. They were pale and classically plain, and so tall that to reach their cornice she had to stand on a chair. When she was a child they were known to be ugly; now she understood they were estimable. Deducing the great-grandmother from the tallboys, she grew up convinced that the great-grandmother had been a dislikeable character, harsh and ungiving, with none of the rich fruit-like glow of the mahogany table under which she and Cecily used to play houses. When she and Cecily set up house together after the parents were dead, Cecily had insisted on the mahogany table. Neither of them wanted the tallboys; but as belated twins at the end of a long family they had to take what was allotted and be grateful for it.

Moving to a small villa in a county without associations, they lived a happy slatternly life till the day in 1918 when Cecily brought in her limping expeditionary American. He was a Californian, large and polite, politely concealing his astonishment at the speed with which Cecily had caught him. Cecily was not in the least astonished. As though she were speaking a part in a play she told Letitia that everything was settled, that she had never been so happy in her life, that as soon as Dexter's new leg had settled in they would marry and leave for California. Dexter hoped that Letitia would visit them.

The invitation ripped open Letitia's sense of injury. 'Will you be taking the mahogany table?' she asked. The words were no sooner out of her mouth than she blushed for them. Cecily appeared to consider. 'Dear old thing . . . no, I don't think so. Dexter swarms with furniture he calls missionary.' Her triumphant satisfaction wadded her against reproach; one might as well be sarcastic to a cat with a bird between its jaws. It was so painful to be alone with her, in surroundings where they had always been together, that Letitia, concentrating her resentment into hating Dexter, was thankful for his company.

One evening after she had farewelled him with an almost genuine 'Must you go already?' Cecily looked up from the night-dress she was embroidering for her trousseau. 'Must he go already? Do you suppose he enjoys sitting here while you mope at him? Can you think of nobody but yourself?' They hurled themselves into a violent quarrel, each knowing where to wound. Cecily won. Having allowed Letitia to rant to a standstill, she remarked cheerfully 'Thank God we shan't have to make this one up,' and went on with her embroidery. To the last, she was conscienceless and Dexter was kindly. At last they were gone and Letitia was alone in a house littered with remains of packing. By the time she had set it to rights, method and economy had fastened on her. On alternate Tuesdays she wrote to Cecily. Cecily's letters came intermittently: she had had a child; she had bobbed her hair; there was wonderful news but it must wait till the next letter. The next letter came from Dexter's mother. Cecily had been killed in a road accident; Dexter had taken an overdose.

Wisps of the past had become entangled in the routine of her days, and recurred as regularly, to be acknowledged and ignored. A chipped dinner plate was Dunkirk; a hearth rug, the first raw misery of being alone. Cecily with her hair in pigtails was an adjunct to polishing the mahogany table. Today, as on every other Wednesday, the act of taking off the heavy tablecloth and folding it, uncovered Cecily waggling the moveable table leg and saying the roof of their house was about to fall. It was a large oblong table the two moveable legs supported its hinged flaps. All four legs were made of an inferior wood, and she always polished these first, looking forward the while to the smooth sweeping pressure and rewarding glow of polishing the top. The glow had again rewarded her, she had seen her face reflected – though wanly; for the day was clouding over. It was working up for rain and presently she would hear the first raindrops patter on the concrete square where the garden had been. It was on such afternoons that she and Cecily were told to stay indoors and played at houses. She had put back the tablecloth and was replacing the cap on the canister of polish when there was a loud rap at the door – so loud, so startling, that her hand shook as she put down the canister.

Village people always knocked instead of ringing the bell, but this crack of doom summons was intolerable. She flung open the front door, too incensed to know what she would say, but knowing it would put the fear of God into whoever had knocked. There was no one in sight, there were no runaway footsteps. Large separate raindrops spotted the concrete. She stood on the threshold long enough to recover her breath and grow chilled. Shrugging her shoulders, she slammed the door, and went back into the house which had lost that much daylight by slamming it. What little was left seemed to exist in the cold pallor of the tallboys, as though the polish she had put on them had turned to ice.

The canister stood on the very edge of the table, so hastily had she set it down. The cap was gone; it must have dropped from her hand. Groaning, she went down on all fours, and groped about for it. The carpet was theadbare; if the cap had fallen on its rim it might have rolled some way. It might have rolled under the table. She poked her head under the table-cloth, and peered. There, lodged against the further leg, was the cap. She crawled in and seized it.

It was not that she was unfamiliar with the underneath of the table; she was there every day with the dustpan and brush. But that was in the morning, and daylight came in with her, for the tablecloth was rolled back. This was in the late afternoon, the tablecloth enclosed a compacter darkness than the dusk of the room, and she had no purpose to be there – only the trivial accident of the strayed canister lid. And she was feeling quite remarkably tired. If she had been one of those women who lie down after lunch ... She subsided, warily; there was still head-room enough. She sat down, amid the smell of polish, under the noise of rain, in the obscurity, holding the little cap, she drooped her head toward her knees and curled herself up and fell asleep. She knew where she was and the little cap was still in her hand when Cecily came by, and remarked, 'Identical twins always quarrel. Think of Jacob and Esau.' Cecily walked on, but the words stayed in the air, and Letitia accepting them in her depth of sleep thought, 'When I wake up everything will be all right,' and saw rancour and remorse detach themselves and rise out of her like two dark bubbles that would burst on the surface of waking and be gone.

By that time Mrs Carrington had poured out the first round of sherry and handed cheese biscuits (the salted almonds had been a failure), stuffed olives, rings of onion, little sausages on sticks, and was retailing the neighbourly deed but for which there would have been a greater variety of things to eat.

'I have no idea how old she is, but she must be well on in her eighties, and getting quite appallingly stiff. And there she is, stuck at the end of that lane like a hermit-crab – or do I mean limpet? – anyway, there she is, without a relation in the world to come and look after her. I lie awake for hours wondering how to make her see sense, and go into a Home. But what can one do, what can one do? Of course, I do my best, but she ought to be in a Home. There's that delightful place at Booton – Sorrento, or something. Mercy Bradshaw says it's ideal.'

About the time when Mrs Carrington's guests were driving homeward, Letitia awoke under the impression she was in Sweden, for nowhere else could it be so cold; yet at the same time she was under the mahogany table, smelling polish and the thick smell of the tablecloth. She stirred. An agonising pain darted up her thigh, nailing her to place and identity. She was that old fool, Letitia Foley, with an attack of cramp; but such knotted cramp that she was afraid to move, could only grit her teeth and wait. One after another her stiffened muscles creaked into anguish. In fragments of reason, she knew she must escape from beneath the table, stand, pull herself together, turn on the light, drink something hot, fill a hot-water bottle, creep into bed with an aspirin. To get up, she must get onto her knees, for that she must have something to haul on. Still sitting, she writhed about directionless till she felt a table leg. Clutching it, she tried to hoist herself. It reeled away from her, the flap of the table fell, and knocked her senseless.

In the lounge of Sorrento, some days later, Marina Wickstead filched the local evening paper from the woman beside her, and read the report of an inquest, headed 'Peculiar Death of an Elderly Recluse'.

'Some people have all the luck!' she exclaimed – so passionately that Matron offered her another cup of tea.

Kate Chopin 1854–1904

Kate Chopin was the child of an Irish immigrant father and a French mother from St Louis. Her father died in a train crash when Kate was very young and she was brought up in an all female household – mother, grandmother and great grand-mother – in the American Deep South.

From the time of her marriage in 1870 Kate lived in New Orleans. She read widely, and she especially admired the stories of the French writer Guy de Maupassant, translating a number of his pieces for American publication.

Kate's own writing began after the death of her husband in 1883. She took her work seriously, bravely picking up and extending themes which less confident writers had tended to pass over. She was especially keen to explore the complex experiences of women in relation to men, family life and the wider world. Her writing was often controversial and many of her stories were refused publication during her lifetime. However, her focus on women's experience and the acces-sibility of her writing style has generated a lot of recent interest in her work. Chopin's short novel *The Awakening* (1899) is now regularly in print, as are several collections of her short stories.

'The Kiss', written in 1895 originally for a magazine read-ership, is a typical Kate Chopin short story. At its centre is a consideration of the choices available to women at this time. Should they be guided by their heads or their hearts? By expectations of romantic fulfilment or the firmer certainties of financial security? Can an independent woman such as Nathalie continue to kiss for pleasure, even after marrying for money?

The Kiss

Kate Chopin

It was still quite light out of doors, but inside with the curtains drawn and the smouldering fire sending out a dim, uncertain glow, the room was full of deep shadows.

Brantain sat in one of these shadows; it had overtaken him and he did not mind. The obscurity lent him courage to keep his eyes fastened as ardently as he liked upon the girl who sat in the firelight.

She was very handsome, with a certain fine, rich colouring that belongs to the healthy brune type. She was quite composed, as she idly stroked the satiny coat of the cat that lay curled in her lap, and she occasionally sent a slow glance into the shadow where her companion sat. They were talking low, of indifferent things which plainly were not the things that occupied their thoughts. She knew that he loved her – a frank, blustering fellow without guile enough to conceal his feelings, and no desire to do so. For two weeks past he had sought her society eagerly and persistently. She was confidently waiting for him to declare himself and she meant to accept him. The rather insignificant and unattractive Brantain was enormously rich; and she liked and required the entourage which wealth could give her.

During one of the pauses between their talk of the last tea and the next reception the door opened and a young man entered whom Brantain knew quite well. The girl turned her face toward him. A stride or two brought him to her side, and bending over her chair – before she could suspect his intention, for she did not realize that he had not seen her visitor – he pressed an ardent, lingering kiss upon her lips.

Brantain slowly arose; so did the girl arise, but quickly, and the newcomer stood between them, a little amusement and some defiance struggling with the confusion in his face.

'I believe,' stammered Brantain, 'I see that I have stayed

too long. I – I had no idea – that is, I must wish you good-bye.'
He was clutching his hat with both hands, and probably did
not perceive that she was extending her hand to him, her
presence of mind had not completely deserted her; but she
could not have trusted herself to speak.

'Hang me if I saw him sitting there, Nattie! I know it's
deuced awkward for you. But I hope you'll forgive me this
once – this very first break. Why, what's the matter?'

'Don't touch me; don't come near me,' she returned angrily.
'What do you mean by entering the house without ringing?'

'I came in with your brother, as I often do,' he answered
coldly, in self-justification. 'We came in the side way. He went
upstairs and I came in here hoping to find you. The explanation is simple enough and ought to satisfy you that the
misadventure was unavoidable. But do say that you forgive
me, Nathalie,' he entreated, softening.

'Forgive you! You don't know what you are talking about.
Let me pass. It depends upon – a good deal whether I ever
forgive you.'

At that next reception which she and Brantain had been
talking about she approached the young man with a delicious
frankness of manner when she saw him there.

'Will you let me speak to you a moment or two, Mr
Brantain?' she asked with an engaging but perturbed smile.
He seemed extremely unhappy; but when she took his arm
and walked away with him, seeking a retired corner, a ray
of hope mingled with the almost comical misery of his
expression. She was apparently very outspoken.

'Perhaps I should not have sought this interview, Mr
Brantain; but – but, oh, I have been very uncomfortable,
almost miserable since that little encounter the other afternoon. When I thought how you might have misinterpreted it,
and believed things' – hope was plainly gaining the ascend-
ancy over misery in Brantain's round, guileless face – 'of
course, I know it is nothing to you, but for my own sake I do
want you to understand that Mr Harvy is an intimate friend
of long standing. Why, we have always been like cousins –
like brother and sister, I may say. He is my brother's most
intimate associate and often fancies that he is entitled to the
same privileges as the family. Oh, I know it is absurd,
uncalled for, to tell you this; undignified even,' she was almost
weeping, 'but it makes so much difference to me what you

think of – of me.' Her voice had grown very low and agitated. The misery had all disappeared from Brantain's face.

'Then you do really care what I think, Miss Nathalie? May I call you Miss Nathalie?' They turned into a long, dim corridor that was lined on either side with tall, graceful plants. They walked slowly to the very end of it. When they turned to retrace their steps Brantain's face was radiant and hers was triumphant.

Harvy was among the guests at the wedding; and he sought her out in a rare moment when she stood alone.

'Your husband,' he said, smiling, 'has sent me over to kiss you.'

A quick blush suffused her face and round polished throat. 'I suppose it's natural for a man to feel and act generously on an occasion of this kind. He tells me he doesn't want his marriage to interrupt wholly that pleasant intimacy which has existed between you and me. I don't know what you've been telling him,' with an insolent smile, 'but he has sent me here to kiss you.'

She felt like a chess player who, by the clever handling of his pieces, sees the game taking the course intended. Her eyes were bright and tender with a smile as they glanced up into his; and her lips looked hungry for the kiss which they invited.

'But, you know,' he went on quietly, 'I didn't tell him so, it would have seemed ungrateful, but I can tell you. I've stopped kissing women; it's dangerous.'

Well, she had Brantain and his million left. A person can't have everything in this world; and it was a little unreasonable of her to expect it.

Ernest Hemingway 1898–1961

Ernest Hemingway was born near Chicago in 1898. His father was a physician who often took the young Hemingway with him on his country visits, but he was also a keen sportsman who gave his son a fishing rod at two and a gun at ten.

Hemingway was educated at local schools and although his father wanted him to study medicine, his academic work was patchy. He ran away from home when he was fifteen but he returned and finally graduated from high school.

His first job was with the *Kansas City Star*, but after a few months he left for Italy to become an ambulance driver in the First World War. Almost immediately, Hemingway was severely wounded and was invalided home in 1919. Back home he found some poorly paid work with a variety of newspapers until the *Toronto Star* agreed to accept a series of Letters from Europe. In 1921, he set off for Paris.

In Paris, Hemingway met a number of writers, Ezra Pound and Gertrude Stein in particular, who were to have a profound effect on his writing career. His first stories and poetry were published there by small literary magazines.

Various journalistic assignments followed: Spain, to report the bull running festival in Pamplona; Italy, to meet with the fascist leader Mussolini whom he considered 'the biggest bluff in Europe'; Istanbul, to report on the territorial disputes of the Balkans. But throughout this time nothing major was published.

In 1925 he broke through, two books were published in America – an important collection of short stories *In Our Time*; and the less influential *The Torrents of Spring*. *In Our Time* was very well received by the critics, who recognized a new, starkly unadorned, objective style of writing. F Scott Fitzgerald thought him 'the real thing'. James Joyce wrote 'He's a good writer, Hemingway. He writes as he is. We like him. He's a big, powerful peasant, as strong as a buffalo. A sportsman. And ready to live the life he writes about.'

His second novel *The Sun Also Rises* – created out of the bull running events he had witnessed in Pamplona – was both a popular and commercial success. He was, by now, quite a well-known international celebrity. He returned to the United States in the late 1920s and bought a house in Key West, Florida which, despite travels to Spain, for the

Civil War, and Africa, for big game hunting, was to be his base for the rest of his life.

Despite considerable public acclaim, Hemingway's private life was often troubled. He married four times and was increasingly subject to bouts of alcoholism and severe depression. The outward show of the tough, adventurous, man of action did not always match with the anxious and gloomily superstitious, private individual.

Other major works followed: *A Farewell to Arms* (1929), *Death in the Afternoon* (1932), *For Whom the Bell Tolls* (1940), *The Old Man and the Sea* (1952). Hemingway was awarded the Pulitzer prize in 1953, and the Nobel Prize in 1954 but was too ill to receive it in person. His health, both mental and physical, continued to decline, and in 1961 he committed suicide, as his father had done thirty years before.

'Hills Like White Elephants' first appeared in magazine form in 1927 and again in the collection *The First Forty-Nine Stories* of 1938. Hemingway was an accomplished short story writer, and in this story the famous 'Hemingway dialogue' is plain for all to see – short, clipped, repetitious and bare – 'the very essence of speech'.

The story is set in Spain, a predominantly Catholic country. A young couple are waiting for a train. They sit in the shade and think about ordering drinks. A series of small arguments flair up but are quickly extinguished by the girl. We gradually realise that these small clashes are part of a larger conflict that centres on the question of an abortion, although Hemingway never uses the word. What are they to do? Which way are they to go? To Madrid and the abortion, or away from Madrid to a more settled, family life? Who will make the final decision?

Hills Like White Elephants

Ernest Hemingway

The hills across the valley of the Ebro were long and white. On this side there was no shade and no trees and the station was between two lines of rails in the sun. Close against the side of the station there was the warm shadow of the building and a curtain, made of strings of bamboo beads, hung across the open door into the bar, to keep out flies. The American and the girl with him sat at a table in the shade, outside the building. It was very hot and the express from Barcelona would come in forty minutes. It stopped at this junction for two minutes and went on to Madrid.

'What should we drink?' the girl asked. She had taken off her hat and put it on the table.

'It's pretty hot,' the man said.

'Let's drink beer.'

'Dos cervezas,' the man said into the curtain.

'Big ones?' a woman asked from the doorway.

'Yes. Two big ones.'

The woman brought two glasses of beer and two felt pads. She put the felt pads and the beer glasses on the table and looked at the man and the girl. The girl was looking off at the line of hills. They were white in the sun and the country was brown and dry.

'They look like white elephants,' she said.

'I've never seen one.' The man drank his beer.

'No, you wouldn't have.'

'I might have,' the man said. 'Just because you say I wouldn't have doesn't prove anything.'

The girl looked at the bead curtain. 'They've painted something on it,' she said. 'What does it say?'

'Anis del Toro. It's a drink.'

'Could we try it?'

The man called 'Listen' through the curtain.

The woman came out from the bar.

'Four reales.'

'We want two Anis del Toros.'

'With water?'

'Do you want it with water?'

'I don't know,' the girl said. 'Is it good with water?'

'It's all right.'

'You want them with water?' asked the woman.

'Yes, with water.'

'It tastes like liquorice,' the girl said and put the glass down.

'That's the way with everything.'

'Yes,' said the girl. 'Everything tastes of liquorice. Especially all the things you've waited so long for, like absinthe.'

'Oh, cut it out.'

'You started it,' the girl said. 'I was being amused. I was having a fine time.'

'Well, let's try and have a fine time.'

'All right. I was trying. I said the mountains looked like white elephants. Wasn't that bright?'

'That was bright.'

'I wanted to try this new drink. That's all we do, isn't it – look at things and try new drinks?'

'I guess so.'

The girl looked across at the hills.

'They're lovely hills,' she said. 'They don't really look like white elephants. I just meant the colouring of their skin through the trees.'

'Should we have another drink?'

'All right.'

The warm wind blew the bead curtain against the table.

'The beer's nice and cool,' the man said.

'It's lovely,' the girl said.

'It's really an awfully simple operation, Jig,' the man said. 'It's not really an operation at all.'

The girl looked at the ground the table legs rested on.

'I know you wouldn't mind it, Jig. It's really not anything. It's just to let the air in.'

The girl did not say anything.

'I'll go with you and I'll stay with you all the time. They just let the air in and then it's all perfectly natural.'

'Then what will we do afterwards?'

'We'll be fine afterwards. Just like we were before.'

'What makes you think so?'

'That's the only thing that bothers us. It's the one thing that's made us unhappy.'

The girl looked at the bead curtain, put her hand out and took hold of two of the strings of beads.

'And you think then we'll be all right and be happy?'

'I know we will. You don't have to be afraid. I've known lots of people that have done it.'

'So have I,' said the girl. 'And afterward they were all so happy.'

'Well,' the man said, 'if you don't want to you don't have to. I wouldn't have you do it if you didn't want to. But I know it's perfectly simple.'

'And you really want to?'

'I think it's the best thing to do. But I don't want you to do it if you don't really want to.'

'And if I do it you'll be happy and things will be like they were and you'll love me?'

'I love you now. You know I love you.'

'I know. But if I do it, then it will be nice again if I say things are like white elephants, and you'll like it?'

'I'll love it. I love it now but I just can't think about it. You know how I get when I worry.'

'If I do it you won't ever worry.'

'I won't worry about that because it's perfectly simple.'

'Then I'll do it. Because I don't care about me.'

'What do you mean?'

'I don't care about me.'

'Well, I care about you.'

'Oh, yes. But I don't care about me. And I'll do it and then everything will be fine.'

'I don't want you to do it if you feel that way.'

The girl stood up and walked to the end of the station. Across, on the other side, were fields of grain and trees along the banks of the Ebro. Far away, beyond the river, were mountains. The shadow of a cloud moved across the field of grain and she saw the river through the trees.

'And we could have all this,' she said. 'And we could have everything and every day we make it more impossible.'

'What did you say?'

'I said we could have everything.'

'We can have everything.'

'No, we can't.'

'We can have the whole world.'

'No, we can't.'

'We can go everywhere.'

'No, we can't. It isn't ours any more.'

'It's ours.'

'No, it isn't. And once they take it away, you never get it back.'

'But they haven't taken it away.'

'We'll wait and see.'

'Come on back in the shade,' he said. 'You mustn't feel that way.'

'I don't feel any way,' the girl said. 'I just know things.'

'I don't want you to do anything that you don't want to do – '

'Nor that isn't good for me,' she said. 'I know. Could we have another beer?'

'All right. But you've got to realize – '

'I realize,' the girl said. 'Can't we maybe stop talking?'

They sat down at the table and the girl looked across at the hills on the dry side of the valley and the man looked at her and at the table.

'You've got to realize,' he said, 'that I don't want you to do it if you don't want to. I'm perfectly willing to go through with it if it means anything to you.'

'Doesn't it mean anything to you? We could get along.'

'Of course it does. But I don't want anybody but you. I don't want anyone else. And I know it's perfectly simple.'

'Yes, you know it's perfectly simple.'

'It's all right for you to say that, but I do know it.'

'Would you do something for me now?'

'I'd do anything for you.'

'Would you please please please please please please please stop talking?'

He did not say anything but looked at the bags against the wall of the station. There were labels on them from all the hotels where they had spent nights.

'But I don't want you to,' he said, 'I don't care anything about it.'

'I'll scream,' the girl said.

The woman came out through the curtains with two glasses of beer and put them down on the damp felt pads.

'The train comes in five minutes,' she said.

'What did she say?' asked the girl.

'That the train is coming in five minutes.'

The girl smiled brightly at the woman, to thank her.

'I'd better take the bags over to the other side of the station,' the man said. She smiled at him.

'All right. Then come back and we'll finish the beer.'

He picked up the two heavy bags and carried them around the station to the other tracks. He looked up the tracks but could not see the train. Coming back, he walked through the bar-room, where people waiting for the train were drinking. He drank an Anis at the bar and looked at the people. They were all waiting reasonably for the train. He went out through the bead curtain. She was sitting at the table and smiled at him.

'Do you feel better?' he asked.

'I feel fine,' she said. 'There's nothing wrong with me. I feel fine.'

Elizabeth Taylor 1912–1975

Elizabeth Taylor was born Elizabeth Coles in Reading, Berkshire in 1912. She was educated at the Abbey School, Reading, a school which carries on the name of an eighteenth-century school where the novelist Jane Austen was a pupil.

As a child Elizabeth Taylor began writing stories and always wanted to be a novelist. However she did not earn anything from her writing until after she was thirty. She became a governess, then worked in a library and wrote in her spare time but commented, 'I learnt so much from these jobs I have never regretted the time I spent on them.'

Elizabeth Taylor married John Taylor, a businessman, when she was 24 and had two children. She wrote her first novel *At Mrs Lippincote's* (1945) during the Second World War while her husband was in the Royal Air Force and she was living a lonely life in the country. She went on to write twelve novels including *A View of the Harbour* (1947), *Angel* (1957) and *Mrs Palfrey at the Claremont* (1971) as well as five collections of short stories. The short story 'The Flypaper' is taken from the best known collection *The Devastating Boys*.

Elizabeth Taylor's writing is careful and precise, dealing not only with the polite surfaces of life, but also with the tensions which lie below the surface. She lived in the country at Penn in Buckinghamshire. She disliked travelling and although she loved London would not have liked to live there. She wrote, 'Village life with its wider differences, in every social sense – seems a better background for a woman novelist, and certainly more congenial to me. In towns, one tends to select one's friends. In the country they are chosen for one – and if they rarely have the same interests as oneself, so much the better; so much the richer.'

So she chose to write about small town or village life, and the sort of characters she knew from her own life. 'I should like to feel that the people in my books are essentially English and set down against a truly English background', was a comment she made about her work. Yet even as Taylor describes these characters and tells of their everyday lives, she is seeking to probe below those surface impressions, to see what lies beneath.

The story 'The Fly-paper' tells of an everyday event. It is a Wednesday afternooon and an eleven-year-old girl is setting out to her weekly piano lesson. However we soon see how oppressive this trip is and what dangers it holds. We also learn that appearances can be deceptive.

The Fly-paper

Elizabeth Taylor

On Wednesdays, after school, Sylvia took the bus to the outskirts of the nearest town for her music lesson. Because of her docile manner, she did not complain of the misery she suffered in Miss Harrison's darkened parlour, sitting at the old-fashioned upright piano with its brass candlesticks and loose, yellowed keys. In the highest register there was not the faintest tinkle of a note, only the hollow sound of the key being banged down. Although that distant octave was out of her range, Sylvia sometimes pressed down one of its notes, listening mutely to Miss Harrison's exasperated railings about her – Sylvia's – lack of aptitude, or even concentration. The room was darkened in winter by a large fir-tree pressing against – in windy weather tapping against – the window, and in summer even more so by holland blinds, half-drawn to preserve the threadbare carpet. To add to all the other miseries, Sylvia had to peer short-sightedly at the music-book, her glance going up and down between it and the keyboard, losing her place, looking hunted, her lips pursed.

It was now the season of the drawn blinds, and she waited in the lane at the bus-stop, feeling hot in her winter coat, which her grandmother insisted on her wearing, just as she insisted on the music lessons. The lane buzzed in the heat of the late afternoon – with bees in the clover, and flies going crazy over some cow-pats on the road.

Since her mother's death, Sylvia had grown glum and sullen. She was a plain child, plump, mature for her eleven years. Her greasy hair was fastened back by a pink plastic slide; her tweed coat, of which, last winter, she had been rather proud, had cuffs and collar of mock ocelot. She carried, beside her music case, a shabby handbag, once her mother's.

The bus seemed to tremble and jingle as it came slowly

down the road. She climbed on, and sat down on the long seat inside the door, where a little air might reach her.

On the other long seat opposite her, was a very tall man; quite old, she supposed, for his hair was carefully arranged over his bald skull. He stared at her. She puffed with the heat and then, to avoid his glance, she slewed round a little to look over her shoulder at the dusty hedges – the leaves all in late summer darkness. She was sure that he was wondering why she wore a winter's coat on such a day, and she unbuttoned it and flapped it a little to air her armpits. The weather had a threat of change in it, her grandmother had said, and her cotton dress was too short. It had already been let down and had a false hem, which she now tried to draw over her thighs.

'Yes, it is very warm,' the man opposite her suddenly said, as if agreeing with someone else's remark.

She turned in surprise, and her face reddened, but she said nothing.

After a while, she began to wonder if it would be worth getting off at the fare-stage before the end of her journey and walk the rest of the way. Then she could spend the money on a lolly. She had to waste half-an-hour before her lesson, and must wander about somewhere to pass the time. It would be better to be wandering about with a lolly to suck. Her grandmother did not allow her to eat sweets – bathing the teeth in acid, she said it was.

'I believe I have seen you before,' the man opposite said. 'Either wending your way to or from a music-lesson, I imagine.' He looked knowingly at her music-case.

'To,' she said sullenly.

'A budding Myra Hess,' he went on. 'I take it that you play the piano, as you seem to have no instrument secreted about your person.'

She did not know what he meant, and stared out of the window, frowning, feeling so hot and anguished.

'And what is your name?' he asked. 'We shall have to keep it in mind for the future when you are famous.'

'Sylvia Wilkinson,' she said under her breath.

'Not bad. Not bad, Sylvia. No doubt one day I shall boast that I met the great Sylvia Wilkinson on a bus one summer's afternoon. Name-dropping, you know. A harmless foible of the humble.'

He was very neat and natty, but his reedy voice had a

nervous tremor. All this time, he had held an unlighted cigarette in his hand, and gestured with it, but made no attempt to find matches.

'I expect at school you sing the beautiful song, "Who is Sylvia?" Do you?'

She shook her head, without looking at him and, to her horror, he began to sing, quaveringly, 'Who is Sylvia? What is she-he?'

A woman sitting a little farther down the bus, turned and looked at him sharply.

He's mad, Sylvia decided. She was embarrassed, but not nervous, not nervous at all, here in the bus with other people, in spite of all her grandmother had said about not getting into conversations with strangers.

He went on singing, wagging his cigarette in time.

The woman turned again and gave him a longer stare. She was homely-looking, Sylvia decided – in spite of fair hair going very dark at the roots. She had a comfortable, protective manner, as if she were keeping an eye on the situation for Sylvia's sake.

Suddenly, he broke off his singing and returned her stare. 'I take it, Madam,' he said, 'that you do not appreciate my singing.'

'I should think it's hardly the place,' she said shortly. 'That's all,' and turned her head away.

'Hardly the place!' he said, in a low voice, as if to himself, and with feigned amazement. 'On a fair summer's afternoon, while we bowl merrily along the lanes. Hardly the place – to express one's joy of living! I am sorry,' he said to Sylvia, in a louder voice. 'I had not realised we were going to a funeral.'

Thankfully, she saw that they were coming nearer to the outskirts of the town. It was not a large town, and its outskirts were quiet.

'I hope you don't mind me chatting to you,' the man said to Sylvia. 'I am fond of children. I am known as being *good* with them. Well known for that. I treat them on my own level, as one should.'

Sylvia stared – almost glared – out of the window, twisted round in her seat, her head aching with the stillness of her eyes.

It was flat country, intersected by canals. On the skyline,

were the clustered chimneys of a brick-works. The only movement out there was the faintest shimmering of heat.

She was filled by misery; for there seemed nothing in her life now but acquiescence to hated things, and her grandmother's old ways setting her apart from other children. Nothing she did was what she wanted to do – school-going, church-going, now this terrible music lesson ahead of her. Since her mother's death, her life had taken a sharp turn for the worse, and she could not see how it would ever be any better. She had no faith in freeing herself from it, even when she was grown-up.

A wasp zigzagged across her and settled on the front of her coat. She was obliged to turn. She sat rigid, her head held back, her chin tucked in, afraid to make a movement.

'Allow me!' The awful man opposite had reached across the bus, and flapped a crumpled handkerchief at her. The wasp began to fuss furiously, darting about her face.

'We'll soon settle you, you little pest,' the man said, making matters worse.

The bus-conductor came between them. He stood carefully still for a moment, and then decisively clapped his hands together, and the wasp fell dead to the ground.

'Thank you,' Sylvia said to him, but not to the other.

They were passing bungalows now, newly-built, and with unmade gardens. Looking directly ahead of her, Sylvia got up, and went to the platform of the bus, standing there in a slight breeze, ready for the stopping-place.

Beyond the bus-shelter, she knew that there was a little general shop. She would comfort herself with a bright red lolly on a stick. She crossed the road and stood looking in the window, at jars of boiled sweets, and packets of detergents and breakfast cereals. There was a notice about ice-creams, but she had not enough money.

She turned to go into the empty, silent shop when the now familiar and dreaded voice came from beside her. 'Would you care to partake of an ice, this hot afternoon?'

He stood between her and the shop, and the embarrassment she had suffered on the bus gave way to terror.

'An ice?' he repeated, holding his head on one side, looking at her imploringly.

She thought that if she said 'yes', she could at least get inside the shop. Someone must be there to serve, someone

whose protection she might depend upon. Those words of
warning from her grandmother came into her head, caution-
ary tales, dark with unpleasant hints.

Before she could move, or reply, she felt a hand lightly but
firmly touch her shoulder. It was the glaring woman from the
bus, she was relieved to see.

'Haven't you ever been told not to talk to strangers?' she
asked Sylvia, quite sharply, but with calm common sense in
her brusqueness. '*You'd* better be careful,' she said to the man
menacingly. 'Now come along, child, and let this be a lesson
to you. Which way were you going?'

Sylvia nodded ahead.

'Well, best foot forward, and keep going. And *you*, my man,
can kindly step in a different direction, or I'll find a
policeman.'

At this last word, Sylvia turned to go, feeling flustered, but
important.

'You should *never*,' the woman began, going along beside
her. 'There's some funny people about these days. Doesn't
your mother warn you?'

'She's dead.'

'Oh, well, I'm sorry about that. My God, it's warm.' She
pulled her dress away from her bosom, fanning it. She had a
shopping-basket full of comforting, homely groceries, and
Sylvia looked into it, as she walked beside her.

'Wednesday's always my day,' the woman said. 'Early-
closing here, so I take the bus up to Horseley. I have a relative
who has the little general store there. It makes a change, but
not in this heat.'

She rambled on about her uninteresting affairs. Once,
Sylvia glanced back, and could see the man still standing
there, gazing after them.

'I shouldn't turn round,' the woman said. 'Which road did
you say?'

Sylvia hadn't, but now did so.

'Well, you can come my way. That would be better, and
there's nothing much in it. Along by the gravel-pits. I'll have
a quick look round before we turn the corner.'

When she did so, she said that she thought they were being
followed, at a distance. 'Oh, it's disgraceful,' she said. 'And
with all the things you read in the papers. You can't be too

careful, and you'll have to remember that in the future. I'm not sure I ought not to inform the police.'

Along this road, there were disused gravel-pits, and chicory and convolvulus. Rusty sorrel and rustier tin-cans gave the place a derelict air. On the other side, there were allotments, and ramshackle tool-sheds among dark nettles.

'It runs into Hamilton Road,' the woman explained.

'But I don't have to be there for another half-hour,' Sylvia said nervously. She could imagine Miss Harrison's face if she turned up on the doorstep all that much too soon, in the middle of a lesson with the bright-looking girl she had often met leaving.

'I'm going to give you a nice cup of tea, and make sure you're all right. Don't you worry.'

Thankfully, she turned in at the gate of a little red brick house at the edge of the waste land. It was ugly, but very neat, and surrounded by hollyhocks. The beautifully shining windows were draped with frilly, looped-up curtains, with plastic flowers arranged between them.

Sylvia followed the woman down a side path to the back door, trying to push her worries from her mind. She was all right this time, but what of all the future Wednesdays, she wondered – with their perilous journeys to be made alone.

She stood in the kitchen and looked about her. It was clean and cool there. A budgerigar hopped in a cage. Rather listlessly, but not knowing what else to do, she went to it and ran her finger-nail along the wires.

'There's my baby boy, my little Joey,' the woman said in a sing-song, automatic way, as she held the kettle under the tap. 'You'll feel better when you've had a cup of tea,' she added, now supposedly addressing Sylvia.

'It's very kind of you.'

'Any woman would do the same. There's a packet of Oval Marie in my basket, if you'd like to open it and put them on this plate.'

Sylvia was glad to do something. She arranged the biscuits carefully on the rose-patterned plate. 'It's very nice here,' she said. Her grandmother's house was so dark and cluttered; Miss Harrison's even more so. Both smelt stuffy, of thick curtains and old furniture. She did not go into many houses, for she was so seldom invited anywhere. She was a dull girl, whom nobody liked very much, and she knew it.

'I must have everything sweet and fresh,' the woman said complacently.

The kettle began to sing.

I've still got to get home, Sylvia thought in a panic. She stared up at a fly-paper hanging in the window – the only disconcerting thing in the room. Some of the flies were still half alive, and striving hopelessly to free themselves. But they were caught forever.

She heard footsteps on the path, and listened in surprise; but the woman did not seem to hear, or lift her head. She was spooning tea from the caddy into the teapot.

'Just in time, Herbert,' she called out.

Sylvia turned round as the door opened. With astonished horror, she saw the man from the bus step confidently into the kitchen.

'Well done, Mabel!' he said, closing the door behind him. 'Don't forget one for the pot.' He smiled, smoothing his hands together, surveying the room.

Sylvia spun round questioningly to the woman, who was now bringing the teapot to the table, and she noticed for the first time that there were three cups and saucers laid there.

'Well, sit down, do,' the woman said, a little impatiently. 'It's all ready.'

Katherine Mansfield 1888–1923

Katherine Mansfield Beauchamp was born in Wellington, New Zealand in 1888, the third daughter in a family of four girls and one boy. She spent her early years in Karori, near Wellington and attended the local county school with other local children where her teachers commented she was 'Good at arithmetic but bad at spelling'. She loved reading and would often read by candlelight until her grandmother came to bed. She won a prize when only eight for English composition with an imaginary description of a sea voyage. Later Katherine Mansfield went to Wellington High School where she wrote for the school magazine and had her first story published.

In 1903, at the age of fifteen, Katherine Mansfield was sent to England with her two older sisters to finish her education. However it was not 'finishing school' she went to, but Queen's College, the first institution to be created in England for the higher education of women. Here she was encouraged to read widely and became an accomplished cello player.

Three years later she returned to New Zealand but hated it, feeling herself cut off from life and writing of the 'narrow, sodden, mean, draggled houses'. At the age of eighteen she had some short prose pieces called *Vignettes* published in an Australian magazine and it was at this stage that she adopted her shortened pen name.

Her return to England in July 1908 saw her continuing to write, but without a market for her sort of writing. She was not interested in stories with a plot and happy endings, but wanted to write about the things she saw around her. Her aim was, 'to intensify the small things so that truly everything was significant.'

1909 proved an unhappy and turbulent year for Katherine Mansfield. Disappointed with one love affair she made a rapid decision to marry George Bowden. 'Suddenly snap!' was how she described her decision to marry, but she changed her mind as quickly after the wedding and left her husband after only a few days. She went to Woerishofen, a Bavarian spa town, where she had a stillbirth. Her time in Bavaria formed the basis for her first collection of stories *In A German Pension* published 1911.

On her return to England Katherine Mansfield met John Middleton Murry, a critic and magazine editor who published her writing in magazines. They soon formed a relationship and married later when a divorce allowed them to do so. Together they collaborated with the writer D. H. Lawrence on the publication of a magazine called *The Signature*. Katherine Mansfield also developed a close correspondence with another writer, Virginia Woolf, each commenting on the other's writing.

The publication of *Bliss and Other Stories* in 1920 brought widespread recognition of Katherine Mansfield's talent. Despite increasing ill-health she continued writing, publishing *The Garden Party and Other Stories* in 1922 and her *Journal* which was published after her death. She died in 1923 when she was only 34 years old.

'Pictures' is a story firmly rooted in the everyday, which also lets us see the dreams of would-be singer and film actress Miss Amy Moss. A fruitless search for work proves to be a depressing experience and she is driven towards the Café de Madrid. Perhaps there she will find the money for rent she so desperately needs?

Pictures

Katherine Mansfield

Eight o'clock in the morning. Miss Ada Moss lay in a black iron bedstead, staring up at the ceiling. Her room, a Bloomsbury top-floor back, smelled of soot and face powder and the paper of fried potatoes she brought in for supper the night before.

'Oh, dear,' thought Miss Moss, 'I am cold. I wonder why it is that I always wake up so cold in the mornings now. My knees and feet and my back – especially my back; it's like a sheet of ice. And I always was such a one for being warm in the old days. It's not as if I was skinny – I'm just the same full figure that I used to be. No, it's because I don't have a good hot dinner in the evenings.'

A pageant of Good Hot Dinners passed across the ceiling, each of them accompanied by a bottle of Nourishing Stout . . .

'Even if I were to get up now,' she thought, 'and have a sensible substantial breakfast . . .' A pageant of Sensible Substantial Breakfasts followed the dinners across the ceiling, shepherded by an enormous, white, uncut ham. Miss Moss shuddered and disappeared under the bedclothes. Suddenly, in bounced the landlady.

'There's a letter for you, Miss Moss.'

'Oh,' said Miss Moss, far too friendly, 'thank you very much, Mrs Pine. It's very good of you, I'm sure, to take the trouble.'

'No trouble at all,' said the landlady. 'I thought perhaps it was the letter you'd been expecting.'

'Why,' said Miss Moss brightly, 'yes, perhaps it is.' She put her head on one side and smiled vaguely at the letter. 'I shouldn't be surprised.'

The landlady's eyes popped. 'Well, I should, Miss Moss,' said she, 'and that's how it is. And I'll trouble you to open it, if you please. Many is the lady in my place as would have done it for you and have been within her rights. For things

can't go on like this, Miss Moss, no indeed they can't. What
with week in week out and first you've got it and then you
haven't, and then it's another letter lost in the post or another
manager down at Brighton but will be back on Tuesday for
certain – I'm fair sick and tired and I won't stand it no more.
Why should I, Miss Moss, I ask you, at a time like this, with
prices flying up in the air and my poor dear lad in France?
My sister Eliza was only saying to me yesterday – "Minnie,"
she says, "you're too soft-hearted. You could have let that
room time and time again," says she, "and if people won't look
after themselves in times like these, nobody else will," she
says. "She may have had a College eddication and sung in
West End concerts," says she, "but if your Lizzie says what's
true," she says, "and she's washing her own wovens and
drying them on the towel rail, it's easy to see where the
finger's pointing. And it's high time you had done with it,"
says she.'

Miss Moss gave no sign of having heard this. She sat up in
bed, tore open her letter, and read:

Dear Madam,
    Yours to hand. Am not producing at present, but have
filed photo for future ref.

Yours truly,
BACKWASH FILM CO.

This letter seemed to afford her peculiar satisfaction; she
read it through twice before replying to the landlady.

'Well, Mrs Pine, I think you'll be sorry for what you said.
This is from a manager, asking me to be there with evening
dress at ten o'clock next Saturday morning.'

But the landlady was too quick for her. She pounced,
secured the letter.

'Oh, is it! Is it indeed!' she cried.

'Give me back that letter. Give it back to me at once, you
bad, wicked woman,' cried Miss Moss, who could not get out
of bed because her nightdress was slit down the back. 'Give
me back my private letter.' The landlady began slowly back-
ing out of the room, holding the letter to her buttoned bodice.

'So it's come to this, has it?' said she. 'Well, Miss Moss, if I
don't get my rent at eight o'clock tonight, we'll see who's a
bad, wicked woman – that's all.' Here she nodded, mysteri-

ously. 'And I'll keep this letter.' Here her voice rose. 'It will be a pretty little bit of evidence!' And here it fell, sepulchral, *'My lady.'*

The door banged and Miss Moss was alone. She flung off the bed clothes, and sitting by the side of the bed, furious and shivering, she stared at her fat white legs with their great knots of greeny-blue veins.

'Cockroach! That's what she is. She's a cockroach!' said Miss Moss. 'I could have her up for snatching my letter – I'm sure I could.' Still keeping on her nightdress she began to drag on her clothes.

'Oh, if I could only pay that woman, I'd give her a piece of my mind that she wouldn't forget. I'd tell her off proper.' She went over to the chest of drawers for a safety-pin, and seeing herself in the glass she gave a vague smile and shook her head. 'Well, old girl,' she murmured, 'you're up against it this time, and no mistake.' But the person in the glass made an ugly face at her.

'You silly thing,' scolded Miss Moss. 'Now what's the good of crying: you'll only make your nose red. No, you get dressed and go out and try your luck – that's what you've got to do.'

She unhooked her vanity bag from the bedpost, rooted in it, shook it, turned it inside out.

'I'll have a nice cup of tea at an A B C to settle me before I go anywhere,' she decided. 'I've got one and thrippence – yes, just one and three.'

Ten minutes later, a stout lady in blue serge, with a bunch of artificial 'parmas' at her bosom, a black hat covered with purple pansies, white gloves, boots with white uppers, and a vanity bag containing one and three, sang in a low contralto voice:

> 'Sweet-heart, remember when days are forlorn
> It al-ways is dar-kest before the dawn.'

But the person in the glass made a face at her, and Miss Moss went out. There were grey crabs all the way down the street slopping water over grey stone steps. With his strange, hawking cry and the jangle of the cans the milk boy went his rounds. Outside Brittweiler's Swiss House he made a splash, and an old brown cat without a tail appeared from nowhere, and began greedily and silently drinking up the spill. It gave

Miss Moss a queer feeling to watch – a sinking – as you might say.

But when she came to the A B C she found the door propped open; a man went in and out carrying trays of rolls, and there was nobody inside except a waitress doing her hair and the cashier unlocking the cash boxes. She stood in the middle of the floor but neither of them saw her.

'My boy came home last night,' sang the waitress.

'Oh, I say – how topping for you!' gurgled the cashier.

'Yes, wasn't it,' sang the waitress. 'He brought me a sweet little brooch. Look, it's got "Dieppe" written on it.'

The cashier ran across to look and put her arm round the waitress's neck.

'Oh, I say – how topping for you.'

'Yes, isn't it,' said the waitress. 'O-oh, he is brahn. "Hullo," I said, "hullo, old mahogany."'

'Oh, I say,' gurgled the cashier, running back into her cage and nearly bumping into Miss Moss on the way. 'You are a *treat*!' Then the man with the rolls came in again, swerving past her.

'Can I have a cup of tea, Miss?' she asked.

But the waitress went on doing her hair. 'Oh,' she sang, 'we're not *open* yet.' She turned round and waved her comb at the cashier.

'*Are* we, dear?'

'Oh, no,' said the cashier. Miss Moss went out.

'I'll go to Charing Cross. Yes, that's what I'll do,' she decided. 'But I won't have a cup of tea. No, I'll have a coffee. There's more of a tonic in coffee . . . Cheeky, those girls are! Her boy came home last night; he brought her a brooch with "Dieppe" written on it.' She began to cross the road . . .

'Look out, Fattie; don't go to sleep!' yelled a taxi driver. She pretended not to hear.

'No, I won't go to Charing Cross,' she decided. 'I'll go straight to Kig and Kadgit. They're open at nine. If I get there early Mr Kadgit may have something by the morning's post . . . I'm very glad you turned up so early, Miss Moss. I've just heard from a manager who wants a lady to play. . . . I think you'll just suit him. I'll give you a card to go and see him. It's three pounds a week and all found. If I were you I'd hop round as fast as I could. Lucky you turned up so early . . .'

But there was nobody at Kig and Kadgit's except the charwoman wiping over the 'lino' in the passage.

'Nobody here yet, Miss,' said the char.

'Oh, isn't Mr Kadgit here?' said Miss Moss, trying to dodge the pail and brush. 'Well, I'll just wait a moment, if I may.'

'You can't wait in the waiting-room, Miss. I 'aven't done it yet. Mr Kadgit's never 'ere before 'leven-thirty Saturdays. Sometimes 'e don't come at all.' And the char began crawling towards her.

'Dear me – how silly of me,' said Miss Moss. 'I forgot it was Saturday.'

'Mind your feet, *please*, Miss,' said the char. And Miss Moss was outside again.

That was one thing about Beit and Bithems; it was lively. You walked into the waiting-room, into a great buzz of conversation, and there was everybody; you knew almost everybody. The early ones sat on chairs and the later ones sat on the early ones' laps, while the gentlemen leaned negligently against the walls or preened themselves in front of the admiring ladies.

'Hello,' said Miss Moss, very gay. 'Here we are again!'

And young Mr Clayton, playing the banjo on his walking-stick sang: 'Waiting for the Robert E. Lee.'

'Mr Bithem here yet?' asked Miss Moss, taking out an old dead powder puff and powdering her nose mauve.

'Oh, yes, dear,' cried the chorus. 'He's been here for ages. We've all been waiting here for more than an hour.'

'Dear me!' said Miss Moss. 'Anything doing, do you think?'

'Oh, a few jobs going for South Africa,' said young Mr Clayton. 'Hundred and fifty a week for two years, you know.'

'Oh!' cried the chorus. 'You *are* weird, Mr Clayton. Isn't he a *cure*? Isn't he a *scream*, dear? Oh, Mr Clayton, you do make me laugh. Isn't he a *comic*?'

A dark mournful girl touched Miss Moss on the arm.

'I just missed a lovely job yesterday,' she said. 'Six weeks in the provinces and then the West End. The manager said I would have got it for certain if only I'd been robust enough. He said if my figure had been fuller, the part was made for me.' She stared at Miss Moss, and the dirty dark red rose under the brim of her hat looked, somehow, as though it shared the blow with her, and was crushed, too.

'Oh, dear, that was hard lines,' said Miss Moss trying to appear indifferent. 'What was it – if I may ask?'

But the dark, mournful girl saw through her and a gleam of spite came into her heavy eyes.

'Oh, no good to you, my dear,' said she. 'He wanted someone young, you know – a dark Spanish type – my style, but more figure, that was all.'

The inner door opened and Mr Bithem appeared in his shirt sleeves. He kept one hand on the door ready to whisk back again, and held up the other.

'Look here, ladies – ' and then he paused, grinned his famous grin before he said – '*and bhoys.*' The waiting-room laughed so loudly at this that he had to hold both hands up. 'It's no good waiting this morning. Come back Monday; I'm expecting several calls on Monday.'

Miss Moss made a desperate rush forward. 'Mr Bithem, I wonder if you've heard from . . .'

'Now let me see,' said Mr Bithem slowly, staring; he had only seen Miss Moss four times a week for the past – how many weeks? 'Now, who are you?'

'Miss Ada Moss.'

'Oh, yes, yes; of course, my dear. Not yet, my dear. Now I had a call for twenty-eight ladies today, but they had to be young and able to hop it a bit – see? And I had another call for sixteen – but they had to know something about sand-dancing. Look here, my dear, I'm up to my eyebrows this morning. Come back on Monday week; it's no good coming before that.' He gave her a whole grin to herself and patted her fat back. 'Hearts of oak, dear lady,' said Mr Bithem, 'hearts of oak!'

At the North-East Film Company the crowd was all the way up the stairs. Miss Moss found herself next to a fair little baby thing about thirty in a white lace hat with cherries round it.

'What a crowd!' said she. 'Anything special on?'

'*Didn't* you know, dear?' said the baby, opening her immense pale eyes. 'There was a call at nine-thirty for *attractive* girls. We've all been waiting for *hours*. Have you played for this company before?' Miss Moss put her head on one side. 'No, I don't think I have.'

'They're a lovely company to play for,' said the baby. 'A

friend of mine has a friend who gets thirty pounds a day . . . Have you *arcted* much for the *fil*-lums?'

'Well, I'm not an actress by profession,' confessed Miss Moss. 'I'm a contralto singer. But things have been so bad lately that I've been doing a little.'

'It's *like* that, isn't it, dear?' said the baby.

'I had a splendid education at the College of Music,' said Miss Moss, 'and I got my silver medal for singing. I've often sung at West End concerts. But I thought, for a change, I'd try my luck . . .'

'Yes, it's *like* that, isn't it, dear?' said the baby.

At that moment a beautiful typist appeared at the top of the stairs.

'Are you all waiting for the North-East call?'

'Yes!' cried the chorus.

'Well, it's off. I've just had a phone through.'

'But look here! What about our expenses?' shouted a voice.

The typist looked down at them, and she couldn't help laughing.

'Oh, you weren't to have been *paid*. The North-East never *pay* their crowds.'

There was only a little round window at the Bitter Orange Company. No waiting-room – nobody at all except a girl, who came to the window when Miss Moss knocked, and said: 'Well?'

'Can I see the producer, please?' said Miss Moss pleasantly. The girl leaned on the window-bar, half-shut her eyes, and seemed to go to sleep for a moment. Miss Moss smiled at her. The girl not only frowned; she seemed to smell something vaguely unpleasant; she sniffed. Suddenly she moved away, came back with a paper, and thrust it at Miss Moss.

'Fill up the form!' said she. And banged the window down.

'Can you aviate – high-dive – drive a car – buck-jump – shoot?' read Miss Moss. She walked along the street asking herself those questions. There was a high, cold wind blowing; it tugged at her, slapped her face, jeered; it knew she could not answer them. In the Square Gardens she found a little wire basket to drop the form into. And then she sat down on one of the benches to powder her nose. But the person in the mirror made a hideous face at her, and that was too much for Miss Moss; she had a good cry. It cheered her wonderfully.

'Well, that's over,' she sighed. 'It's one comfort to be off my

feet. And my nose will soon get cool in the air . . . It's very
nice in here. Look at the sparrows. Cheep. Cheep. How close
they come. I expect somebody feeds them. No, I've nothing for
you, you cheeky little things . . .' She looked away from them.
What was the big building opposite – the Café de Madrid? My
goodness, what a smack that little child came down! Poor
little mite! Never mind – up again . . . By eight o'clock tonight
. . . Café de Madrid. 'I could just go in and sit there and have
a coffee, that's all,' thought Miss Moss. 'It's such a place for
artists too. I might just have a stroke of luck . . . A dark
handsome gentleman in a fur coat comes in with a friend, and
sits at my table, perhaps. "No, old chap, I've searched London
for a contralto and I can't find a soul. You see, the music is
difficult; have a look at it."' And Miss Moss heard herself
saying: 'Excuse me, I happen to be a contralto, and I have
sung that part many times . . . Extraordinary! "Come back to
my studio and I'll try your voice now." . . . Ten pounds a week
. . . Why should I feel nervous? It's not nervousness. Why
shouldn't I go to the Café de Madrid? I'm a respectable woman
– I'm a contralto singer. And I'm only trembling because I've
had nothing to eat today . . . "A nice little piece of evidence,
my lady." . . . Very well, Mrs Pine. Café de Madrid. They have
concerts there in the evenings . . . "Why don't they begin?"
The contralto has not arrived . . . "Excuse me, I happen to be
a contralto; I have sung that music many times."'

It was almost dark in the café. Men, palms, red plush seats,
white marble tables, waiters in aprons, Miss Moss walked
through them all. Hardly had she sat down when a very stout
gentleman wearing a very small hat that floated on the top of
his head like a little yacht flopped into the chair opposite
hers.

'Good evening!' said he.

Miss Moss said, in her cheerful way: 'Good evening!'

'Fine evening,' said the stout gentleman.

'Yes, very fine. Quite a treat, isn't it?' said she.

He crooked a sausage finger at the waiter – 'Bring me a
large whisky' – and turned to Miss Moss. 'What's yours?'

'Well, I think I'll take a brandy if it's all the same.'

Five minutes later the stout gentleman leaned across the
table and blew a puff of cigar smoke full in her face.

'That's a tempting bit o' ribbon!' said he.

Miss Moss blushed until a pulse at the top of her head that she never had felt before pounded away.

'I always was one for pink,' said she.

The stout gentleman considered her, drumming with her fingers on the table.

'I like 'em firm and well covered,' said he.

Miss Moss, to her surprise, gave a loud snigger.

Five minutes later the stout gentleman heaved himself up. 'Well, am I goin' your way, or are you comin' mine?' he asked.

'I'll come with you, if it's all the same,' said Miss Moss. And she sailed after the little yacht out of the café.

Bessie Head 1937–1986

Bessie Head was born in Pietermaritzburg, South Africa, in 1937. As the child of a white mother and a black father, Bessie Head suffered under South Africa's apartheid laws which said that her parents' relationship was illegal. After a traumatic early life she went into voluntary exile in Botswana in 1964. She spent fifteen years as a refugee in her adopted country before being granted citizenship in 1979. She worked as a teacher and novelist until her death in 1986.

Bessie Head's writing looks at the conflict between tradition and change in African society. She also explores the situation of women and the pressures they face. She published three novels, all of them set in Botswana, her country of exile. *When Rain Clouds Gather* was published in 1969 and was widely recognized as being the work of an important new writer. *Maru*, her second novel, published in 1971, told the story of a Masarwa woman brought up by a white missionary's wife in her own image and taught the meaning of pride. *A Question of Power*, her final novel, published in 1974, is a shattering story of a woman undergoing mental breakdown. Ronald Blythe, reviewing the novel in *The Sunday Times*, wrote, 'Bessie Head's vision of the separation of the mentally sick, and her ability to give mind-suffering a kind of picture language, convey a positively mediaeval horror.'

Botswana also provided the setting for Bessie Head's two collections of short stories: *The Collector of Treasures* and *Serowe: The Village of the Rain-Wind*. In this latter collection the history of an African community is reconstructed by a series of interviews with people living in the village.

In the story 'Looking for a Rain God' we see the desperation brought about by seven long years of drought. 'Tragedy was in the air' as the family of Mokgobja see their crops fail in the burning heat. The old man seeks an escape from this terrible pressure in memories of ancient customs from his youth.

Looking for a Rain God

Bessie Head

It is lonely at the lands where the people go to plough. These
lands are vast clearings in the bush, and the wild bush is
lonely too. Nearly all the lands are within walking distance
from the village. In some parts of the bush where the under-
ground water is very near the surface, people made little rest
camps for themselves and dug shallow wells to quench their
thirst while on their journey to their own lands. They experienced all kinds of things once they left the village. They could
rest at shady watering places full of lush, tangled trees with
delicate pale-gold and purple wild flowers springing up
between soft green moss and the children could hunt around
for wild figs and any berries that might be in season. But
from 1958, a seven-year drought fell upon the land and even
the watering places began to look as dismal as the dry open
thorn-bush country; the leaves of the trees curled up and
withered; the moss became dry and hard and, under the shade
of the tangled trees, the ground turned a powdery black and
white, because there was no rain. People said rather humor-
ously that if you tried to catch the rain in a cup it would only
fill a teaspoon. Towards the beginning of the seventh year of
drought, the summer had become an anguish to live through.
The air was so dry and moisture-free that it burned the skin.
No one knew what to do to escape the heat and tragedy was
in the air. At the beginning of that summer, a number of men
just went out of their homes and hung themselves to death
from trees. The majority of the people had lived off crops,
but for two years past they had all returned from the lands
with only their rolled-up skin blankets and cooking utensils.
Only the charlatans, incanters, and witch-doctors made a
pile of money during this time because people were always
turning to them in desperation for little talismans and

herbs to rub on the plough for the crops to grow and the rain to fall.

The rains were late that year. They came in early November, with a promise of good rain. It wasn't the full, steady downpour of the years of good rain, but thin, scanty, misty rain. If softened the earth and a rich growth of green things sprang up everywhere for the animals to eat. People were called to the village kgotla to hear the proclamation of the beginning of the ploughing season; they stirred themselves and whole families began to move off to the lands to plough.

The family of the old man, Mokgobja, were among those who left early for the lands. They had a donkey cart and piled everything onto it, Mokgobja – who was over seventy years old; two little girls, Neo and Boseyong; their mother Tiro and an unmarried sister, Nesta; and the father and supporter of the family, Ramadi, who drove the donkey cart. In the rush of the first hope of rain, the man, Ramadi, and the two women, cleared the land of thorn-bush and then hedged their vast ploughing area with this same thorn-bush to protect the future crop from the goats they had brought along for milk. They cleared out and deepened the old well with its pool of muddy water and still in this light, misty rain, Ramadi inspanned two oxen and turned the earth over with a hand plough.

The land was ready and ploughed, waiting for the crops. At night, the earth was alive with insects singing and rustling about in search of food. But suddenly, by mid-November, the rain fled away; the rain-clouds fled away and left the sky bare. The sun danced dizzily in the sky, with a strange cruelty. Each day the land was covered in a haze of mist as the sun sucked up the last drop of moisture out of the earth. The family sat down in despair, waiting and waiting. Their hopes had run so high; the goats had started producing milk, which they had eagerly poured on their porridge, now they ate plain porridge with no milk. It was impossible to plant the corn, maize, pumpkin and water-melon seeds in the dry earth. They sat the whole day in the shadow of the huts and even stopped thinking, for the rain had fled away. Only the children, Neo and Boseyong, were quite happy in their little girl world. They carried on with their game of making house like their mother and chattered to each other in light, soft tones. They made children from sticks around which they tied rags, and scolded them severely in an exact imitation of their own mother. Their voices could be heard scolding the day long: 'You stupid thing, when I send you to draw water, why do you spill half of it out of the bucket!' 'You stupid thing! Can't you mind the porridge-pot without letting the porridge burn!' And then they would beat the rag-dolls on their bottoms with severe expressions.

The adults paid no attention to this; they did not even hear the funny chatter; they sat waiting for rain; their nerves were stretched to breaking-point willing the rain to fall out of the sky. Nothing was important, beyond that. All their animals had been sold during the bad years to purchase food, and of all their herd only two goats were left. It was the women of the family who finally broke down under the strain of waiting for rain. It was really the two women who caused the death of the little girls. Each night they started a weird, high-pitched wailing that began on a low, mournful note and whipped up to a frenzy. Then they would stamp their feet and shout as though they had lost their heads. The men sat quiet and self-controlled; it was important for men to maintain their self-control at all times but their nerve was breaking too. They knew the women were haunted by the starvation of the coming year.

Finally, an ancient memory stirred in the old man, Mok-gobja. When he was very young and the customs of the ancestors still ruled the land, he had been witness to a rain-making ceremony. And he came alive a little, struggling to recall the details which had been buried by years and years of prayer in a Christian church. As soon as the mists cleared a little, he began consulting in whispers with his youngest son, Ramadi. There was, he said, a certain rain god who accepted only the sacrifice of the bodies of children. Then the rain would fall; then the crops would grow, he said. He explained the ritual and as he talked, his memory became a conviction and he began to talk with unshakable authority. Ramadi's nerves were smashed by the nightly wailing of the women and soon the two men began whispering with the two women. The children continued their game: 'You stupid thing! How could you have lost the money on the way to the shop! You must have been playing again!'

After it was all over and the bodies of the two little girls had been spread across the land, the rain did not fall. Instead, there was a deathly silence at night and the devouring heat of the sun by day. A terror, extreme and deep, overwhelmed the whole family. They packed, rolling up their skin blankets and pots, and fled back to the village.

People in the village soon noted the absence of the two little girls. They had died at the lands and were buried there, the family said. But people noted their ashen, terror-stricken faces and a murmur arose. What had killed the children, they wanted to know? And the family replied that they had just died. And people said amongst themselves that it was strange that the two deaths had occurred at the same time. And there was a feeling of great unease at the unnatural looks of the family. Soon the police came around. The family told them the same story of death and burial at the lands. They did not know what the children had died of. So the police asked to see the graves. At this, the mother of the children broke down and told everything.

Throughout that terrible summer the story of the children hung like a dark cloud of sorrow over the village, and the sorrow was not assuaged when the old man and Ramadi were sentenced to death for ritual murder. All they had on the statute books was that ritual murder was against the law and must be stamped out with the death penalty. The subtle story of strain and starvation and breakdown was inadmissible evidence at court; but all the people who lived off crops knew in their hearts that only a hair's breadth had saved them from sharing a fate similar to that of the Mokgobja family. They could have killed something to make the rain fall.

Charlotte Perkins Gilman 1860–1935

When Charlotte Perkins Gilman died in 1935 she left a huge legacy of writing – a volume of poetry (and hundreds of uncollected poems), nearly 200 short stories, nine novels and an enormous number of articles and essays. As a young woman she had determined that her life would be one of independence and work, and that work would be about improving the world. Running through all of her work is a deep-seated concern about injustice and inequality; throughout her life she worked for the trade union movement, for the cause of women's suffrage and for more equal treatment of men and women in all aspects of their home and working lives.

Born Charlotte Anna Perkins in Connecticut, USA, in 1860, she was brought up by her mother after her father left the family. She studied at art school and for a time made her living by designing greetings cards. In January 1882, she met Charles Walter Stetson, an artist well known for his charm and good looks. For some years she was unsure about marrying him. She worried particularly about whether she would be able to match what was expected of a wife and mother in American society at that time, and how she would be able to continue the political and artistic work she considered so important. In May 1884 she married and later gave birth to a daughter.

From the start of her marriage Charlotte Stetson was prone to depression; after Katharine's birth she fell into a post-natal depression so deep that her husband insisted on consulting a doctor famous for his treatment of women's nervous disorders. The doctor prescribed a 'rest cure': 'Live as domestic a life as possible ... Lie down an hour after each meal. Have but two hours intellectual life a day. And never touch pen, brush or pencil as long as you live.'

This 'cure' almost drove Charlotte Stetson mad. Her depression arose, at least in part, from her sense of being restricted and unable to work creatively. The 'treatment' made things so bad that she felt that she never fully recovered and that she was left to live 'a crippled life'. She wrote 'The Yellow Wallpaper' in 1892 to show how destructive such attitudes towards women could be.

Charlotte Stetson separated from her husband and

devoted herself to her work. She wrote and lectured, shared the care of her daughter and looked after her mother until her death. In 1900 she remarried – George Gilman, a first cousin. In 1932 Charlotte Perkins Gilman found that she had an inoperable cancer; in 1935, when the end was in sight, she committed suicide, preferring, as she explained in her note, 'chloroform to cancer'.

'Turned' is a story unusual for its time. Published first in 1911, it is typical of Gilman's sharp eye for the difficulties of marriage and her belief in the power of solidarity.

Turned

Charlotte Perkins Gilman

In her soft-carpeted, thick-curtained, richly furnished chamber, Mrs Marroner lay sobbing on the wide, soft bed.

She sobbed bitterly, chokingly, despairingly; her shoulders heaved and shook convulsively; her hands were tight-clenched. She had forgotten her elaborate dress, the more elaborate bed-cover; forgotten her dignity, her self-control, her pride. In her mind was an overwhelming, unbelievable horror, an immeasurable loss, a turbulent, struggling mass of emotion.

In her reserved, superior, Boston-bred life, she had never dreamed that it would be possible for her to feel so many things at once, and with such trampling intensity.

She tried to cool her feelings into thoughts; to stiffen them into words; to control herself – and could not. It brought vaguely to her mind an awful moment in the breakers at York Beach, one summer in girlhood when she had been swimming under water and could not find the top.

In her uncarpeted, thin-curtained, poorly furnished chamber on the top floor, Gerta Petersen lay sobbing on the narrow, hard bed.

She was of larger frame than her mistress, grandly built and strong; but all her proud young womanhood was prostrate now, convulsed with agony, dissolved in tears. She did not try to control herself. She wept for two.

If Mrs Marroner suffered more from the wreck and ruin of a longer love – perhaps a deeper one; if her tastes were finer, her ideals loftier; if she bore the pangs of bitter jealousy and outraged pride, Gerta had personal shame to meet, a hopeless future, and a looming present which filled her with unreasoning terror.

She had come like a meek young goddess into that perfectly ordered house, strong, beautiful, full of goodwill and eager obedience, but ignorant and childish – a girl of eighteen.

Mr Marroner had frankly admired her, and so had his wife. They discussed her visible perfections and as visible limitations with that perfect confidence which they had so long enjoyed. Mrs Marroner was not a jealous woman. She had never been jealous in her life – till now.

Gerta had stayed and learned their ways. They had both been fond of her. Even the cook was fond of her. She was what is called 'willing,' was unusually teachable and plastic; and Mrs Marroner, with her early habits of giving instruction, tried to educate her somewhat.

'I never saw anyone so docile,' Mrs Marroner had often commented. 'It is perfection in a servant, but almost a defect in character. She is so helpless and confiding.'

She was precisely that: a tall, rosy-cheeked baby; rich womanhood without, helpless infancy within. Her braided wealth of dead-gold hair, her grave blue eyes, her mighty shoulders and long, firmly moulded limbs seemed those of a primal earth spirit; but she was only an ignorant child, with a child's weaknesses.

When Mr Marroner had to go abroad for his firm, unwillingly, hating to leave his wife, he had told her he felt quite safe to leave her in Gerta's hands – she would take care of her.

'Be good to your mistress, Gerta,' he told the girl that last morning at breakfast. 'I leave her to you to take care of. I shall be back in a month at latest.'

Then he turned, smiling, to his wife. 'And you must take care of Gerta, too,' he said. 'I expect you'll have her ready for college when I get back.'

This was seven months ago. Business had delayed him from week to week, from month to month. He wrote to his wife, long, loving, frequent letters, deeply regretting the delay, explaining how necessary, how profitable it was, congratulating her on the wide resources she had, her well-filled, well-balanced mind, her many interests.

'If I should be eliminated from your scheme of things, by any of those "acts of God" mentioned on the tickets, I do not feel that you would be an utter wreck,' he said. 'That is very comforting to me. Your life is so rich and wide that no one loss, even a great one, would wholly cripple you. But nothing of the sort is likely to happen, and I shall be home again in three weeks – if this thing gets settled. And you will be looking so lovely, with that eager light in your eyes and the changing flush I know so well – and love so well! My dear wife! We shall have to have a new honeymoon – other moons come every month, why shouldn't the mellifluous kind?'

He often asked after 'little Gerta,' sometimes enclosed a picture postcard to her, joked his wife about her laborious efforts to educate 'the child,' was so loving and merry and wise –

All this was racing through Mrs Marroner's mind as she lay there with the broad, hemstitched border of fine linen sheeting crushed and twisted in one hand, and the other holding a sodden handkerchief.

She had tried to teach Gerta, and had grown to love the patient, sweet-natured child, in spite of her dullness. At work with her hands, she was clever, if not quick, and could keep small accounts from week to week. But to the woman who held a Ph.D., who had been on the faculty of a college, it was like baby-tending.

Perhaps having no babies of her own made her love the big child the more, though the years between them were but fifteen.

To the girl she seemed quite old, of course; and her young heart was full of grateful affection for the patient care which made her feel so much at home in this new land.

And then she had noticed a shadow on the girl's bright face. She looked nervous, anxious, worried. When the bell rang, she seemed startled, and would rush hurriedly to the door. Her peals of frank laughter no longer rose from the area gate as she stood talking with the always admiring tradesmen.

Mrs Marroner had labored long to teach her more reserve with men, and flattered herself that her words were at last effective. She suspected the girl of homesickness, which was denied. She suspected her of illness, which was denied also. At last she suspected her of something which could not be denied.

For a long time she refused to believe it, waiting. Then she had to believe it, but schooled herself to patience and understanding. 'The poor child,' she said. 'She is here without a mother – she is so foolish and yielding – I must not be too stern with her.' And she tried to win the girl's confidence with wise, kind words.

But Gerta had literally thrown herself at her feet and begged her with streaming tears not to turn her away. She would admit nothing, explain nothing, but frantically promised to work for Mrs Marroner as long as she lived – if only she would keep her.

Revolving the problem carefully in her mind, Mrs Marroner thought she would keep her, at least for the present. She tried to repress her sense of ingratitude in one she had so sincerely tried to help, and the cold, contemptuous anger she had always felt for such weakness.

'The thing to do now,' she said to herself, 'is to see her through this safely. The child's life should not be hurt any more than is unavoidable. I will ask Dr Bleet about it – what a comfort a woman doctor is! I'll stand by the poor, foolish thing till it's over, and then get her back to Sweden somehow with her baby. How they do come where they are not wanted – and don't come where they are wanted!' And Mrs Marroner, sitting alone in the quiet, spacious beauty of the house, almost envied Gerta.

Then came the deluge.

She had sent the girl out for needed air toward dark. The late mail came; she took it in herself. One letter for her – her husband's letter. She knew the postmark, the stamp, the kind of typewriting. She impulsively kissed it in the dim hall. No one would suspect Mrs Marroner of kissing her husband's letters – but she did, often.

She looked over the others. One was for Gerta, and not from Sweden. It looked precisely like her own. This struck her as a little odd, but Mr Marroner had several times sent messages and cards to the girl. She laid the letter on the hall table and took hers to her room.

'My poor child,' it began. What letter of hers had been sad enough to warrant that?

'I am deeply concerned at the news you send.' What news to so concern him had she written? 'You must bear it bravely, little girl. I shall be home soon, and will take care of you, of course. I hope there is not immediate anxiety – you do not say. Here is money, in case you need it. I expect to get home in a month at latest. If you have to go, be sure to leave your address at my office. Cheer up – be brave – I will take care of you.'

The letter was typewritten, which was not unusual. It was unsigned, which was unusual. It enclosed an American bill – fifty dollars. It did not seem in the least like any letter she had ever had from her husband, or any letter she could imagine him writing. But a strange, cold feeling was creeping over her, like a flood rising around a house.

She utterly refused to admit the ideas which began to bob and push about outside her mind, and to force themselves in. Yet under the pressure of these repudiated thoughts she went downstairs and brought up the other letter – the letter to Gerta. She laid them side by side on a smooth dark space on the table; marched to the piano and played, with stern precision, refusing to think, till the girl came back. When she came in, Mrs Marroner rose quietly and came to the table. 'Here is a letter for you,' she said.

The girl stepped forward eagerly, saw the two lying together there, hesitated, and looked at her mistress.

'Take yours, Gerta. Open it, please.'

The girl turned frightened eyes upon her.

'I want you to read it, here,' said Mrs Marroner.

'Oh, ma'am – No! Please don't make me!'

'Why not?'

There seemed to be no reason at hand, and Gerta flushed more deeply and opened her letter. It was long; it was evidently puzzling to her; it began 'My dear wife.' She read it slowly.

'Are you sure it is your letter?' asked Mrs Marroner. 'Is not this one yours? Is not that one – mine?'

She held out the other letter to her.

'It is a mistake,' Mrs Marroner went on, with a hard quietness. She had lost her social bearings somehow, lost her usual keen sense of the proper thing to do. This was not life; this was a nightmare.

'Do you not see? Your letter was put in my envelope and my letter was put in your envelope. Now we understand it.'

But poor Gerta had no antechamber to her mind, no trained forces to preserve order while agony entered. The thing swept over her, resistless, overwhelming. She cowered before the outraged wrath she expected; and from some hidden cavern that wrath arose and swept over her in pale flame.

'Go and pack your trunk,' said Mrs Marroner. 'You will leave my house tonight. Here is your money.'

She laid down the fifty-dollar bill. She put with it a month's wages. She had no shadow of pity for those anguished eyes, those tears which she heard drop on the floor.

'Go to your room and pack,' said Mrs Marroner. And Gerta, always obedient, went.

Then Mrs Marroner went to hers, and spent a time she never counted, lying on her face on the bed.

But the training of the twenty-eight years which had elapsed before her marriage; the life at college, both as student and teacher; the independent growth which she had made, formed a very different background for grief from that in Gerta's mind.

After a while Mrs Marroner arose. She administered to herself a hot bath, a cold shower, a vigorous rubbing. 'Now I can think,' she said.

First she regretted the sentence of instant banishment. She went upstairs to see if it had been carried out. Poor Gerta! The tempest of her agony had worked itself out at last as in a child, and left her sleeping, the pillow wet, the lips still grieving, a big sob shuddering itself off now and then.

Mrs Marroner stood and watched her, and as she watched she considered the helpless sweetness of the face; the defenseless, unformed character; the docility and habit of obedience which made her so attractive – and so easily a victim. Also she thought of the mighty force which had swept over her; of the great process now working itself out through her; of how pitiful and futile seemed any resistance she might have made.

She softly returned to her own room, made up a little fire, and sat by it, ignoring her feelings now, as she had before ignored her thoughts.

Here were two women and a man. One woman was a wife: loving, trusting, affectionate. One was a servant: loving, trusting, affectionate – a young girl, an exile, a dependent; grateful for any kindness; untrained, uneducated, childish. She ought, of course, to have resisted temptation; but Mrs Marroner was wise enough to know how difficult temptation is to recognize when it comes in the guise of friendship and from a source one does not suspect.

Gerta might have done better in resisting the grocer's clerk; had, indeed, with Mrs Marroner's advice, resisted several.

But where respect was due, how could she criticize? Where obedience was due, how could she refuse – with ignorance to hold her blinded – until too late?

As the older, wiser woman forced herself to understand and extenuate the girl's misdeed and foresee her ruined future, a new feeling rose in her heart, strong, clear, and overmastering: a sense of measureless condemnation for the man who had done this thing. He knew. He understood. He could fully foresee and measure the consequences of his act. He appreciated to the full the innocence, the ignorance, the grateful affection, the habitual docility, of which he deliberately took advantage.

Mrs Marroner rose to icy peaks of intellectual apprehension, from which her hours of frantic pain seemed far indeed removed. He had done this thing under the same roof with her – his wife. He had not frankly loved the younger woman, broken with his wife, made a new marriage. That would have been heart-break pure and simple. This was something else.

That letter, that wretched, cold, carefully guarded, unsigned letter, that bill – far safer than a check – these did not speak of affection. Some men can love two women at one time. This was not love.

Mrs Marroner's sense of pity and outrage for herself, the wife, now spread suddenly into a perception of pity and outrage for the girl. All that splendid, clean young beauty, the hope of a happy life, with marriage and motherhood, honorable independence, even – these were nothing to that man. For his own pleasure he had chosen to rob her of her life's best joys.

He would 'take care of her,' said the letter. How? In what capacity?

And then, sweeping over both her feelings for herself, the wife, and Gerta, his victim, came a new flood, which literally lifted her to her feet. She rose and walked, her head held high. 'This is the sin of man against woman,' she said. 'The offense is against womanhood. Against motherhood. Against – the child.'

She stopped.

The child. His child. That, too, he sacrificed and injured – doomed to degradation.

Mrs Marroner came of stern New England stock. She was not a Calvinist, hardly even a Unitarian, but the iron of

Calvinism was in her soul: of that grim faith which held that most people had to be damned 'for the glory of God.'

Generations of ancestors who both preached and practiced stood behind her; people whose lives had been sternly moulded to their highest moments of religious conviction. In sweeping bursts of feeling, they achieved 'conviction,' and afterward they lived and died according to that conviction.

When Mr Marroner reached home a few weeks later, following his letters too soon to expect an answer to either, he saw no wife upon the pier, though he had cabled, and found the house closed darkly. He let himself in with his latch-key, and stole softly upstairs, to surprise his wife.

No wife was there.

He rang the bell. No servant answered it.

He turned up light after light, searched the house from top to bottom; it was utterly empty. The kitchen wore a clean, bald, unsympathetic aspect. He left it and slowly mounted the stairs, completely dazed. The whole house was clean, in perfect order, wholly vacant.

One thing he felt perfectly sure of – she knew.

Yet was he sure? He must not assume too much. She might have been ill. She might have died. He started to his feet. No, they would have cabled him. He sat down again.

For any such change, if she had wanted him to know, she would have written. Perhaps she had, and he, returning so suddenly, had missed the letter. The thought was some comfort. It must be so. He turned to the telephone and again hesitated. If she had found out – if she had gone – utterly gone, without a word – should he announce it himself to friends and family?

He walked the floor; he searched everywhere for some letter, some word of explanation. Again and again he went to the telephone – and always stopped. He could not bear to ask: 'Do you know where my wife is?'

The harmonious, beautiful rooms reminded him in a dumb, helpless way of her – like the remote smile on the face of the dead. He put out the lights, could not bear the darkness, turned them all on again.

It was a long night –

In the morning he went early to the office. In the accumulated mail was no letter from her. No one seemed to know of anything unusual. A friend asked after his wife – 'Pretty glad to see you, I guess?' He answered evasively.

About eleven a man came to see him: John Hill, her lawyer. Her cousin, too. Mr Marroner had never liked him. He liked him less now, for Mr Hill merely handed him a letter, remarked, 'I was requested to deliver this to you personally,' and departed, looking like a person who is called on to kill something offensive.

'I have gone. I will care for Gerta. Good-bye. Marion.'

That was all. There was no date, no address, no postmark, nothing but that.

In his anxiety and distress, he had fairly forgotten Gerta and all that. Her name aroused in him a sense of rage. She had come between him and his wife. She had taken his wife from him. That was the way he felt.

At first he said nothing, did nothing, lived on alone in his house, taking meals where he chose. When people asked him about his wife, he said she was traveling – for her health. He would not have it in the newspapers. Then, as time passed, as no enlightenment came to him, he resolved not to bear it any longer, and employed detectives. They blamed him for not having put them on the track earlier, but set to work, urged to the utmost secrecy.

What to him had been so blank a wall of mystery seemed not to embarrass them in the least. They made careful inquiries as to her 'past,' found where she had studied, where taught, and on what lines; that she had some little money of her own, that her doctor was Josephine L. Bleet, M.D., and many other bits of information.

As a result of careful and prolonged work, they finally told him that she had resumed teaching under one of her old professors, lived quietly, and apparently kept boarders; giving him town, street, and number, as if it were a matter of no difficulty whatever.

He had returned in early spring. It was autumn before he found her.

A quiet college town in the hills, a broad, shady street, a pleasant house standing in its own lawn, with trees and flowers about it. He had the address in his hand, and the number showed clear on the white gate. He walked up the straight gravel path and rang the bell. An elderly servant opened the door.

'Does Mrs Marroner live here?'

'No, sir.'

'This is number twenty-eight?'

'Yes, sir.'

'Who does live here?'

'Miss Wheeling, sir.'

Ah! Her maiden name. They had told him, but he had forgotten.

He stepped inside. 'I would like to see her,' he said.

He was ushered into a still parlor, cool and sweet with the scent of flowers, the flowers she had always loved best. It almost brought tears to his eyes. All their years of happiness rose in his mind again – the exquisite beginnings; the days of eager longing before she was really his; the deep, still beauty of her love.

Surely she would forgive him – she must forgive him. He would humble himself; he would tell her of his honest remorse – his absolute determination to be a different man.

Through the wide doorway there came in to him two women. One like a tall Madonna, bearing a baby in her arms.

Marion, calm, steady, definitely impersonal, nothing but a clear pallor to hint of inner stress.

Gerta, holding the child as a bulwark, with a new intelligence in her face, and her blue, adoring eyes fixed on her friend – not upon him.

He looked from one to the other dumbly.

And the woman who had been his wife asked quietly:

'What have you to say to us?'

D. H. Lawrence 1885–1930

David Herbert Richards Lawrence was born in Eastwood, Nottinghamshire, on 11 September 1885. He was the fourth child of Arthur Lawrence, a miner, and Lydia, who had been a teacher. Lawrence was the first boy from his primary school, Beauvale Board School, to win a scholarship to Nottingham High School, which he attended until 1901. When he left school he began work as a clerk at Haywood's surgical appliances factory, but had to leave when his older brother died and he himself contracted a severe attack of pneumonia.

Lawrence worked as a pupil–teacher in Eastwood until he began his teachers' certificate course at Nottingham University College in 1906. He wrote his first poems and stories at this time and began his first novel. From 1908 to 1911 he worked as a teacher in Croydon. He wrote prolifically, and his poems and stories began to be published. His first novel, *The White Peacock*, was published in 1911.

In 1910 Lawrence's mother died of cancer. After giving up teaching, he worked on a range of literary projects, including writing the novel *Sons and Lovers*, in which he drew upon his own experiences of growing up, particularly his relationships with his mother and father, and his active love life. In 1912 Lawrence met Frieda Weekly, the wife of his former modern languages professor; six weeks later he eloped with her to Germany. They walked over the Alps into Italy and settled there while Lawrence finished *Sons and Lovers*.

Lawrence led an unsettled life over the next decade, travelling, between England and Italy mainly, but writing prolifically. He became a controversial figure. His politics, his novels and his life-style were considered outrageous by some; he gave joint lectures with Bertrand Russell against war, made plans for an ideal community, and tried to set up a revolutionary anti-war political party. His novel *The Rainbow* was published and then immediately suppressed in 1914; in 1917 he was ordered out of Cornwall on suspicion of spying.

In the early 1920s Lawrence travelled further afield, visiting Ceylon and Australia and settling for some time on a ranch in New Mexico. He continued to write poetry, short stories, novels and non-fiction pieces, but he suffered from periodic

D. H. Lawrence

bouts of ill health and depression. In 1925 a doctor in Mexico City told Frieda that Lawrence was dying of tuberculosis, but he rallied and fought against ill health for another five years, during which time he continued to write and to travel, and took up painting seriously. In 1928 his novel *Lady Chatterley's Lover*, which was more sexually explicit than was common at the time, caused a furore in the press and was confiscated; in 1929 a show of his paintings was raided by the police and a collection of his poems was seized in the mail. He died of tuberculosis in 1930. He was buried in France until 1935 when his body was exhumed and cremated, and his ashes were taken to his ranch in Taos, where Frieda lived with her third husband until her death in 1956.

Lawrence's prolific writing included nearly one thousand poems, as well as travel books, plays, essays and novels. He was interested in exploring the internal lives of his characters and often concentrated on episodes of great intensity. His uncompromising frankness and refusal to conform to social and literary conventions led to censorship and the banning of some of his books during his lifetime – notably *Lady Chatterley's Lover* which was not published in Britain in its unexpurgated form until 1960, after a famous trial. His short story 'Strike-pay' draws upon themes that are familiar in Lawrence's work: life in a mining village and tensions within the family.

Strike-pay

D. H. Lawrence

Strike-money is paid in the Primitive Methodist Chapel. The crier was round quite early on Wednesday morning to say that paying would begin at ten o'clock.

The Primitive Methodist Chapel is a big barn of a place, built, designed, and paid for by the colliers themselves. But it threatened to fall down from its first form, so that a professional architect had to be hired at last to pull the place together.

It stands in the Square. Forty years ago, when Bryan and Wentworth opened their pits, they put up the 'squares' of miners' dwellings. They are two great quadrangles of houses, enclosing a barren stretch of ground, littered with broken pots and rubbish, which forms a square, a great, sloping, lumpy playground for the children, a drying-ground for many women's washing.

Wednesday is still wash-day with some women. As the men clustered round the Chapel, they heard the thud-thud-thud of many pouches, women pounding away at the wash-tub with a wooden pestle. In the Square the white clothes were waving in the wind from a maze of clothes-lines, and here and there women were pegging out, calling to the miners, or to the children who dodged under the flapping sheets.

Ben Townsend, the Union agent, has a bad way of paying. He takes the men in order of his round, and calls them by name. A big, oratorical man with a grey beard, he sat at the table in the Primitive school-room, calling name after name. The room was crowded with colliers, and a great group pushed up outside. There was much confusion. Ben dodged from the Scargill Street list to the Queen Street. For this Queen Street men were not prepared. They were not to the fore.

'Joseph Grooby – Joseph Grooby! Now, Joe, where are you?'

'Hold on a bit, Sorry!' cried Joe from outside. 'I'm shovin' up.'

There was a great noise from the men.

'I'm takin' Queen Street. All you Queen Street men should be ready. Here you are, Joe,' said the Union agent loudly.

'Five children!' said Joe, counting the money suspiciously.

'That's right, I think,' came the mouthing voice. 'Fifteen shillings, is it not?'

'A bob a kid,' said the collier.

'Thomas Sedgwick – How are you, Tom? Missis better?'

'Ay, 'er's shapin' nicely. Tha'rt hard at work to-day, Ben.' This was sarcasm on the idleness of a man who had given up the pit to become a Union agent.

'Yes. I rose at four to fetch the money.'

'Dunna hurt thysen,' was the retort, and the men laughed.

'No – John Merfin!'

But the colliers, tired with waiting, excited by the strike spirit, began to rag. Merfin was young and dandiacal. He was choir-master at the Wesleyan Chapel.

'Does your collar cut, John?' asked a sarcastic voice out of the crowd.

'Hymn Number Nine.

> "Diddle-diddle dumpling, my son John
> Went to bed with his best suit on,"'

came the solemn announcement.

Mr Merfin, his white cuffs down to his knuckles, picked up his half-sovereign, and walked away loftily.

'Sam Coutts!' cried the paymaster.

'Now, lad, reckon it up,' shouted the voice of the crowd, delighted.

Mr Coutts was a straight-backed ne'er-do-well. He looked at his twelve shillings sheepishly.

'Another two-bob – he had twins a-Monday night – get thy money, Sam, tha's earned it – tha's addled it, Sam; dunna go be-out it. Let him ha' the two bob for 'is twins, mister,' came the clamour from the men around.

Sam Coutts stood grinning awkwardly.

'You should ha' given us notice, Sam,' said the paymaster suavely. 'We can make it all right for you next week – '

'Nay, nay, nay,' shouted a voice. 'Pay on delivery – the goods is there right enough.'

'Get thy money, Sam, tha's addled it,' became the universal cry, and the Union agent had to hand over another florin, to prevent a disturbance. Sam Coutts grinned with satisfaction.

'Good shot, Sam,' the men exclaimed.

'Ephraim Wharmby,' shouted the pay-man.

A lad came forward.

'Gi' him sixpence for what's on t'road,' said a sly voice.

'Nay, nay,' replied Ben Townsend; 'pay on delivery.'

There was a roar of laughter. The miners were in high spirits.

In the town they stood about in gangs, talking and laughing. Many sat on their heels in the market-place. In and out of the public-houses they went, and on every bar the half-sovereigns clicked.

'Comin' ter Nottingham wi' us, Ephraim?' said Sam Coutts to the slender, pale young fellow of about twenty-two.

'I'm non walkin' that far of a gleamy day like this.'

'He has na got the strength,' said somebody, and a laugh went up.

'How's that?' asked another pertinent voice.

'He's a married man, mind yer,' said Chris Smitheringale, 'an' it ta'es a bit o' keepin' up.'

The youth was teased in this manner for some time.

'Come on ter Nottingham wi's; tha'll be safe for a bit,' said Coutts.

A gang set off, although it was only eleven o'clock. It was a nine-mile walk. The road was crowded with colliers travelling on foot to see the match between Notts and Aston Villa. In Ephraim's gang were Sam Coutts, with his fine shoulders and his extra florin, Chris Smitheringale, fat and smiling, and John Wharmby, a remarkable man, tall, erect as a soldier, black-haired and proud; he could play any musical instrument, he declared.

'I can play owt from a comb up'ards. If there's music to be got outer a thing, I back I'll get it. No matter what shape or form of instrument you set before me, it doesn't signify if I nivir clapped eyes on it before, I's warrant I'll have a tune out of it in five minutes.'

He beguiled the first two miles so. It was true, he had caused a sensation by introducing the mandoline into the

townlet, filling the hearts of his fellow-colliers with pride as
he sat on the platform in evening dress, a fine soldierly man,
bowing his black head, and scratching the mewing mandoline
with hands that had only to grasp the 'instrument' to crush it
entirely.

Chris stood a can round at the 'White Bull' at Gilt Brook.
John Wharmby took his turn at Kimberley top.

'We wunna drink again,' they decided, 'till we're at Cinder
Hill. We'll non stop i' Nuttall.'

They swung along the high-road under the budding trees.
In Nuttall churchyard the crocuses blazed with yellow at the
brim of the balanced, black yews. White and purple crocuses
clipt up over the graves, as if the churchyard were bursting
out in tiny tongues of flame.

'Sithee,' said Ephraim, who was an ostler down pit, 'sithee,
here comes the Colonel. Sithee at his 'osses how they pick
their toes up, the beauties!'

The Colonel drove past the men, who took no notice of him.

'Hast heard, Sorry,' said Sam, 'as they're com'n out i'
Germany, by the thousand, an' begun riotin'?'

'An' comin' out i' France simbitar,' cried Chris.

The men all gave a chuckle.

'Sorry,' shouted John Wharmby, much elated, 'we oughtna
ter go back under a twenty per cent rise.'

'We should get it,' said Chris.

'An' easy! They can do nowt bi-out us, we'n on'y ter stop out
long enough.'

'I'm willin',' said Sam, and there was a laugh. The colliers
looked at one another. A thrill went through them as if an
electric current passed.

'We'n on'y ter stick out, an' we s'll see who's gaffer.'

'Us!' cried Sam. 'Why, what can they do again' us, if we
come out all over th' world?'

'Nowt!' said John Wharmby. 'Th' mesters is bobbin' about
like corks on a cassivoy a'ready.' There was a large natural
reservoir, like a lake, near Bestwood, and this supplied the
simile.

Again there passed through the men that wave of elation,
quickening their pulses. They chuckled in their throats.
Beyond all consciousness was this sense of battle and triumph
in the hearts of the working-men at this juncture.

It was suddenly suggested at Nuttall that they should go

over the fields to Bulwell, and into Nottingham that way. They went single file across the fallow, past the wood, and over the railway, where now no trains were running. Two fields away was a troop of pit ponies. Of all colours, but chiefly of red or brown, they clustered thick in the field, scarcely moving, and the two lines of trodden earth patches showed where fodder was placed down the field.

'Theer's the pit 'osses,' said Sam. 'Let's run 'em.'

'It's like a circus turned out. See them skewbawd 'uns – seven skewbawd,' said Ephraim.

The ponies were inert, unused to freedom. Occasionally one walked round. But there they stood, two thick lines of ruddy brown and piebald and white, across the trampled field. It was a beautiful day, mild, pale blue, a 'growing day', as the men said, when there was the silence of swelling sap everywhere.

'Let's ha'e a ride,' said Ephraim.

The younger men went up to the horses.

'Come on – co-oop, Taffy – co-oop, Ginger.'

The horses tossed away. But having got over the excitement of being above-ground, the animals were feeling dazed and rather dreary. They missed the warmth and the life of the pit. They looked as if life were a blank to them.

Ephraim and Sam caught a couple of steeds, on whose backs they went careering round, driving the rest of the sluggish herd from end to end of the field. The horses were good specimens, on the whole, and in fine condition. But they were out of their element.

Performing too clever a feat, Ephraim went rolling from his mount. He was soon up again, chasing his horse. Again he was thrown. Then the men proceeded on their way.

They were drawing near to miserable Bulwell, when Ephraim, remembering his turn was coming to stand drinks, felt in his pocket for his beloved half-sovereign, his strike-pay. It was not there. Through all his pockets he went, his heart sinking like lead.

'Sam,' he said, 'I believe I'n lost that ha'ef a sovereign.'

'Tha's got it somewheer about thee,' said Chris.

They made him take off his coat and waistcoat. Chris examined the coat, Sam the waistcoat, whilst Ephraim searched his trousers.

'Well,' said Chris, 'I'n foraged this coat, an' it's non theer.'

'An' I'll back my life as th' on'y bit a metal on this wa'scoat is the buttons,' said Sam.

'An' it's non in my breeches,' said Ephraim. He took off his boots and his stockings. The half-sovereign was not there. He had not another coin in his possession.

'Well,' said Chris, 'we mun go back an' look for it.'

Back they went, four serious-hearted colliers, and searched the field, but in vain.

'Well,' said Chris, 'we s'll ha'e ter share wi' thee, that's a'.'

'I'm willin',' said John Wharmby.

'An' me,' said Sam.

'Two bob each,' said Chris.

Ephraim, who was in the depths of despair, shamefully accepted their six shillings.

In Bulwell they called in a small public-house, which had one long room with a brick floor, scrubbed benches and scrubbed tables. The central space was open. The place was full of colliers, who were drinking. There was a great deal of drinking during the strike, but not a vast amount drunk. Two men were playing skittles, and the rest were betting. The seconds sat on either side the skittle-board, holding caps of money, sixpences and coppers, the wagers of the 'backers'.

Sam, Chris, and John Wharmby immediately put money on the man who had their favour. In the end Sam declared himself willing to play against the victor. He was the Bestwood champion. Chris and John Wharmby backed him heavily, and even Ephraim the Unhappy ventured sixpence.

In the end, Sam won half a crown, with which he promptly stood drinks and bread and cheese for his comrades. At half-past one they set off again.

It was a good match between Notts and Villa – no goals at half-time, two-none for Notts at the finish. The colliers were hugely delighted, especially as Flint, the forward for Notts, who was an Underwood man well known to the four comrades, did some handsome work, putting the two goals through.

Ephraim determined to go home as soon as the match was over. He knew John Wharmby would be playing the piano at the 'Punch Bowl', and Sam, who had a good tenor voice, singing, while Chris cut in with witticisms, until evening. So he bade them farewell, as he must get home. They, finding him somewhat of a damper on their spirits, let him go.

He was the sadder for having witnessed an accident near

the football-ground. A navvy, working at some drainage, carting an iron tip-tub of mud and emptying it, had got with his horse on to the deep deposit of ooze which was crusted over. The crust had broken, the man had gone under the horse, and it was some time before the people had realised he had vanished. When they found his feet sticking out, and hauled him forth, he was dead, stifled dead in the mud. The horse was at length hauled out, after having its neck nearly pulled from the socket.

Ephraim went home vaguely impressed with a sense of death, and loss, and strife. Death was loss greater than his own, the strike was a battle greater than that he would presently have to fight.

He arrived home at seven o'clock, just when it had fallen dark. He lived in Queen Street with his young wife, to whom he had been married two months, and with his mother-in-law, a widow of sixty-four. Maud was the last child remaining unmarried, the last of eleven.

Ephraim went up the entry. The light was burning in the kitchen. His mother-in-law was a big, erect woman, with wrinkled, loose face, and cold blue eyes. His wife was also large, with very vigorous fair hair, frizzy like unravelled rope. She had a quiet way of stepping, a certain cat-like stealth, in spite of her large build. She was five months pregnant.

'Might we ask wheer you've been to?' inquired Mrs Marriott, very erect, very dangerous. She was only polite when she was very angry.

'I'n bin ter th' match.'

'Oh, indeed!' said the mother-in-law. 'And why couldn't we be told as you thought of jaunting off?'

'I didna know mysen,' he answered, sticking to his broad Derbyshire.

'I suppose it popped into your mind, an' so you darted off,' said the mother-in-law dangerously.

'I didna. It wor Chris Smitheringale who exed me.'

'An' did you take much invitin'?'

'I didna want ter goo.'

'But wasn't there enough man beside your jacket to say no?'

He did not answer. Down at the bottom he hated her. But he was, to use his own words, all messed up with having lost his strike-pay and with knowing the man was dead. So he was more helpless before his mother-in-law, whom he feared.

His wife neither looked at him nor spoke, but kept her head bowed. He knew she was with her mother.

'Our Maud's been waitin' for some money, to get a few things,' said the mother-in-law.

In silence, he put five-and-sixpence on the table.

'Take that up, Maud,' said the mother.

Maud did so.

'You'll want it for us board, shan't you?' she asked, furtively, of her mother.

'Might I ask if there's nothing you want to buy yourself, first?'

'No, there's nothink I want,' answered the daughter.

Mrs Marriott took the silver and counted it.

'And do you,' said the mother-in-law, towering upon the shrinking son, but speaking slowly and statelily, 'do you think I'm going to keep you and your wife for five and sixpence a week?'

'It's a' I've got,' he answered sulkily.

'You've had a good jaunt, my sirs, if it's cost four and sixpence. You've started your game early, haven't you?'

He did not answer.

'It's a nice thing! Here's our Maud an' me been sitting since eleven o'clock this morning! Dinner waiting and cleared away, tea waiting and washed up; then in he comes crawling with five and sixpence. Five and sixpence for a man an' wife's board for a week, if you please!'

Still he did not say anything.

'You must think something of yourself, Ephraim Wharmby!' said his mother-in-law. 'You must think something of yourself. You suppose, do you, *I'm* going to keep you an' your wife, while you make a holiday, off on the nines to Nottingham, drink an' women.'

'I've neither had drink nor women, as you know right well,' he said.

'I'm glad we know summat about you. For you're that close, anybody'd think we was foreigners to you. You're a pretty little jockey, aren't you? Oh, it's a gala time for you, the strike is. That's all men strike for, indeed. They enjoy themselves, they do that. Ripping and racing and drinking, from morn till night, my sirs!'

'Is there on'y tea for me?' he asked, in a temper.

'Hark at him! Hark-ye! Should I ask you whose house you

think you're in? Kindly order me about, do. Oh, it makes him big, the strike does. See him land home after being out on the spree for hours, and give his orders, my sirs! Oh, strike sets the men up, it does. Nothing have they to do but guzzle and gallivant to Nottingham. Their wives'll keep them, oh yes. So long as they get something to eat at home, what more do they want! What more *should* they want, prithee? Nothing! Let the women and children starve and scrape, but fill the man's belly, and let him have his fling. My sirs, indeed, I think so! Let tradesmen go – what do they matter! Let rent go. Let children get what they can catch. Only the man will see *he's* all right. But not here, though!'

'Are you goin' ter gi'e me ony bloody tea?'

His mother-in-law started up.

'If tha dares ter swear at me, I'll lay thee flat.'

'Are yer – goin' ter – gi'e me – any blasted, rotten, còssed, blòody tèa?' he bawled, in a fury, accenting every other word deliberately.

'Maud!' said the mother-in-law, cold and stately, 'If you gi'e him any tea after that, you're a trollops.' Whereupon she sailed out to her other daughters.

Maud quietly got the tea ready.

'Shall y'ave your dinner warmed up?' she asked.

'Ay.'

She attended to him. Not that she was really meek. But – he was *her* man, not her mother's.

Thomas Hardy 1840–1928

Thomas Hardy was born in 1840, the son of a builder in the rural county of Dorset. Hardy is sometimes thought of as a 'self-educated' man; in fact he went to Dorchester High School and then trained as an architect, spending some time in London. His main interest, though, was in the countryside and people of Wessex – that area of southern England made up of Dorset and its neighbouring counties. In his novels, such as *Tess of the d'Urbervilles* (1891) and *Jude the Obscure* (1895), he set out to observe and describe the lives of ordinary people. He wrote about their life and work, about the making and breaking of relationships.

Although Hardy's work is still widely read and enjoyed today, with many film adaptations of his novels, his writing was poorly received in its day. The novel *Jude the Obscure* was viciously attacked as 'immoral', making Hardy comment, 'The experience completely cured me of further interest in novel writing.' He stopped writing novels in 1895 but continued writing poetry until his death in 1928.

'The Winters and the Palmleys' is taken from *Life's Little Ironies* (1895). A group of people on a carrier van take it in turns to tell a story about someone they know to John Lackland, who is returning to the village after an absence of 35 years.

In this story the 'groceress' tells of what happened to two families, the Winters and the Palmleys. It is a tale of jealous rivalry, love and disappointment. It also shows that good handwriting can sometimes be a matter of life or death!

The Winters and the Palmleys

Thomas Hardy

'To go back to the beginning – if one must – there were two women in the parish when I was a child, who were to a certain extent rivals in good looks. Never mind particulars, but in consequence of this they were at daggers-drawn, and they did not love each other any better when one of them tempted the other's lover away from her and married him. He was a young man of the name of Winter, and in due time they had a son.

'The other woman did not marry for many years: but when she was about thirty a quiet man named Palmley asked her to be his wife, and she accepted him. You don't mind when the Palmleys were Longpuddle folk, but I do well. She had a son also, who was, of course, nine or ten years younger than the son of the first. The child proved to be of rather weak intellect, though his mother loved him as the apple of her eye.

'This woman's husband died when the child was eight years old, and left his widow and boy in poverty. Her former rival, also a widow now, but fairly well provided for, offered for pity's sake to take the child as errand-boy, small as he was, her own son, Jack, being hard upon seventeen. Her poor neighbour could do no better than let the child go there. And to the richer woman's house little Palmley straightway went.

'Well, in some way or other – how, it was never exactly known, the thriving woman, Mrs Winter, sent the little boy with a message to the next village one December day, much against his will. It was getting dark, and the child prayed to be allowed not to go, because he would be afraid coming home. But the mistress insisted, more out of thoughtlessness than cruelty, and the child went. On his way back he had to pass through Yalbury Wood, and something came out from behind a tree and frightened him into fits. The child was quite ruined by it; he became quite a drivelling idiot, and soon afterward died.

'Then the other woman had nothing left to live for, and vowed vengeance against that rival who had first won away her lover, and now had been the cause of her bereavement. This last affliction was certainly not intended by her thriving acquaintance, though it must be owned that when it was done she seemed but little concerned. Whatever vengeance poor Mrs Palmley felt, she had no opportunity of carrying it out, and time might have softened her feelings into forgetfulness of her supposed wrongs as she dragged on her lonely life. So matters stood when, a year after the death of the child, Mrs Palmley's niece, who had been born and bred in the city of Exonbury, came to live with her.

'This young woman – Miss Harriet Palmley – was a proud and handsome girl, very well brought up, and more stylish and genteel than the people of our village, as was natural, considering where she came from. She regarded herself as much above Mrs Winter and her son in position as Mrs Winter and her son considered themselves above poor Mrs Palmley. But love is an unceremonious thing, and what in the world should happen but that young Jack Winter must fall wofully and wildly in love with Harriet Palmley almost as soon as he saw her.

'She, being better educated than he, and caring nothing for the village notion of his mother's superiority to her aunt, did not give him much encouragement. But Longpuddle being no very large world, the two could not help seeing a good deal of each other while she was staying there, and, disdainful young woman as she was, she did seem to take a little pleasure in his attentions and advances.

'One day when they were picking apples together, he asked her to marry him. She had not expected anything so practical as that at so early a time, and was led by her surprise into a half-promise; at any rate she did not absolutely refuse him, and accepted some little presents that he made her.

'But he saw that her view of him was rather as a simple village lad than as a young man to look up to, and he felt that he must do something bold to secure her. So he said one day, "I am going away, to try to get into a better position than I can get here." In two or three weeks he wished her good-bye, and went away to Monksbury, to superintend a farm, with a view to start as a farmer himself; and from there he wrote regularly to her, as if their marriage were an understood thing.

'Now Harriet liked the young man's presents and the admiration of his eyes; but on paper he was less attractive to her. Her mother had been a schoolmistress, and Harriet had besides a natural aptitude for pen-and-ink work, in days when to be a ready writer was not such a common thing as it is now, and when actual handwriting was valued as an accomplishment in itself. Jack Winter's performances in the shape of love-letters quite jarred her city nerves and her finer taste, and when she answered one of them, in the lovely running hand that she took such pride in, she very strictly and loftily bade him to practise with a pen and spelling-book if he wished to please her. Whether he listened to her request or not nobody knows, but his letters did not improve. He ventured to tell her in his clumsy way that if her heart were more warm towards him she would not be so nice about his handwriting and spelling; which indeed was true enough.

'Well, in Jack's absence the weak flame that had been set alight in Harriet's heart soon sank low, and at last went out altogether. He wrote and wrote, and begged and prayed her to give a reason for her coldness; and then she told him plainly that she was town born, and he was not sufficiently well educated to please her.

'Jack Winter's want of pen-and-ink training did not make him less thin-skinned than others; in fact, he was terribly tender and touchy about anything. This reason that she gave for finally throwing him over grieved him, shamed him, and mortified him more than can be told in these times, the pride of that day in being able to write with beautiful flourishes, and the sorrow at not being able to do so, raging so high. Jack replied to her with an angry note, and then she hit back with smart little stings, telling him how many words he had misspelt in his last letter, and declaring again that this alone was sufficient justification for any woman to put an end to an understanding with him. Her husband must be a better scholar.

'He bore her rejection of him in silence, but his suffering was sharp – all the sharper in being untold. She communicated with Jack no more; and as his reason for going out into the world had been only to provide a home worthy of her, he had no further object in planning such a home now that she was lost to him. He therefore gave up the farming occupation by which he had hoped to make himself a master-farmer, and left the spot to return to his mother.

'As soon as he got back to Longpuddle he found that Harriet had already looked wi' favour upon another lover. He was a young road-contractor, and Jack could not but admit that his rival was both in manners and scholarship much ahead of him. Indeed, a more sensible match for the beauty who had been dropped into the village by fate could hardly have been found than this man, who could offer her so much better a chance than Jack could have done, with his uncertain future and narrow abilities for grappling with the world. The fact was so clear to him that he could hardly blame her.

'One day by accident Jack saw on a scrap of paper the handwriting of Harriet's new beloved. It was flowing like a stream, well spelt, the work of a man accustomed to the ink-bottle and the dictionary, of a man already called in the parish a good scholar. And then it struck all of a sudden into Jack's mind what a contrast the letters of this young man must make to his own miserable old letters, and how ridiculous they must make his lines appear. He groaned and wished he had never written to her, and wondered if she had ever kept his poor performances. Possibly she had kept them, for women are in the habit of doing that, he thought, and whilst they were in her hands there was always a chance of his honest, stupid love-assurances to her being joked over by Harriet with her present lover, or by anybody who should accidentally uncover them.

'The nervous, moody young man could not bear the thought of it, and at length decided to ask her to return them, as was proper when engagements were broken off. He was some hours in framing, copying, and recopying the short note in which he made his request, and having finished it he sent it to her house. His messenger came back with the answer, by word of mouth, that Miss Palmley bade him say she should not part with what was hers, and wondered at his boldness in troubling her.

'Jack was much affronted at this, and determined to go for his letters himself. He chose a time when he knew she was at home, and knocked and went in without much ceremony; for though Harriet was so high and mighty, Jack had small respect for her aunt, Mrs Palmley, whose little child had been his boot-cleaner in earlier days. Harriet was in the room, this being the first time they had met since she had jilted him. He asked for his letters with a stern and bitter look at her.

'At first she said he might have them for all that she cared, and took them out of the bureau where she kept them. Then she glanced over the outside one of the packet, and suddenly altering her mind, she told him shortly that his request was a silly one, and slipped the letters into her aunt's work-box, which stood open on the table, locking it, and saying with a bantering laugh that of course she thought it best to keep 'em, since they might be useful to produce as evidence that she had good cause for declining to marry him.

'He blazed up hot. "Give me those letters!" he said. "They are mine!"

'"No, they are not," she replied; "they are mine."

'"Whos'ever they are I want them back," says he. "I don't want to be made sport of for my penmanship: you've another young man now! He has your confidence, and you pour all your tales into his ear. You'll be showing them to him!"

'"Perhaps," said my lady Harriet, with calm coolness, like the heartless woman that she was.

'Her manner so maddened him that he made a step towards the work-box, but she snatched it up, locked it in the bureau, and turned upon him triumphant. For a moment he seemed to be going to wrench the key of the bureau out of her hand; but he stopped himself, and swung round upon his heel and went away.

'When he was out-of-doors alone, and it got night, he walked about restless, and stinging with the sense of being beaten at all points by her. He could not help fancying her telling her new lover or her acquaintances of this scene with himself, and laughing with them over those poor blotted, crooked lines of his that he had been so anxious to obtain. As the evening passed on he worked himself into a dogged resolution to have them back at any price, come what might.

'At the dead of night he came out of his mother's house by the back door, and creeping through the garden hedge went along the field adjoining till he reached the back of her aunt's dwelling. The moon struck bright and flat upon the walls, 'twas said, and every shiny leaf of the creepers was like a little looking-glass in the rays. From long acquaintance Jack knew the arrangement and position of everything in Mrs

Palmley's house as well as in his own mother's. The back window close to him was a casement with little leaded squares, as it is to this day, and was, as now, one of two lighting the sitting-room. The other, being in front, was closed up with shutters, but this back one had not even a blind, and the moonlight as it streamed in showed every article of the furniture to him outside. To the right of the room is the fireplace, as you may remember; to the left was the bureau at that time; inside the bureau was Harriet's work-box, as he supposed (though it was really her aunt's), and inside the work-box were his letters. Well, he took out his pocket-knife, and without noise lifted the leading of one of the panes, so that he could take out the glass, and putting his hand through the hole he unfastened the casement, and climbed in through the opening. All the household – that is to say, Mrs Palmley, Harriet, and the little maidservant – were asleep. Jack went straight to the bureau, so he said, hoping it might have been unfastened again – it not being kept locked in ordinary – but Harriet had never unfastened it since she secured her letters there the day before. Jack told afterward how he thought of her asleep upstairs, caring nothing for him, and of the way she had made sport of him and of his letters; and having advanced so far, he was not to be hindered now. By forcing the large blade of his knife under the flap of the bureau, he burst the weak lock; within was the rosewood work-box just as she had placed it in her hurry to keep it from him. There being no time to spare for getting the letters out of it then, he took it under his arm, shut the bureau, and made the best of his way out of the house, latching the casement behind him, and refixing the pane of glass in its place.

'Winter found his way back to his mother's as he had come, and being dog-tired, crept upstairs to bed, hiding the box till he could destroy its contents. The next morning early he set about doing this, and carried it to the linhay at the back of his mother's dwelling. Here by the hearth he opened the box, and began burning one by one the letters that had cost him so much labour to write and shame to think of, meaning to return the box to Harriet, after repairing the slight damage he had caused it by opening it without a key, with a note – the last she would ever receive from him – telling her triumphantly that in refusing to return what he had asked for she had calculated too surely upon his submission to her whims.

'But on removing the last letter from the box he received a shock; for underneath it, at the very bottom, lay money – several golden guineas – "Doubtless Harriet's pocket-money," he said to himself; though it was not, but Mrs Palmley's. Before he had got over his qualms at this discovery he heard footsteps coming through the house-passage to where he was. In haste he pushed the box and what was in it under some brushwood which lay in the linhay; but Jack had been already seen. Two constables entered the out-house, and seized him as he knelt before the fireplace, securing the work-box and all it contained at the same moment. They had come to appre-hend him on a charge of breaking into the dwelling-house of Mrs Palmley on the night preceding; and almost before the lad knew what had happened to him they were leading him along the lane that connects that end of the village with this turnpike-road, and along they marched him between 'em all the way to Casterbridge jail.

'Jack's act amounted to night burglary – though he had never thought of it – and burglary was felony, and a capital offence in those days. His figure had been seen by some one against the bright wall as he came away from Mrs Palmley's back window, and the box and money were found in his possession, while the evidence of the broken bureau-lock and tinkered windowpane was more than enough for circumstan-tial detail. Whether his protestation that he went only for his letters, which he believed to be wrongfully kept from him, would have availed him anything if supported by other evidence I do not know; but the one person who could have borne it out was Harriet, and she acted entirely under the sway of her aunt. That aunt was deadly towards Jack Winter. Mrs Palmley's time had come. Here was her revenge upon the woman who had first won away her lover, and next ruined and deprived her of her heart's treasure – her little son. When the assize week drew on, and Jack had to stand his trial, Harriet did not appear in the case at all, which was allowed to take its course, Mrs Palmley testifying to the general facts of the burglary. Whether Harriet would have come forward if Jack had appealed to her is not known; possibly she would have done it for pity's sake; but Jack was too proud to ask a single favour of a girl who had jilted him; and he let her alone. The trial was a short one, and the death sentence was passed.

'The day o' young Jack's execution was a cold dusty Saturday in March. He was so boyish and slim that they were obliged in mercy to hang him in the heaviest fetters kept in the jail, lest his heft should not break his neck, and they weighed so upon him that he could hardly drag himself up to the drop. At that time the gover'ment was not strict about burying the body of an executed person within the precincts of the prison, and at the earnest prayer of his poor mother his body was allowed to be brought home. All the parish waited at their cottage doors in the evening for its arrival: I remember how, as a very little girl, I stood by my mother's side. About eight o'clock, as we hearkened on our door-stones in the cold bright starlight, we could hear the faint crackle of a waggon from the direction of the turnpike-road. The noise was lost as the waggon dropped into a hollow, then it was plain again as it lumbered down the next long incline, and presently it entered Longpuddle. The coffin was laid in the belfry for the night, and the next day, Sunday, between the services, we buried him. A funeral sermon was preached the same afternoon, the text chosen being, "He was the only son of his mother, and she was a widow." . . . Yes, they were cruel times!

'As for Harriet, she and her lover were married in due time; but by all account her life was no jocund one. She and her good-man found that they could not live comfortably at Longpuddle, by reason of her connection with Jack's misfortunes, and they settled in a distant town, and were no more heard of by us; Mrs Palmley, too, found it advisable to join 'em shortly after. The dark-eyed, gaunt old Mrs Winter, remembered by the emigrant gentleman here, was, as you will have foreseen, the Mrs Winter of this story; and I can well call to mind how lonely she was, how afraid the children were of her, and how she kept herself as a stranger among us, though she lived so long.'

'Longpuddle has had her sad experiences as well as her sunny ones,' said Mr Lackland.

'Yes, yes. But I am thankful to say not many like that, though good and bad have lived among us.'

'There was Georgy Crookhill – he was one of the shady sort,

as I have reason to know,' observed the registrar, with the manner of a man who would like to have his say also.

'I used to hear what he was as a boy at school.'

'Well, as he began so he went on. It never got so far as a hanging matter with him, to be sure; but he had some narrow escapes of penal servitude; and once it was a case of the biter bit.'

Wilkie Collins 1824–1889

Wilkie Collins was the elder son of the landscape painter William Collins. He was educated for a few years at private schools but at the age of twelve he set off with his family on a two-year painting tour of Italy. He always later claimed that this journey was far more educational than school. On his return to an English boarding school, Wilkie Collins was severely bullied, but managed to get the older boys to protect him in exchange for his telling them ghostly and frightening stories at night in the dormitory.

After a short time working as a tea importer, Collins went on to study the law before finally becoming a writer, beginning with a biography of his father. He became a close friend and collaborator of the novelist Charles Dickens, writing articles and stories for his magazines *Household Words* and *All the Year Round*, and acting in the Dickens company Splendid Strollers.

Wilkie Collins was fascinated by mystery, suspense and crime and wrote the first full-length detective stories in English. He was extremely popular with the general public and there were usually crowds outside the *All the Year Round* magazine office eagerly waiting for the next instalment of his serials or for his latest short story.

His most famous novel, *The Woman in White*, was first serialized in the magazine *All the Year Round* and achieved a record circulation. It was based on the transcript of a real-life trial which Collins discovered on a trip to Paris. The story is told through a number of different viewpoints, giving the reader a succession of mysteries to unravel. When the serialization was later published as a novel in 1860 it proved equally popular and went into five editions within two months. Such was the popularity that there were even perfumes, cloaks, bonnets and music named 'Woman in White'.

Wilkie Collins was a prolific writer and went on to publish twenty-four novels as well as a number of plays and collections of short stories. Besides *The Woman in White*, his best-known novels are *No Name* (1862), *Armadale* (1866) and *The Moonstone* (1868).

Although Wilkie Collins never married he lived with Caroline Graves, whom he first met in a mysterious midnight encounter which he used in *The Woman in White*. He also had three children by another woman, Martha Rudd. In his later life he became ill with gout and rheumatism and became addicted to the opium he took to relieve his pain.

The story 'The Biter Bit' shows Wilkie Collins's fascination with form. He liked to experiment in his storytelling, trying out diaries and, in this case, letters. It tells the story of a very amateurish detective bungling his way through his first and only case.

The Biter Bit

Wilkie Collins

*From Chief Inspector Theakstone, of the Detective Police, to
Sergeant Bulmer of the same force*

LONDON, *4th July* 18—.

SERGEANT BULMER, – This is to inform you that you are
wanted to assist in looking up a case of importance, which
will require all the attention of an experienced member of the
force. The matter of the robbery on which you are now
engaged, you will please to shift over to the young man who
brings you this letter. You will tell him all the circumstances
of the case, just as they stand; you will put him up to the
progress you have made (if any) towards detecting the person
or persons by whom the money has been stolen; and you will
leave him to make the best he can of the matter now in your
hands. He is to have the whole responsibility of the case, and
the whole credit of his success, if he brings it to a proper issue.

So much for the orders that I am desired to communicate to
you.

A word in your ear, next, about this new man who is to
take your place. His name is Matthew Sharpin; and he is to
have the chance given him of dashing into our office at a jump
– supposing he turns out strong enough to take it. You will
naturally ask me how he comes by this privilege. I can only
tell you that he has some uncommonly strong interest to back
him in certain high quarters which you and I had better not
mention except under our breaths. He has been a lawyer's
clerk; and he is wonderfully conceited in his opinion of
himself, as well as mean and underhand to look at. According
to his own account, he leaves his old trade, and joins ours of
his own free will and preference. You will no more believe
that than I do. My notion is, that he has managed to ferret
out some private information in connection with the affairs of

one of his master's clients, which makes him rather an awkward customer to keep in the office for the future, and which, at the same time, gives him hold enough over his employer to make it dangerous to drive him into a corner by turning him away. I think the giving him this unheard-of chance among us, is, in plain words, pretty much like giving him hush-money to keep him quiet. However that may be, Mr Matthew Sharpin is to have the case now in your hands; and if he succeeds with it, he pokes his ugly nose into our office, as sure as fate. I put you up to this, sergeant, so that you may not stand in your own light by giving the new man any cause to complain of you at headquarters, and remain yours,

FRANCIS THEAKSTONE.

From Mr Matthew Sharpin to Chief Inspector Theakstone,

LONDON, *5th July* 18—.

DEAR SIR, – Having now been favoured with the necessary instructions from Sergeant Bulmer, I beg to remind you of certain directions which I have received, relating to the report of my future proceedings which I am to prepare for examination at headquarters.

The object of my writing, and of your examining what I have written, before you send it in to the higher authorities, is, I am informed, to give me, as an untried hand, the benefit of your advice, in case I want it (which I venture to think I shall not) at any stage of my proceedings. As the extraordinary circumstances of the case on which I am now engaged, make it impossible for me to absent myself from the place where the robbery was committed, until I have made some progress towards discovering the thief, I am necessarily precluded from consulting you personally. Hence the necessity of my writing down the various details, which might, perhaps, be better communicated by word of mouth. This, if I am not mistaken, is the position in which we are now placed. I state my own impressions on the subject, in writing, in order that we may clearly understand each other at the outset; and have the honour to remain, your obedient servant,

MATTHEW SHARPIN.

From Chief Inspector Theakstone to Mr Matthew Sharpin

LONDON, 5th July 18—.

SIR, – You have begun by wasting time, ink, and paper. We both of us perfectly well knew the position we stood in towards each other, when I sent you with my letter to Sergeant Bulmer. There was not the least need to repeat it in writing. Be so good as to employ your pen, in future, on the business actually in hand.

You have now three separate matters on which to write to me. First, you have to draw up a statement of your instructions received from Sergeant Bulmer, in order to show us that nothing has escaped your memory, and that you are thoroughly acquainted with all the circumstances of the case which has been entrusted to you. Secondly, you are to inform me what it is you propose to do. Thirdly, you are to report every inch of your progress (if you make any) from day to day, and, if need be, from hour to hour as well. This is *your* duty. As to what *my* duty may be, when I want you to remind me of it, I will write and tell you so. In the meantime, I remain, yours,

FRANCIS THEAKSTONE.

From Mr Matthew Sharpin to Chief Inspector Theakstone

LONDON, *6th July* 18—.

SIR, – You are rather an elderly person, and, as such, naturally inclined to be a little jealous of men like me, who are in the prime of their lives and their faculties. Under these circumstances, it is my duty to be considerate towards you, and not to bear too hardly on your small failings. I decline, therefore, altogether, to take offence at the tone of your letter; I give you the full benefit of the natural generosity of my nature; I sponge the very existence of your surly communication out of my memory – in short, Chief Inspector Theakstone, I forgive you, and proceed to business.

My first duty is to draw up a full statement of the instructions I have received from Sergeant Bulmer. Here they are at your service, according to my version of them.

At number 13 Rutherford Street, Soho, there is a stationer's shop. It is kept by one Mr Yatman. He is a married man, but has no family. Besides Mr and Mrs Yatman, the other inmates in the house are a young single man named Jay, who lodges in the front room on the second floor – a shopman, who sleeps in one of the attics – and a servant-of-all-work, whose bed is in the back-kitchen. Once a week a charwoman comes for a few hours in the morning only, to help this servant. These are all the persons who, on ordinary occasions, have means of access to the interior of the house, placed, as a matter of course, at their disposal.

Mr Yatman has been in business for many years, carrying on his affairs prosperously enough to realize a handsome independence for a person in his position. Unfortunately for himself, he endeavoured to increase the amount of his property by speculating. He ventured boldly in his investments, luck went against him, and rather less than two years ago he found himself a poor man again. All that was saved out of the wreck of his property was the sum of two hundred pounds.

Although Mr Yatman did his best to meet his altered circumstances, by giving up many of the luxuries and comforts to which he and his wife had been accustomed, he found it impossible to retrench so far as to allow of putting by any money from the income produced by the shop. The business has been declining of late years – the cheap advertising stationers having done it injury with the public. Consequently, up to the last week the only surplus property possessed by Mr Yatman consisted of the two hundred pounds which had been recovered from the wreck of his fortune. This sum was placed as a deposit in a joint-stock bank of the highest possible character.

Eight days ago, Mr Yatman and his lodger, Mr Jay, held a conversation on the subject of the commercial difficulties which are hampering trade in all directions at the present time. Mr Jay (who lives by supplying the newspapers with short paragraphs relating to accidents, offences, and brief records of remarkable occurrences in general – who is, in short, what they call a penny-a-liner) told his landlord that he had been in the city that day, and had heard unfavourable rumours on the subject of the joint-stock banks. The rumours to which he alluded had already reached the ears of Mr Yatman from other quarters; and the confirmation of them by his lodger had such an effect on his mind – predisposed as it was to alarm by the experience of his former losses – that he resolved to go at once to the bank and withdraw his deposit.

It was then getting on towards the end of the afternoon; and he arrived just in time to receive his money before the bank closed.

He received the deposit in bank-notes of the following amounts: one fifty-pound note, three twenty-pound notes, six ten-pound notes, and six five-pound notes. His object in drawing the money in this form was to have it ready to lay out immediately in trifling loans, on good security, among the small tradespeople of his district, some of whom are sorely pressed for the very means of existence at the present time. Investments of this kind seemed to Mr Yatman to be the most safe and the most profitable on which he could now venture.

He brought the money back in an envelope placed in his breast-pocket; and asked his shopman, on getting home, to look for a small flat tin cash-box, which had not been used for years, and which, as Mr Yatman remembered it, was exactly the right size to hold the bank-notes. For some time the cash-box was searched for in vain. Mr Yatman called to his wife to know if she had any idea where it was. The question was overheard by the servant-of-all-work, who was taking up the tea-tray at the time, and by Mr Jay, who was coming downstairs on his way out to the theatre. Ultimately the cash-box was found by the shopman. Mr Yatman placed the bank-notes in it, secured them by a padlock, and put the box in his coat-pocket. It stuck out of the coat-pocket a very little, but enough to be seen. Mr Yatman remained at home, upstairs, all the evening. No visitors called. At eleven o'clock he went to bed, and put the cash-box along with his clothes, on a chair by the bed-side.

When he and his wife woke the next morning, the box was gone. Payment of the notes was immediately stopped at the Bank of England; but no news of the money has been heard of since that time.

So far, the circumstances of the case are perfectly clear. They point unmistakably to the conclusion that the robbery must have been committed by some person living in the house. Suspicion falls, therefore, upon the servant-of-all-work, upon the shopman, and upon Mr Jay. The two first knew that the cash-box was being inquired for by their master, but did not know what it was he wanted to put into it. They would assume, of course, that it was money. They both had opportunities (the servant, when she took away the tea – and the shopman, when he came, after shutting up, to give the keys of the till to his master) of seeing the cash-box in Mr Yatman's pocket, and of inferring naturally, from its position there, that he intended to take it into his bedroom with him at night.

Mr Jay, on the other hand, had been told, during the afternoon's conversation on the subject of joint-stock banks, that his landlord had a deposit of two hundred pounds in one of them. He also knew that Mr Yatman left him with the intention of drawing that money out; and he heard the inquiry for the cash-box, afterwards, when he was coming downstairs. He must, therefore, have inferred that the money was in the house, and that the cash-box was the receptacle intended to contain it. That he could have had any idea, however, of the place in which Mr Yatman intended to keep it for the night, is impossible, seeing that he went out before the box was found, and did not return till his landlord was in bed. Consequently, if he committed the robbery, he must have gone into the bedroom purely on speculation.

Speaking of the bedroom reminds me of the necessity of noticing the situation of it in the house, and the means that exist of gaining easy access to it at any hour of the night.

The room in question is the back room on the first floor. In consequence of Mrs Yatman's constitutional nervousness on the subject of fire (which makes her apprehend being burnt alive in her room, in case of accident, by the hampering of the lock if the key is turned in it) her husband has never been accustomed to lock the bedroom door. Both he and his wife are, by their own admission, heavy sleepers. Consequently, the risk to be run by any evil-disposed persons wishing to plunder the bedroom, was of the most trifling kind. They could enter the room by merely turning the handle of the door; and if they moved with ordinary caution, there was no fear of their waking the sleepers inside. This fact is of importance. It strengthens our conviction that the money must have been taken by one of the inmates of the house, because it tends to show that the robbery, in this case, might have been committed by persons not possessed of the superior vigilance and cunning of the experienced thief.

Such are the circumstances, as they were related to

Sergeant Bulmer, when he was first called in to discover the guilty parties, and, if possible, to recover the lost bank-notes. The strictest inquiry which he could institute, failed of producing the smallest fragment of evidence against any of the persons on whom suspicion naturally fell. Their language and behaviour, on being informed of the robbery, was perfectly consistent with the language and behaviour of innocent people. Sergeant Bulmer felt from the first that this was a case for private inquiry and secret observation. He began by recommending Mr and Mrs Yatman to affect a feeling of perfect confidence in the innocence of the persons living under their roof; and he then opened the campaign by employing himself in following the goings and comings, and in discovering the friends, the habits, and the secrets of the maid-of-all-work.

Three days and nights of exertions on his own part, and on that of others who were competent to assist his investigations, were enough to satisfy him that there was no sound cause for suspicion against the girl.

He next practised the same precaution in relation to the shopman. There was more difficulty and uncertainty in privately clearing up this person's character without his knowledge, but the obstacles were at last smoothed away with tolerable success; and though there is not the same amount of certainty, in this case, which there was in that of the girl, there is still fair reason for supposing that the shopman has had nothing to do with the robbery of the cash-box.

As a necessary consequence of these proceedings, the range of suspicion now becomes limited to the lodger, Mr Jay.

When I presented your letter of introduction to Sergeant Bulmer, he had already made some inquiries on the subject of this young man. The result, so far, has not been at all favourable. Mr Jay's habits are irregular; he frequents public-houses, and seems to be familiarly acquainted with a great many dissolute characters; he is in debt to most of the tradespeople whom he employs; he has not paid his rent to Mr Yatman for the last month; yesterday evening he came home excited by liquor, and last week he was seen talking to a prize-fighter. In short, though Mr Jay does call himself a journalist, in virtue of his penny-a-line contributions to the newspapers, he is a young man of low tastes, vulgar manners, and bad habits. Nothing has yet been discovered in relation to him, which redounds to his credit in the smallest degree.

I have now reported, down to the very last details, all the particulars communicated to me by Sergeant Bulmer. I believe you will not find an omission anywhere; and I think you will admit, though you are prejudiced against me, that a clearer statement of facts was never laid before you than the statement I have now made. My next duty is to tell you what I propose to do, now that the case is confided to my hands.

In the first place, it is clearly my business to take up the case at the point where Sergeant Bulmer has left it. On his authority, I am justified in assuming that I have no need to trouble myself about the maid-of-all-work and the shopman. Their characters are now to be considered as cleared up. What remains to be privately investigated is the question of the guilt or innocence of Mr Jay. Before we give up the notes for lost, we must make sure, if we can, that he knows nothing about them.

This is the plan that I have adopted, with the full approval of Mr and Mrs Yatman, for discovering whether Mr Jay is or is not the person who has stolen the cash-box:

I propose, to-day, to present myself at the house in the character of a young man who is looking for lodgings. The back room on the second floor will be shown to me as the room to let; and I shall establish myself there to-night, as a person from the country who has come to London to look for a situation in a respectable shop or office.

By this means I shall be living next to the room occupied by Mr Jay. The partition between us is mere lath and plaster. I shall make a small hole in it, near the cornice, through which I can see what Mr Jay does in his room, and hear every word that is said when any friend happens to call on him. Whenever he is at home, I shall be at my post of observation. Whenever he goes out, I shall be after him. By employing these means of watching him, I believe I may look forward to the discovery of his secret – if he knows anything about the lost bank-notes – as to a dead certainty.

What you may think of my plan of observation I cannot undertake to say. It appears to me to unite the invaluable merits of boldness and simplicity. Fortified by this conviction, I close the present communication with feelings of the most sanguine description in regard to the future, and remain your obedient servant,

MATTHEW SHARPIN.

From the Same to the Same

7th July.

SIR, – As you have not honoured me with any answer to my last communication, I assume that, in spite of your prejudices against me, it has produced the favourable impression on your mind which I ventured to anticipate. Gratified beyond measure by the token of approval which your eloquent silence conveys to me, I proceed to report the progress that has been made in the course of the last twenty-four hours.

I am now comfortably established next door to Mr Jay; and I am delighted to say that I have two holes in the partition, instead of one. My natural sense of humour has led me into the pardonable extravagance of giving them appropriate names. One I call my peep-hole, and the other my pipe-hole. The name of the first explains itself; the name of the second refers to a small tin pipe, or tube, inserted in the hole, and twisted so that the mouth of it comes close to my ear, while I am standing at my post of observation. Thus, while I am looking at Mr Jay through my peep-hole, I can hear every word that may be spoken in his room through my pipe-hole.

Perfect candour – a virtue which I have possessed from my childhood – compels me to acknowledge, before I go any further, that the ingenious notion of adding a pipe-hole to my proposed peep-hole originated with Mrs Yatman. This lady – a most intelligent and accomplished person, simple, and yet distinguished, in her manners – has entered into all my little plans with an enthusiasm and intelligence which I cannot too highly praise. Mr Yatman is so cast down by his loss, that he is quite incapable of affording me any assistance. Mrs Yatman, who is evidently most tenderly attached to him, feels her husband's sad condition of mind even more acutely than she feels the loss of the money; and is mainly stimulated to exertion by her desire to assist in raising him from the miserable state of prostration into which he has now fallen.

'The money, Mr Sharpin,' she said to me yesterday evening, with tears in her eyes, 'the money may be regained by rigid economy and strict attention to business. It is my husband's wretched state of mind that makes me so anxious for the discovery of the thief. I may be wrong, but I felt hopeful of success as soon as you entered the house; and I believe, if the wretch who has robbed us is to be found, you are the man to discover him.' I accepted this gratifying compliment in the spirit in which it was offered – firmly believing that I shall be found, sooner or later, to have thoroughly deserved it.

Let me now return to business; that is to say, to my peep-hole and my pipe-hole.

I have enjoyed some hours of calm observation of Mr Jay. Though rarely at home, as I understand from Mrs Yatman, on ordinary occasions, he has been indoors the whole of this day. That is suspicious, to begin with. I have to report, further, that he rose at a late hour this morning (always a bad sign in a young man), and that he lost a great deal of time, after he was up, in yawning and complaining to himself of headache. Like other debauched characters, he ate little or nothing for breakfast. His next proceeding was to smoke a pipe – a dirty clay pipe, which a gentleman would have been ashamed to put between his lips. When he had done smoking, he took out pen, ink, and paper, and sat down to write with a groan – whether of remorse for having taken the bank-notes, or of disgust at the task before him, I am unable to say. After writing a few lines (too far away from my peep-hole to give me a chance of reading over his shoulder), he leaned back in his chair, and amused himself by humming the tunes of certain popular songs. Whether these do, or do not, represent secret signals by which he communicates with his accomplices remains to be seen. After he had amused himself for some time by humming, he got up and began to walk about the room, occasionally stopping to add a sentence to the paper on his desk. Before long, he went to a locked cupboard and opened it. I strained my eyes eagerly, in expectation of making a discovery. I saw him take something carefully out of the cupboard – he turned round – and it was only a pint bottle of brandy! Having drunk some of the liquor, this extremely indolent reprobate lay down on his bed again, and in five minutes was fast asleep.

After hearing him snoring for at least two hours, I was recalled to my peep-hole by a knock at his door. He jumped up and opened it with suspicious activity.

A very small boy, with a very dirty face, walked in, said:

'Please, sir, they're waiting for you,' sat down on a chair, with his legs a long way from the ground, and instantly fell asleep! Mr Jay swore an oath, tied a wet towel round his head, and going back to his paper, began to cover it with writing as fast as his fingers could move the pen. Occasionally getting up to dip the towel in water and tie it on again, he continued at this employment for nearly three hours; then folded up the leaves of writing, woke the boy, and gave them to him, with this remarkable expression: 'Now, then, young sleepy-head, quick – march! If you see the governor, tell him to have the money ready when I call for it.' The boy grinned, and disappeared. I was sorely tempted to follow 'sleepy-head,' but, on reflection, considered it safest still to keep my eye on the proceedings of Mr Jay.

In half an hour's time, he put on his hat and walked out. Of course, I put on my hat and walked out also. As I went downstairs, I passed Mrs Yatman going up. The lady has been kind enough to undertake, by previous arrangement between us, to search Mr Jay's room, while he is out of the way, and while I am necessarily engaged in the pleasing duty of following him wherever he goes. On the occasion to which I now refer, he walked straight to the nearest tavern, and ordered a couple of mutton chops for his dinner. I placed myself in the next box to him, and ordered a couple of mutton chops for my dinner. Before I had been in the room a minute, a young man of highly suspicious manners and appearance, sitting at a table opposite, took his glass of porter in his hand and joined Mr Jay. I pretended to be reading the newspaper, and listened, as in duty bound, with all my might.

'Jack has been here inquiring after you,' says the young man.

'Did he leave any message?' asks Mr Jay.

'Yes,' says the other. 'He told me, if I met with you, to say that he wished very particularly to see you to-night; and that he would give you a look in, at Rutherford Street, at seven o'clock.'

'All right,' says Mr Jay. 'I'll get back in time to see him.'

Upon this, the suspicious-looking young man finished his porter, and saying that he was rather in a hurry, took leave of his friend (perhaps I should not be wrong if I said his accomplice) and left the room.

At twenty-five minutes and a half past six – in these serious cases it is important to be particular about time – Mr Jay finished his chops and paid his bill. At twenty-six minutes and three-quarters I finished my chops and paid mine. In ten minutes more I was inside the house in Rutherford Street, and was received by Mrs Yatman in the passage. That charming woman's face exhibited an expression of melancholy and disappointment which it quite grieved me to see.

'I am afraid, ma'am,' says I, 'that you have not hit on any little criminating discovery in the lodger's room?'

She shook her head and sighed. It was a soft, languid, fluttering sigh; and, upon my life, it quite upset me. For the moment I forgot business, and burned with envy of Mr Yatman.

'Don't despair, ma'am,' I said, with an insinuating mildness which seemed to touch her. 'I have heard a mysterious conversation – I know of a guilty appointment – and I expect great things from my peep-hole and my pipe-hole to-night. Pray, don't be alarmed, but I think we are on the brink of a discovery.'

Here my enthusiastic devotion to business got the better of my tender feelings. I looked – winked – nodded – left her.

When I got back to my observatory, I found Mr Jay digesting his mutton chops in an arm-chair, with his pipe in his mouth. On his table were two tumblers, a jug of water, and the pint bottle of brandy. It was then close upon seven o'clock. As the hour struck, the person described as 'Jack' walked in.

He looked agitated – I am happy to say he looked violently agitated. The cheerful glow of anticipated success diffused itself (to use a strong expression) all over me, from head to foot. With breathless interest I looked through my peep-hole, and saw the visitor – the 'Jack' of this delightful case – sit down, facing me, at the opposite side of the table to Mr Jay. Making allowance for the difference in expression which their countenances just now happened to exhibit, these two abandoned villains were so much alike in other respects as to lead at once to the conclusion that they were brothers. Jack was the cleaner man and the better dressed of the two. I admit that, at the outset. It is, perhaps, one of my failings to push justice and impartiality to their utmost limits. I am no Pharisee; and where vice has its redeeming point, I say, let vice have its due – yes, yes, by all manner of means, let vice have its due.

'What's the matter now, Jack?' says Mr Jay.

'Can't you see it in my face?' says Jack. 'My dear fellow, delays are dangerous. Let us have done with suspense, and risk it the day after to-morrow.'

'So soon as that?' cried Mr Jay, looking very much astonished. 'Well, I'm ready, if you are. But, I say, Jack, is Somebody Else ready too? Are you quite sure of that?'

He smiled as he spoke – a frightful smile – and laid a very strong emphasis on those two words, 'Somebody Else.' There is evidently a third ruffian, a nameless desperado, concerned in the business.

'Meet us to-morrow,' says Jack, 'and judge for yourself. Be in the Regent's Park at eleven in the morning, and look out for us at the turning that leads to the Avenue Road.'

'I'll be there,' says Mr Jay. 'Have a drop of brandy and water? What are you getting up for? You're not going already?'

'Yes, I am,' says Jack. 'The fact is, I'm so excited and agitated that I can't sit still anywhere for five minutes together. Ridiculous as it may appear to you, I'm in a perpetual state of nervous flutter. I can't, for the life of me, help fearing that we shall be found out. I fancy that every man who looks twice at me in the street is a spy – '

At those words, I thought my legs would have given way under me. Nothing but strength of mind kept me at my peephole – nothing else, I give you my word of honour.

'Stuff and nonsense!' cried Mr Jay, with all the effrontery of a veteran in crime. 'We have kept the secret up to this time, and we will manage cleverly to the end. Have a drop of brandy and water, and you will feel as certain about it as I do.'

Jack steadily refused the brandy and water, and steadily persisted in taking his leave.

'I must try if I can't walk it off,' he said. 'Remember to-morrow morning – eleven o'clock, Avenue Road side of the Regent's Park.'

With those words he went out. His hardened relative laughed desperately, and resumed the dirty clay pipe.

I sat down on the side of my bed, actually quivering with excitement.

It is clear to me that no attempt has yet been made to

change the stolen bank-notes; and I may add that Sergeant Bulmer was of that opinion also, when he left the case in my hands. What is the natural conclusion to draw from the conversation which I have just set down? Evidently, that the confederates meet to-morrow to take their respective shares in the stolen money, and to decide on the safest means of getting the notes changed the day after. Mr Jay is, beyond a doubt, the leading criminal in this business, and he will probably run the chief risk – that of changing the fifty-pound note. I shall, therefore, still make it my busines to follow him – attending at the Regent's Park to-morrow, and doing my best to hear what is said there. If another appointment is made the day after, I shall, of course, go to it. In the meantime, I shall want the immediate assistance of two competent persons (supposing the rascals separate after their meeting) to follow the two minor criminals. It is only fair to add, that, if the rogues all retire together, I shall probably keep my subordinates in reserve. Being naturally ambitious, I desire, if possible, to have the whole credit of discovering this robbery to myself.

8th July.

I have to acknowledge, with thanks, the speedy arrival of my two subordinates – men of very average abilities, I am afraid; but, fortunately, I shall always be on the spot to direct them.

My first business this morning was, necessarily, to prevent mistakes by accounting to Mr and Mrs Yatman for the presence of two strangers on the scene. Mr Yatman (between ourselves, a poor feeble man) only shook his head and groaned. Mrs Yatman (that superior woman) favoured me with a charming look of intelligence.

'Oh, Mr Sharpin!' she said, 'I am so sorry to see those two men! Your sending for their assistance looks as if you were beginning to be doubtful of success.'

I privately winked at her (she is very good in allowing me to do so without taking offence), and told her, in my facetious way, that she laboured under a slight mistake.

'It is because I am sure of success, ma'am, that I send for them. I am determined to recover the money, not for my own sake only, but for Mr Yatman's sake – and for yours.'

I laid a considerable amount of stress on those last three words. She said: 'Oh, Mr Sharpin!' again – and blushed of a heavenly red – and looked down at her work. I could go to the world's end with that woman, if Mr Yatman would only die.

I sent off the two subordinates to wait, until I wanted them, at the Avenue Road gate of the Regent's Park. Half an hour afterwards I was following in the same direction myself, at the heels of Mr Jay.

The two confederates were punctual to the appointed time. I blush to record it, but it is nevertheless necessary to state, that the third rogue – the nameless desperado of my report, or if you prefer it, the mysterious 'Somebody Else' of the conversation between the two brothers – is a Woman! and, what is worse, a young woman! and what is more lamentable still, a nice-looking woman! I have long resisted a growing conviction, that, wherever there is mischief in this world, an individual of the fair sex is inevitably certain to be mixed up in it. After the experience of this morning, I can struggle against that sad conclusion no longer. I give up the sex – excepting Mrs Yatman, I give up the sex.

The man named 'Jack' offered the woman his arm. Mr Jay placed himself on the other side of her. The three then walked away slowly among the trees. I followed them at a respectful distance. My two subordinates, at a respectful distance also, followed me.

It was, I deeply regret to say, impossible to get near enough to them to overhear their conversation, without running too great a risk of being discovered. I could only infer from their gestures and actions that they were all three talking with extraordinary earnestness on some subject which deeply interested them. After having been engaged in this way a full quarter of an hour, they suddenly turned round to retrace their steps. My presence of mind did not forsake me in this emergency. I signed to the two subordinates to walk on carelessly and pass them, while I myself slipped dexterously behind a tree. As they came by me, I heard 'Jack' address these words to Mr Jay:

'Let us say half-past ten to-morrow morning. And mind you come in a cab. We had better not risk taking one in this neighbourhood.'

Mr Jay made some brief reply, which I could not overhear. They walked back to the place at which they had met, shaking hands there with an audacious cordiality which it quite sickened me to see. They then separated. I followed Mr Jay. My subordinates paid the same delicate attention to the other two.

Instead of taking me back to Rutherford Street, Mr Jay led me to the Strand. He stopped at a dingy, disreputable-looking house, which, according to the inscription over the door, was a newspaper office, but which, in my judgment, had all the external appearance of a place devoted to the reception of stolen goods.

After remaining inside for a few minutes, he came out, whistling, with his fingers and thumb in his waistcoat pocket. A less discreet man than myself would have arrested him on the spot. I remembered the necessity of catching the two confederates, and the importance of not interfering with the appointment that had been made for the next morning. Such coolness as this, under trying circumstances, is rarely to be found, I should imagine, in a young beginner, whose reputation as a detective policeman is still to make.

From the house of suspicious appearance, Mr Jay betook himself to a cigar-divan, and read the magazines over a cheroot. I sat at a table near him, and read the magazines likewise over a cheroot. From the divan he strolled to the tavern and had his chops. I strolled to the tavern and had my chops. When he had done, he went back to his lodging. When I had done, I went back to mine. He was overcome with drowsiness early in the evening, and went to bed. As soon as I heard him snoring, I was overcome with drowsiness, and went to bed also.

Early in the morning my two subordinates came to make their report.

They had seen the man named 'Jack' leave the woman near the gate of an apparently respectable villa-residence, not far from the Regent's Park. Left to himself, he took a turning to the right, which led to a sort of suburban street, principally inhabited by shopkeepers. He stopped at the private door of one of the houses, and let himself in with his own key – looking about him as he opened the door, and staring suspiciously at my men as they lounged along on the opposite side of the way. These were all the particulars which the subordinates had to communicate. I kept them in my room to attend on me, if needful, and mounted to my peep-hole to have a look at Mr Jay.

He was occupied in dressing himself, and was taking extraordinary pains to destroy all traces of the natural slovenliness of his appearance. This was precisely what I expected. A vagabond like Mr Jay knows the importance of giving himself a respectable look when he is going to run the risk of changing a stolen bank-note. At five minutes past ten o'clock, he had given the last brush to his shabby hat and the last scouring with bread-crumb to his dirty gloves. At ten minutes past ten he was in the street, on his way to the nearest cab-stand, and I and my subordinates were close on his heels.

He took a cab, and we took a cab. I had not overheard them appoint a place of meeting, when following them in the park on the previous day; but I soon found that we were proceeding in the old direction of the Avenue Road gate.

The cab in which Mr Jay was riding turned into the park slowly. We stopped outside, to avoid exciting suspicion. I got out to follow the cab on foot. Just as I did so, I saw it stop, and detected the two confederates approaching it from among the trees. They got in, and the cab was turned about directly. I ran back to my own cab, and told the driver to let them pass him, and then to follow as before.

The man obeyed my directions, but so clumsily as to excite their suspicions. We had been driving after them about three minutes (returning along the road by which we had advanced) when I looked out of the window to see how far they might be ahead of us. As I did this, I saw two hats popped out of the windows of their cab, and two faces looking back at me. I sank into my place in a cold sweat; the expression is coarse, but no other form of words can describe my condition at that trying moment.

'We are found out!' I said faintly to my two subordinates. They stared at me in astonishment. My feelings changed instantly from the depth of despair to the height of indignation.

'It is the cabman's fault. Get out, one of you,' I said, with dignity – 'get out and punch his head.'

Instead of following my directions (I should wish this act of disobedience to be reported at headquarters) they both looked out of the window. Before I could pull them back, they both

sat down again. Before I could express my just indignation,
they both grinned, and said to me: 'Please to look out, sir!'

I did look out. The thieves' cab had stopped.

Where?

At a church door!!!

What effect this discovery might have had upon the ordinary
run of men, I don't know. Being of a strong religious turn
myself, it filled me with horror. I have often read of the
unprincipled cunning of criminal persons; but I never before
heard of three thieves attempting to double on their pursuers
by entering a church! The sacrilegious audacity of that proceeding is, I should think, unparalleled in the annals of crime.

I checked my grinning subordinates by a frown. It was easy
to see what was passing in their superficial minds. If I had
not been able to look below the surface, I might, on observing
two nicely dressed men and one nicely dressed woman enter a
church before eleven in the morning on a weekday, have come
to the same hasty conclusion at which my inferiors had
evidently arrived. As it was, appearances had no power to
impose on *me*. I got out, and, followed by one of my men,
entered the church. The other man I sent round to watch the
vestry door. You may catch a weasel asleep – but not your
humble servant, Matthew Sharpin!

We stole up the gallery stairs, diverged to the organ loft,
and peered through the curtains in front. There they were all
three, sitting in a pew below – yes, incredible as it may
appear, sitting in a pew below!

Before I could determine what to do, a clergyman made his
appearance in full canonicals, from the vestry door, followed
by a clerk. My brain whirled, and my eyesight grew dim.
Dark remembrances of robberies committed in vestries floated
through my mind. I trembled for the excellent man in full
canonicals – I even trembled for the clerk.

The clergyman placed himself inside the altar rails. The
three desperadoes approached him. He opened his book, and
began to read. What? – you will ask.

I answer, without the slightest hesitation, the first lines of
the Marriage Service.

My subordinate had the audacity to look at me, and then to
stuff his pocket-handkerchief into his mouth. I scorned to pay
any attention to him. After I had discovered that the man
'Jack' was the bridegroom, and that the man Jay acted the

part of father, and gave away the bride, I left the church, followed by my man, and joined the other subordinate outside the vestry door. Some people in my position would now have felt rather crestfallen, and would have begun to think that they had made a very foolish mistake. Not the faintest misgiving of any kind troubled me. I did not feel in the slightest degree depreciated in my own estimation. And even now, after a lapse of three hours, my mind remains, I am happy to say, in the same calm and hopeful condition.

As soon as I and my subordinates were assembled together outside the church, I intimated my intention of still following the other cab, in spite of what had occurred. My reason for deciding on this course will appear presently. The two subordinates were astonished at my resolution. One of them had the impertinence to say to me:

'If you please, sir, who is it that we are after? A man who has stolen money, or a man who has stolen a wife?'

The other low person encouraged him by laughing. Both have deserved an official reprimand; and both, I sincerely trust, will be sure to get it.

When the marriage ceremony was over, the three got into their cab; and once more our vehicle (neatly hidden round the corner of the church, so that they could not suspect it to be near them) started to follow theirs.

We traced them to the terminus of the South-Western Railway. The newly married couple took tickets for Richmond – paying their fare with a half-sovereign, and so depriving me of the pleasure of arresting them, which I should certainly have done, if they had offered a bank-note. They parted from Mr Jay, saying: 'Remember the address – 14 Babylon Terrace. You dine with us to-morrow week.' Mr Jay accepted the invitation, and added, jocosely, that he was going home at once to get off his clean clothes, and to be comfortable and dirty again for the rest of the day. I have to report that I saw him home safely, and that he is comfortable and dirty again (to use his own disgraceful language) at the present moment.

Here the affair rests, having by this time reached what I may call its first stage.

I know very well what persons of hasty judgment will be inclined to say of my proceedings thus far. They will assert that I have been deceiving myself all through, in the most absurd way; they will declare that the suspicious conver-

sations which I have reported, referred solely to the difficulties and dangers of successfully carrying out a runaway match;
and they will appeal to the scene in the church, as offering
undeniable proof of the correctness of their assertions. So let
it be. I dispute nothing up to this point. But I ask a question,
out of the depths of my own sagacity as a man of the world,
which the bitterest of my enemies will not, I think, find it
particularly easy to answer.

Granted the fact of the marriage, what proof does it afford
me of the innocence of the three persons concerned in that
clandestine transaction? It gives me none. On the contrary, it
strengthens my suspicions against Mr Jay and his confederates, because it suggests a distinct motive for their stealing
the money. A gentleman who is going to spend his honeymoon
at Richmond wants money; and a gentleman who is in debt to
all his tradespeople wants money. Is this an unjustifiable
imputation of bad motives? In the name of outraged morality,
I deny it. These men have combined together, and have stolen
a woman. Why should they not combine together, and steal a
cash-box? I take my stand on the logic of rigid virtue; and I
defy all the sophistry of vice to move me an inch out of my
position.

Speaking of virtue, I may add that I have put this view of
the case to Mr and Mrs Yatman. That accomplished and
charming woman found it difficult, at first, to follow the close
chain of my reasoning. I am free to confess that she shook her
head, and shed tears, and joined her husband in premature
lamentation over the loss of the two hundred pounds. But a
little careful explanation on my part, and a little attentive
listening on hers, ultimately changed her opinion. She now
agrees with me, that there is nothing in this unexpected
circumstance of the clandestine marriage which absolutely
tends to divert suspicion from Mr Jay, or Mr 'Jack,' or the
runaway lady. 'Audacious hussy' was the term my fair friend
used in speaking of her, but let that pass. It is more to the
purpose to record that Mrs Yatman has not lost confidence in
me and that Mr Yatman promises to follow her example, and
do his best to look hopefully for future results.

I have now, in the new turn that circumstances have taken,
to await advice from your office. I pause for fresh orders with
all the composure of a man who had got two strings to his
bow. When I traced the three confederates from the church

door to the railway terminus, I had two motives for doing so. First, I followed them as a matter of official business, believing them still to have been guilty of the robbery. Secondly, I followed them as a matter of private speculation, with a view of discovering the place of refuge to which the runaway couple intended to retreat, and of making my information a marketable commodity to offer to the young lady's family and friends. Thus, whatever happens, I may congratulate myself beforehand on not having wasted my time. If the office approves of my conduct, I have my plan ready for further proceedings. If the office blames me, I shall take myself off, with my marketable information, to the genteel villa-residence in the neighbourhood of the Regent's Park. Anyway, the affair puts money into my pocket, and does credit to my penetration as an uncommonly sharp man.

I have only one word more to add, and it is this: If any individual ventures to assert that Mr Jay and his confederates are innocent of all share in the stealing of the cash-box, I, in return, defy that individual – though he may even be Chief Inspector Theakstone himself – to tell me who has committed the robbery at Rutherford Street, Soho.

> I have the honour to be,
> Your very obedient servant,
> MATTHEW SHARPIN.

From Chief Inspector Theakstone to Sergeant Bulmer

BIRMINGHAM, *9th July*.

SERGEANT BULMER, – That empty-headed puppy, Mr Matthew Sharpin, has made a mess of the case at Rutherford Street, exactly as I expected he would. Business keeps me in this town; so I write to you to set the matter straight. I enclose, with this, the pages of feeble scribble-scrabble which the creature, Sharpin, calls a report. Look them over; and when you have made your way through all the gabble, I think you will agree with me that the conceited booby has looked for the thief in every direction but the right one. You can lay your hand on the guilty person in five minutes, now. Settle the case at once; forward your report to me at this place; and tell Mr Sharpin that he is suspended till further notice.

> Yours,
> FRANCIS THEAKSTONE.

From Sergeant Bulmer to Chief Inspector Theakstone

LONDON, *10th July.*

INSPECTOR THEAKSTONE, – Your letter and enclosure came safe to hand. Wise men, they say, may always learn something, even from a fool. By the time I had got through Sharpin's maundering report of his own folly, I saw my way clear enough to the end of the Rutherford Street case, just as you thought I should. In half an hour's time I was at the house. The first person I saw there was Mr Sharpin himself.

'Have you come to help me?' says he.

'Not exactly,' says I. 'I've come to tell you that you are suspended till further notice.'

'Very good,' says he, not taken down, by so much as a single peg, in his own estimation. 'I thought you would be jealous of me. It's very natural; and I don't blame you. Walk in, pray, and make yourself at home. I'm off to do a little detective business on my own account, in the neighbourhood of the Regent's Park. Ta-ta, sergeant, ta-ta!'

With those words he took himself out of the way – which was exactly what I wanted him to do.

As soon as the maid-servant had shut the door, I told her to inform her master that I wanted to say a word to him in private. She showed me into the parlour behind the shop; and there was Mr Yatman, all alone, reading the newspaper.

'About this matter of the robbery, sir,' says I.

He cut me short, peevishly enough – being naturally a poor, weak, womanish sort of man. 'Yes, yes, I know,' says he. 'You have come to tell me that your wonderfully clever man, who has bored holes in my second-floor partition, has made a mistake, and is off the scent of the scoundrel who has stolen my money.'

'Yes, sir,' says I. 'That *is* one of the things I came to tell you. But I have got something else to say, besides that.'

'Can you tell me who the thief is?' says he, more pettish than ever.

'Yes, sir,' says I, 'I think I can.'

He put down the newspaper, and began to look rather anxious and frightened.

'Not my shopman?' says he. 'I hope, for the man's own sake, it's not my shopman.'

'Guess again, sir,' says I.

'That idle slut, the maid?' says he.

'She is idle, sir,' says I, 'and she is also a slut; my first inquiries about her proved as much as that. But she's not the thief.'

'Then in the name of Heaven, who is?' says he.

'Will you please to prepare yourself for a very disagreeable surprise, sir?' says I. 'And in case you lose your temper, will you excuse my remarking that I am the stronger man of the two, and that, if you allow yourself to lay hands on me, I may unintentionally hurt you, in pure self-defence?'

He turned as pale as ashes, and pushed his chair two or three feet away from me.

'You have asked me to tell you, sir, who has taken your money,' I went on. 'If you insist on my giving you an answer – '

'I do insist,' he said faintly. 'Who has taken it?'

'Your wife has taken it,' I said very quietly, and very positively at the same time.

He jumped out of the chair as if I had put a knife into him, and struck his fist on the table, so heavily that the wood cracked again.

'Steady, sir,' says I. 'Flying into a passion won't help you to the truth.'

'It's a lie!' says he, with another smack of his fist on the table – 'a base, vile, infamous lie! How dare you – '

He stopped, and fell back into the chair again, looked about him in a bewildered way, and ended by bursting out crying.

'When your better sense comes back to you, sir,' says I, 'I am sure you will be gentleman enough to make an apology for the language you have just used. In the meantime, please to listen, if you can, to a word of explanation. Mr Sharpin has sent in a report to our inspector, of the most irregular and ridiculous kind; setting down, not only all his own foolish doings and sayings, but the doings and sayings of Mrs Yatman as well. In most cases, such a document would have been fit for the waste-paper basket; but, in this particular case, it so happens that Mr Sharpin's budget of nonsense leads to a certain conclusion, which the simpleton of a writer has been quite innocent of suspecting from the beginning to the end. Of that conclusion I am so sure, that I will forfeit my place, if it does not turn out that Mrs Yatman has been practising upon the folly and conceit of this young man, and

that she has tried to shield herself from discovery by pur-
posely encouraging him to suspect the wrong persons. I tell
you that confidently; and I will even go further. I will
undertake to give a decided opinion as to why Mrs Yatman
took the money, and what she has done with it, or with a part
of it. Nobody can look at that lady, sir, without being struck
by the great taste and beauty of her dress – '

As I said those last words, the poor man seemed to find his
powers of speech again. He cut me short directly, as haughtily
as if he had been a duke instead of a stationer.

'Try some other means of justifying your vile calumny
against my wife,' says he. 'Her milliner's bill for the past year
is on my file of receipted accounts at this moment.'

'Excuse me, sir,' says I, 'but that proves nothing. Milliners,
I must tell you, have a certain rascally custom which comes
within the daily experience of our office. A married lady who
wishes it, can keep two accounts at her dressmaker's; one is
the account which her husband sees and pays; the other is the
private account, which contains all the extravagant items,
and which the wife pays secretly, by instalments, whenever
she can. According to our usual experience, these instalments
are mostly squeezed out of the housekeeping money. In your
case, I suspect no instalments have been paid; proceedings
have been threatened; Mrs Yatman, knowing your altered
circumstances, has felt herself driven into a corner; and she
has paid her private account out of your cash-box.'

'I won't believe it,' says he. 'Every word you speak is an
abominable insult to me and to my wife.'

'Are you man enough, sir,' says I, taking him up short, in
order to save time and words, 'to get that receipted bill you
spoke of just now off the file, and come with me at once to the
milliner's shop where Mrs Yatman deals?'

He turned red in the face at that, got the bill directly, and
put on his hat. I took out of my pocket-book the list containing
the numbers of the lost notes, and we left the house together
immediately.

Arrived at the milliner's (one of the expensive West End
houses, as I expected), I asked for a private interview, on important business, with the mistress of the concern. It was not the
first time that she and I had met over the same delicate inves-
tigation. The moment she set eyes on me, she sent for her husband. I mentioned who Mr Yatman was, and what we wanted.

'This is strictly private?' inquires her husband. I nodded my head.

'And confidential?' says the wife. I nodded again.

'Do you see any objection, dear, to obliging the sergeant with a sight of the books?' says the husband.

'None in the world, love, if you approve of it,' says the wife.

All this while poor Mr Yatman sat looking the picture of astonishment and distress, quite out of place at our polite conference. The books were brought – and one minute's look at the pages in which Mrs Yatman's name figured was enough, and more than enough, to prove the truth of every word I had spoken.

There, in one book, was the husband's account, which Mr Yatman had settled. And there, in the other, was the private account, crossed off also; the date of settlement being the very day after the loss of the cash-box. This said private account amounted to the sum of a hundred and seventy-five pounds, odd shillings; and it extended over a period of three years. Not a single instalment had been paid on it. Under the last line was an entry to this effect: 'Written to for the third time, 23rd June.' I pointed to it, and asked the milliner if that meant 'last June.' Yes, it did mean last June; and she now deeply regretted to say that it had been accompanied by a threat of legal proceedings.

'I thought you gave good customers more than three years credit?' says I.

The milliner looks at Mr Yatman, and whispers to me – 'Not when a lady's husband gets into difficulties.'

She pointed to the account as she spoke. The entries after the time when Mr Yatman's circumstances became involved were just as extravagant, for a person in his wife's situation, as the entries for the year before that period. If the lady had economized in other things, she had certainly not economized in the matter of dress.

There was nothing left now but to examine the cash-book, for form's sake. The money had been paid in notes, the amounts and numbers of which exactly tallied with the figures set down in my list.

After that, I thought it best to get Mr Yatman out of the house immediately. He was in such a pitiable condition, that I called a cab and accompanied him home in it. At first he cried and raved like a child: but I soon quieted him – and I must add, to his credit, that he made me a most handsome apology for his language, as the cab drew up at his house door. In return, I tried to give him some advice about how to set matters right, for the future, with his wife. He paid very little attention to me, and went upstairs muttering to himself about a separation. Whether Mrs Yatman will come cleverly out of the scrape or not seems doubtful. I should say, myself, that she will go into screeching hysterics, and so frighten the poor man into forgiving her. But this is no business of ours. So far as we are concerned, the case is now at an end; and the present report may come to a conclusion along with it.

I remain, accordingly, yours to command,

THOMAS BULMER.

PS. I have to add that, on leaving Rutherford Street, I met Mr Matthew Sharpin coming to pack up his things.

'Only think!' says he, rubbing his hands in great spirit, 'I've been to the genteel villa-residence; and the moment I mentioned my business, they kicked me out directly. There were two witnesses of the assault; and it's worth a hundred pounds to me, if it's worth a farthing.'

'I wish you joy of your luck,' says I.

'Thank you,' says he. 'When may I pay you the same compliment on finding the thief?'

'Whenever you like,' says I, 'for the thief is found.'

'Just what I expected,' says he. 'I've done all the work; and now you cut in, and claim all the credit – Mr Jay of course?'

'No,' says I.

'Who is it, then?' says he.

'Ask Mrs Yatman,' says I. 'She's waiting to tell you.'

'All right! I'd much rather hear it from that charming woman than from you,' says he, and goes into the house in a mighty hurry.

What do you think of that, Inspector Theakstone? Would you like to stand in Mr Sharpin's shoes? I shouldn't, I can promise you!

From Chief Inspector Theakstone to Mr Matthew Sharpin

12th July.

SIR, – Sergeant Bulmer has already told you to consider yourself suspended until further notice. I have now authority to add, that your services as a member of the Detective Police are positively declined. You will please to take this letter as notifying officially your dismissal from the force.

I may inform you, privately, that your rejection is not intended to cast any reflection on your character. It merely implies that you are not quite sharp enough for our purpose. If we *are* to have a new recruit among us, we should infinitely prefer Mrs Yatman.

Your obedient servant,

FRANCIS THEAKSTONE.

Note on the preceding correspondence, added by Mr Theakstone

The Inspector is not in a position to append any explanations of importance to the last of the letters. It has been discovered that Mr Matthew Sharpin left the house in Rutherford Street five minutes after his interview outside of it with Sergeant Bulmer – his manner expressing the liveliest emotions of terror and astonishment, and his left cheek displaying a bright patch of red, which might have been the result of a slap on the face from a female hand. He was also heard, by the shopman at Rutherford Street, to use a very shocking expression in reference to Mrs Yatman; and was seen to clench his fist vindictively, as he ran round the corner of the street. Nothing more has been heard of him; and it is conjectured that he has left London with the intention of offering his valuable services to the provincial police.

On the interesting domestic subject of Mr and Mrs Yatman still less is known. It has, however, been positively ascertained that the medical attendant of the family was sent for in a great hurry, on the day when Mr Yatman returned from the milliner's shop. The neighbouring chemist received, soon afterwards, a prescription of a soothing nature to make up for Mrs Yatman. The day after, Mr Yatman purchased some smelling-salts at the shop, and afterwards appeared at the circulating library to ask for a novel, descriptive of high life, that would amuse an invalid lady. It has been inferred from these circumstances, that he has not thought it desirable to carry out his threat of separating himself from his wife – at least in the present (presumed) condition of that lady's sensitive nervous system.

Oscar Wilde 1854–1900

Oscar Fingal O'Flahertie Wills Wilde was born in Dublin in 1854. He was educated at Trinity College, Dublin, and Magdalen College, Oxford, where he showed himself to be a brilliant scholar and a great wit. He kept people entertained with his stories which were so interesting they could 'charm toothache away'. 'He had one of the most alluring voices that I have listened to, round and soft and full of variety of expression, and the cleverness of his remarks received added value from his manner of delivering them,' said Lillie Langtry, a famous English actress and friend of the Prince of Wales.

At first Wilde wrote little, but was a great performer and went on a tour of the United States and Canada, making a name for himself as a poet and art lecturer with an extravagant taste in clothes. After his marriage to Constance and the birth of two sons, Wilde needed to earn money and became editor of the magazine *Woman's World* from 1887 to 1889. He also wrote down many of the stories which had begun life as oral tales and went on to write highly successful plays such as *Lady Windermere's Fan* and *The Importance of Being Earnest*, as well as the more sombre novel *The Picture of Dorian Gray*.

At the height of his success Wilde was involved in a court case over a homosexual affair with Lord Alfred Douglas. Wilde was found guilty and given a sentence of two years' hard labour. After his release from prison he lived in France, physically and psychologically broken. His final work was the powerful poem about capital punishment, 'The Ballad of Reading Gaol'. Wilde died in Paris in November 1900 quipping, 'If another century began and I was still alive it really would be more than the English could stand.'

'The Canterville Ghost' shows Oscar Wilde's great sense of fun. It tells of how an American family moves into a grand English country house, complete with its centuries-old ghost. Their no-nonsense approach, coupled with a fine selection of patent remedies, soon has the ghost in quite a fix.

The Canterville Ghost

Oscar Wilde

A Hylo-Idealistic Romance

I

When Mr Hiram B. Otis, the American Minister, bought Canterville Chase, every one told him he was doing a very foolish thing, as there was no doubt at all that the place was haunted. Indeed, Lord Canterville himself, who was a man of the most punctilious honour, had felt it his duty to mention the fact to Mr Otis when they came to discuss terms.

'We have not cared to live in the place ourselves,' said Lord Canterville, 'since my grand-aunt, the Dowager Duchess of Bolton, was frightened into a fit, from which she never really recovered, by two skeleton hands being placed on her shoulders as she was dressing for dinner, and I feel bound to tell you, Mr Otis, that the ghost has been seen by several living members of my family, as well as by the rector of the parish, the Rev. Augustus Dampier, who is a Fellow of King's College, Cambridge. After the unfortunate accident to the Duchess, none of our younger servants would stay with us, and Lady Canterville often got very little sleep at night, in consequence of the mysterious noises that came from the corridor and the library.'

'My Lord,' answered the Minister, 'I will take the furniture and the ghost at a valuation. I come from a modern country, where we have everything that money can buy; and with all our spry young fellows painting the Old World red, and carrying off your best actors and prima-donnas, I reckon that if there were such a thing as a ghost in Europe, we'd have it at home in a very short time in one of our public museums, or on the road as a show.'

'I fear that the ghost exists,' said Lord Canterville, smiling, 'though it may have resisted the overtures of your enterprising impresarios. It has been well known for three centuries, since 1584 in fact, and always makes its appearance before the death of any member of our family.'

'Well, so does the family doctor for that matter, Lord Canterville. But there is no such thing, sir, as a ghost, and I guess the laws of Nature are not going to be suspended for the British aristocracy.'

'You are certainly very natural in America,' answered Lord Canterville, who did not quite understand Mr Otis's last observation, 'and if you don't mind a ghost in the house, it is all right. Only you must remember I warned you.'

A few weeks after this, the purchase was concluded, and at the close of the season the Minister and his family went down to Canterville Chase. Mrs Otis, who, as Miss Lucretia R. Tappen, of West 53rd Street, had been a celebrated New York belle, was now a very handsome, middle-aged woman with fine eyes, and a superb profile. Many American ladies on leaving their native land adopt an appearance of chronic ill-health, under the impression that it is a form of European refinement, but Mrs Otis had never fallen into this error. She had a magnificent constitution, and a really wonderful amount of animal spirits. Indeed, in many respects, she was quite English, and was an excellent example of the fact that we have really everything in common with America nowadays, except, of course, language. Her eldest son, christened Washington by his parents in a moment of patriotism, which he never ceased to regret, was a fair-haired, rather good-looking young man, who had qualified himself for American diplomacy by leading the German at the Newport Casino for three successive seasons, and even in London was well known as an excellent dancer. Gardenias and the peerage were his only weaknesses. Otherwise he was extremely sensible. Miss Virginia E. Otis was a little girl of fifteen, lithe and lovely as a fawn, and with a fine freedom in her large blue eyes. She was a wonderful amazon, and had once raced old Lord Bilton on her pony twice round the park, winning by a length and a half, just in front of the Achilles statue, to the huge delight of the young Duke of Cheshire, who proposed for her on the spot, and was sent back to Eton that very night by his guardians, in floods of tears. After Virginia came the twins, who were usually called 'The Stars and Stripes,' as they were always getting swished. They were delightful boys, and with the exception of the worthy Minister the only true republicans of the family.

As Canterville Chase is seven miles from Ascot, the nearest railway station, Mr Otis had telegraphed for a waggonette to meet them, and they started on their drive in high spirits. It was a lovely July evening, and the air was delicate with the scent of the pinewoods. Now and then they heard a wood pigeon brooding over its own sweet voice, or saw, deep in the rustling fern, the burnished breast of the pheasant. Little squirrels peered at them from the beech-trees as they went by, and the rabbits scudded away through the brushwood and over the mossy knolls, with their white tails in the air. As they entered the avenue of Canterville Chase, however, the sky became suddenly overcast with clouds, a curious stillness seemed to hold the atmosphere, a great flight of rooks passed silently over their heads, and, before they reached the house, some big drops of rain had fallen.

Standing on the steps to receive them was an old woman, neatly dressed in black silk, with a white cap and apron. This was Mrs Umney, the housekeeper, whom Mrs Otis, at Lady Canterville's earnest requst, had consented to keep on in her former position. She made them each a low curtsey as they alighted, and said in a quaint, old-fashioned manner, 'I bid you welcome to Canterville Chase.' Following her, they passed through the fine Tudor hall into the library, a long, low room, panelled in black oak, at the end of which was a large stained-glass window. Here they found tea laid out for them, and, after taking off their wraps, they sat down and began to look round, while Mrs Umney waited on them.

Suddenly Mrs Otis caught sight of a dull red stain on the floor just by the fireplace and, quite unconscious of what it really signified, said to Mrs Umney, 'I am afraid something has been spilt there.'

'Yes, madam,' replied the old housekeeper in a low voice, 'blood has been spilt on that spot.'

'How horrid,' cried Mrs Otis; 'I don't at all care for blood-stains in a sitting-room. It must be removed at once.'

The old woman smiled, and answered in the same low, mysterious voice, 'It is the blood of Lady Eleanore de Canterville, who was murdered on that very spot by her own husband, Sir Simon de Canterville, in 1575. Sir Simon survived her nine years, and disappeared suddenly under very mysterious circumstances. His body has never been discovered, but his guilty spirit still haunts the Chase. The blood-stain has been much admired by tourists and others, and cannot be removed.'

'That is all nonsense,' cried Washington Otis; 'Pinkerton's Champion Stain Remover and Paragon Detergent will clean it up in no time,' and before the terrified housekeeper could interfere he had fallen upon his knees, and was rapidly scouring the floor with a small stick of what looked like a black cosmetic. In a few moments no trace of the blood-stain could be seen.

'I knew Pinkerton would do it,' he exclaimed triumphantly, as he looked round at his admiring family; but no sooner had he said these words than a terrible flash of lightning lit up the sombre room, a fearful peal of thunder made them all start to their feet, and Mrs Umney fainted.

'What a monstrous climate!' said the American Minister calmly, as he lit a long cheroot. 'I guess the old country is so over-populated that they have not enough decent weather for everybody. I have always been of the opinion that emigration is the only thing for England.'

'My dear Hiram,' cried Mrs Otis, 'what can we do with a woman who faints?'

'Charge it to her like breakages,' answered the Minister; 'she won't faint after that;' and in a few moments Mrs Umney certainly came to. There was no doubt, however, that she was extremely upset, and she sternly warned Mr Otis to beware of some trouble coming to the house.

'I have seen things with my own eyes, sir,' she said, 'that would make any Christian's hair stand on end, and many and many a night I have not closed my eyes in sleep for the awful things that are done here.' Mr Otis, however, and his wife warmly assured the honest soul that they were not afraid of ghosts, and, after invoking the blessings of Providence on her new master and mistress, and making arrangements for an increase of salary, the old housekeeper tottered off to her own room.

II

The storm raged fiercely all that night, but nothing of particular note occurred. The next morning, however, when they came down to breakfast, they found the terrible stain of blood once again on the floor. 'I don't think it can be the fault of the Paragon Detergent,' said Washington, 'for I have tried it with everything. It must be the ghost.' He accordingly rubbed out the stain a second time, but the second morning it appeared again. The third morning also it was there, though the library had been locked up at night by Mr Otis himself, and the key carried upstairs. The whole family were now quite interested; Mr Otis began to suspect that he had been too dogmatic in his denial of the existence of ghosts, Mrs Otis expressed her intention of joining the Psychical Society, and Washington prepared a long letter to Messrs Myers and Podmore on the subject of the Permanence of Sanguineous Stains when connected with Crime. That night all doubts about the objective existence of phantasmata were removed for ever.

The day had been warm and sunny; and, in the cool of the evening, the whole family went out to drive. They did not return home till nine o'clock, when they had a light supper. The conversation in no way turned upon ghosts, so there were not even those primary conditions of receptive expectation which so often precede the presentation of psychical phenomena. The subjects discussed, as I have since learned from Mr Otis, were merely such as form the ordinary conversation of cultured Americans of the better class, such as the immense superiority of Miss Fanny Davenport over Sara Bernhardt as an actress; the difficulty of obtaining green corn, buckwheat cakes, and hominy, even in the best English houses; the importance of Boston in the development of the world-soul; the advantages of the baggage check system in railway travelling; and the sweetness of the New York accent as compared to the London drawl. No mention at all was made of the supernatural, nor was Sir Simon de Canterville alluded to in any way. At eleven o'clock the family retired, and by half-past all the lights were out. Some time after, Mr Otis was awakened by a curious noise in the corridor, outside his room. It sounded like the clank of metal, and seemed to be coming nearer every moment. He got up at once, struck a match, and looked at the time. It was exactly one o'clock. He was quite calm, and felt his pulse, which was not at all feverish. The strange noise still continued, and with it he heard distinctly the sound of footsteps. He put on his slippers, took a small oblong phial out of his dressing-case, and opened the door. Right in front of him he saw, in the wan moonlight, an old man of terrible aspect. His eyes were as red burning coals; long grey hair fell over his shoulders in matted coils; his garments, which were of antique cut, were soiled and ragged, and from his wrists and ankles hung heavy manacles and rusty gyves.

'My dear sir,' said Mr Otis, 'I really must insist on your oiling those chains, and have brought you for that purpose a small bottle of the Tammany Rising Sun Lubricator. It is said to be completely efficacious upon one application, and there are several testimonials to that effect on the wrapper from some of our most eminent native divines. I shall leave it here for you by the bedroom candles, and will be happy to supply you with more should you require it.' With these words the United States Minister laid the bottle down on a marble table, and, closing his door, retired to rest.

For a moment the Canterville ghost stood quite motionless in natural indignation; then, dashing the bottle violently upon the polished floor, he fled down the corridor, uttering hollow groans, and emitting a ghastly green light. Just, however, as he reached the top of the great oak staircase, a door was flung open, two little white-robed figures appeared, and a large pillow whizzed past his head! There was evidently no time to be lost, so, hastily adopting the Fourth Dimension of Space as a means of escape, he vanished through the wainscoting, and the house became quite quiet.

On reaching a small secret chamber in the left wing, he leaned up against a moonbeam to recover his breath, and began to try and realise his position. Never, in a brilliant and uninterrupted career of three hundred years, had he been so grossly insulted. He thought of the Dowager Duchess, whom he had frightened into a fit as she stood before the glass in her lace and diamonds; of the four housemaids, who had gone off into hysterics when he merely grinned at them through the curtains of one of the spare bedrooms; of the rector of the parish, whose candle he had blown out as he was coming late one night from the library, and who had been under the care of Sir William Gull ever since, a perfect martyr to nervous disorders; and of old Madame de Tremouillac, who, having wakened up one morning early and seen a skeleton seated in an armchair by the fire reading her diary, had been confined to her bed for six weeks with an attack of brain fever, and, on her recovery, had become reconciled to the Church, and broken off her connection with that notorious sceptic Monsieur de Voltaire. He remembered the terrible night when the wicked Lord Canterville was found choking in his dressing-room, with the knave of diamonds half-way down his throat, and confessed, just before he died, that he had cheated Charles James Fox out of £50,000 at Crockford's by means of that very card, and swore that the ghost had made him swallow it. All his great achievements came back to him again, from the butler who had shot himself in the pantry because he had seen a green hand tapping at the window pane, to the beautiful Lady Stutfield, who was always obliged to wear a black velvet band round her throat to hide the mark of five fingers burnt upon her white skin, and who drowned herself at last in the carp-pond at the end of the King's Walk. With the enthusiastic egotism of the true artist he went over his most celebrated performances, and smiled bitterly to himself as he recalled to mind his last appearance as 'Red Reuben, or the Strangled Babe,' his *début* as 'Gaunt Gibeon, the Bloodsucker of Bexley Moor,' and the *furore* he had excited one lovely June evening by merely playing ninepins with his own bones upon the lawn-tennis ground. And after all this, some wretched modern Americans were to come and offer him the Rising Sun Lubricator, and throw pillows at his head! It was quite unbearable. Besides, no ghost in history had ever been treated in this manner. Accordingly, he determined to have vengeance, and remained till daylight in an attitude of deep thought.

III

The next morning, when the Otis family met at breakfast, they discussed the ghost at some length. The United States Minister was naturally a little annoyed to find that his present had not been accepted. 'I have no wish,' he said, 'to do the ghost any personal injury, and I must say that, considering the length of time he has been in the house, I don't think it is at all polite to throw pillows at him' – a very just remark, at which, I am sorry to say, the twins burst into shouts of laughter. 'Upon the other hand,' he continued, 'if he really declines to use the Rising Sun Lubricator, we shall have to take his chains from him. It would be quite impossible to sleep, with such a noise going on outside the bedrooms.'

For the rest of the week, however, they were undisturbed, the only thing that excited any attention being the continual renewal of the blood-stain on the library floor. This certainly was very strange, as the door was always locked at night by Mr Otis, and the windows kept closely barred. The chameleon-like colour, also, of the stain excited a good deal of comment. Some mornings it was a dull (almost Indian) red, then it would be vermilion, then a rich purple, and once when they came down for family prayers, according to the simple rites of the Free American Reformed Episcopalian Church, they found it a bright emerald-green. These kaleidoscopic changes naturally amused the party very much, and bets on the subject were freely made every evening. The only person who did not enter into the joke was little Virginia, who, for some unexplained reason, was always a good deal distressed at the sight of the blood-stain, and very nearly cried the morning it was emerald-green.

The second appearance of the ghost was on Sunday night. Shortly after they had gone to bed they were suddenly alarmed by a fearful crash in the hall. Rushing downstairs, they found that a large suit of old armour had become detached from its stand, and had fallen on the stone floor, while, seated in a high-backed chair, was the Canterville ghost, rubbing his knees with an expression of acute agony on his face. The twins, having brought their pea-shooters with them, at once discharged two pellets on him, with that accuracy of aim which can only be attained by long and careful practice on a writing-master, while the United States Minister covered him with his revolver, and called upon him, in accordance with Californian etiquette, to hold up his hands! The ghost started up with a wild shriek of rage, and swept through them like a mist, extinguishing Washington Otis's candle as he passed, and so leaving them all in total darkness. On reaching the top of the staircase he recovered himself, and determined to give his celebrated peal of demoniac laughter. This he had on more than one occasion found extremely useful. It was said to have turned Lord Raker's wig grey in a single night, and had certainly made three of Lady Canterville's French governesses give warning before their month was up. He accordingly laughed his most horrible laugh, till the old vaulted roof rang and rang again, but hardly had the fearful echo died away when a door opened, and Mrs Otis came out in a light blue dressing-gown. 'I am afraid you are far from well,' she said, 'and have brought you a bottle of Dr Dobell's tincture. If it is indigestion, you will find it a most excellent remedy.' The ghost glared at her in fury, and began at once to make preparations for turning himself into a large black dog, an accomplishment for which he was justly renowned, and to which the family doctor always attributed the permanent idiocy of Lord Canterville's uncle, the Hon. Thomas Horton. The sound of approaching footsteps, however, made him hesitate in his fell purpose, so he contented himself with becoming faintly phosphorescent, and vanished with a deep churchyard groan, just as the twins had come up to him.

On reaching his room he entirely broke down, and became a prey to the most violent agitation. The vulgarity of the twins, and the gross materialism of Mrs Otis, were naturally extremely annoying, but what really distressed him most was, that he had been unable to wear the suit of mail. He had hoped that even modern Americans would be thrilled by the sight of a Spectre In Armour, if for no more sensible reason, at least out of respect for their national poet Longfellow, over whose graceful and attractive poetry he himself had whiled away many a weary hour when the Cantervilles were up in town. Besides, it was his own suit. He had worn it with great success at the Kenilworth tournament, and had been highly complimented on it by no less a person than the Virgin Queen herself. Yet when he had put it on, he had been completely overpowered by the weight of the huge breastplate and steel casque, and had fallen heavily on the stone pavement, barking both his knees severely, and bruising the knuckles of his right hand.

For some days after this he was extremely ill, and hardly stirred out of his room at all, except to keep the blood-stain in proper repair. However, by taking great care of himself, he recovered, and resolved to make a third attempt to frighten the United States Minister and his family. He selected Friday, the 17th of August, for his appearance, and spent most of that day in looking over his wardrobe, ultimately deciding in favour of a large slouched hat with a red feather, a winding-sheet frilled at the wrists and neck, and a rusty dagger. Towards evening a violent storm of rain came on, and the

wind was so high that all the windows and doors in the old
house shook and rattled. In fact, it was just such weather as
he loved. His plan of action was this. He was to make his way
quietly to Washington Otis's room, gibber at him from the
foot of the bed, and stab himself three times in the throat to
the sound of low music. He bore Washington a special grudge,
being quite aware that it was he who was in the habit of
removing the famous Canterville blood-stain, by means of
Pinkerton's Paragon Detergent. Having reduced the reckless
and foolhardy youth to a condition of abject terror, he was
then to proceed to the room occupied by the United States
Minister and his wife, and there to place a clammy hand on
Mrs Otis's forehead, while he hissed into her trembling
husband's ear the awful secrets of the charnel-house. With
regard to little Virginia, he had not quite made up his mind.
She had never insulted him in any way, and was pretty and
gentle. A few hollow groans from the wardrobe, he thought,
would be more than sufficient, or, if that failed to wake her,
he might grabble at the counterpane with palsy-twitching
fingers. As for the twins, he was quite determined to teach
them a lesson. The first thing to be done was, of course, to sit
upon their chests, so as to produce the stifling sensation of
nightmare. Then, as their beds were quite close to each other,
to stand between them in the form of a green, icy-cold corpse,
till they became paralysed with fear, and finally, to throw off
the winding-sheet, and crawl round the room, with white,
bleached bones and one rolling eyeball, in the character of
'Dumb Daniel, or the Suicide's Skeleton,' a *rôle* in which he
had on more than one occasion produced a great effect, and
which he considered quite equal to his famous part of 'Martin
the Maniac, or the Masked Mystery.'

At half-past ten he heard the family going to bed. For some
time he was disturbed by wild shrieks of laughter from the
twins, who, with the light-hearted gaiety of schoolboys, were
evidently amusing themselves before they retired to rest, but
at a quarter past eleven all was still, and, as midnight
sounded, he sallied forth. The owl beat against the window
pane, the raven croaked from the old yew-tree, and the wind
wandered moaning round the house like a lost soul; but the
Otis family slept unconscious of their doom, and high above
the rain and storm he could hear the steady snoring of the
Minister for the United States. He stepped stealthily out of

the wainscoting, with an evil smile on his cruel, wrinkled
mouth, and the moon hid her face in a cloud as he stole past
the great oriel window, where his own arms and those of his
murdered wife were blazoned in azure and gold. On and on he
glided, like an evil shadow, the very darkness seeming to
loathe him as he passed. Once he thought he heard something
call, and stopped; but it was only the baying of a dog from the
Red Farm, and he went on, muttering strange sixteenth-
century curses, and ever and anon brandishing the rusty
dagger in the midnight air. Finally he reached the corner of
the passage that led to luckless Washington's room. For a
moment he paused there, the wind blowing his long grey
locks about his head, and twisting into grotesque and fantastic folds the nameless horror of the dead man's shroud. Then
the clock struck the quarter, and he felt the time was come.
He chuckled to himself, and turned the corner; but no sooner
had he done so, than, with a piteous wail of terror, he fell
back, and hid his blanched face in his long, bony hands. Right
in front of him was standing a horrible spectre, motionless as
a carven image, and monstrous as a madman's dream! Its
head was bald and burnished; its face round, and fat, and
white; and hideous laughter seemed to have writhed its
features into an eternal grin. From the eyes streamed rays
of scarlet light, the mouth was a wide well of fire, and a
hideous garment, like to his own, swathed with its silent
snows the Titan form. On its breast was a placard with
strange writing in antique characters, some scroll of shame it
seemed, some record of wild sins, some awful calendar of
crime, and, with its right hand, it bore aloft a falchion of
gleaming steel.

Never having seen a ghost before, he naturally was terribly
frightened, and, after a second hasty glance at the awful
phantom, he fled back to his room, tripping up in his long
winding sheet as he sped down the corridor, and finally
dropping the rusty dagger into the Minister's jack-boots,
where it was found in the morning by the butler. Once in the
privacy of his own apartment, he flung himself down on a
small pallet-bed, and hid his face under the clothes. After a
time, however, the brave old Canterville spirit asserted itself,
and he determined to go and speak to the other ghost as soon
as it was daylight. Accordingly, just as the dawn was touching
the hills with silver, he returned towards the spot where he

had first laid eyes on the grisly phantom, feeling that, after all, two ghosts were better than one, and that, by the aid of his new friend, he might safely grapple with the twins. On reaching the spot, however, a terrible sight met his gaze. Something had evidently happened to the spectre, for the light had entirely faded from its hollow eyes, the gleaming falchion had fallen from its hand, and it was leaning up against the wall in a strained and uncomfortable attitude. He rushed forward and seized it in his arms, when, to his horror, the head slipped off and rolled on the floor, the body assumed a recumbent posture, and he found himself clasping a white dimity bedcurtain, with a sweeping-brush, a kitchen cleaver, and a hollow turnip lying at his feet! Unable to understand this curious transformation, he clutched the placard with feverish haste, and there, in the grey morning light, he read these fearful words:—

> *YE OTIS GHOSTE.*
> *Ye Onlie True and Originale Spook.*
> *Beware of Ye Imitationes.*
> *All others are Counterfeite.*

The whole thing flashed across him. He had been tricked, foiled, and outwitted! The old Canterville look came into his eyes; he ground his toothless gums together; and, raising his withered hands high above his head, swore, according to the picturesque phraseology of the antique school, that when Chanticleer had sounded twice his merry horn, deeds of blood would be wrought, and Murder walk abroad with silent feet.

Hardly had he finished this awful oath when, from the red-tiled roof of a distant homestead, a cock crew. He laughed a long, low, bitter laugh, and waited. Hour after hour he waited, but the cock, for some strange reason, did not crow again. Finally, at half-past seven, the arrival of the housemaids made him give up his fearful vigil, and he stalked back to his room, thinking of his vain oath and baffled purpose. There he consulted several books of ancient chivalry, of which he was exceedingly fond, and found that, on every occasion on which this oath had been used, Chanticleer had always crowed a

second time. 'Perdition seize the naughty fowl,' he muttered,
'I have seen the day when, with my stout spear, I would have
run him through the gorge, and made him crow for me an
'twere in death!' He then retired to a comfortable lead coffin,
and stayed there till evening.

IV

The next day the ghost was very weak and tired. The terrible
excitement of the last four weeks was beginning to have its
effect. His nerves were completely shattered, and he started
at the slightest noise. For five days he kept his room, and at
last made up his mind to give up the point of the blood-stain
on the library floor. If the Otis family did not want it, they
clearly did not deserve it. They were evidently people on a
low, material plane of existence, and quite incapable of
appreciating the symbolic value of sensuous phenomena. The
question of phantasmic apparitions, and the development of
astral bodies, was of course quite a different matter, and
really not under his control. It was his solemn duty to appear
in the corridor once a week, and to gibber from the large oriel
window on the first and third Wednesdays in every month,
and he did not see how he could honourably escape from his
obligations. It is quite true that his life had been very evil,
but, upon the other hand, he was most conscientious in all
things connected with the supernatural. For the next three
Saturdays, accordingly, he traversed the corridor as usual
between midnight and three o'clock, taking every possible
precaution against being either heard or seen. He removed
his boots, trod as lightly as possible on the old worm-eaten
boards, wore a large black velvet cloak, and was careful to
use the Rising Sun Lubricator for oiling his chains. I am
bound to acknowledge that it was with a good deal of difficulty
that he brought himself to adopt this last mode of protection.
However, one night, while the family were at dinner, he
slipped into Mr Otis's bedroom and carried off the bottle. He
felt a little humiliated at first, but afterwards was sensible
enough to see that there was a great deal to be said for the
invention, and, to a certain degree, it served his purpose.
Still, in spite of everything, he was not left unmolested.
Strings were continually being stretched across the corridor,
over which he tripped in the dark, and on one occasion, while

dressed for the part of 'Black Isaac, or the Huntsman of Hogley Woods,' he met with a severe fall, through treading on a butter-slide, which the twins had constructed from the entrance of the Tapestry Chamber to the top of the oak staircase. This last insult so enraged him, that he resolved to make one final effort to assert his dignity and social position, and determined to visit the insolent young Etonians the next night in his celebrated character of 'Reckless Rupert, or the Headless Earl.'

He had not appeared in this disguise for more than seventy years: in fact, not since he had so frightened pretty Lady Barbara Modish by means of it, that she suddenly broke off her engagement with the present Lord Canterville's grandfather, and ran away to Gretna Green with handsome Jack Castletown, declaring that nothing in the world would induce her to marry into a family that allowed such a horrible phantom to walk up and down the terrace at twilight. Poor Jack was afterwards shot in a duel by Lord Canterville on Wandsworth Common, and Lady Barbara died of a broken heart at Tunbridge Wells before the year was out, so, in every way, it had been a great success. It was, however, an extremely difficult 'make-up,' if I may use such a theatrical expression in connection with one of the greatest mysteries of the supernatural, or, to employ a more scientific term, the higher-natural world, and it took him fully three hours to make his preparations. At last everything was ready, and he was very pleased with his appearance. The big leather riding-boots that went with the dress were just a little too large for him, and he could only find one of the two horse-pistols, but, on the whole, he was quite satisfied, and at a quarter past one he glided out of the wainscoting and crept down the corridor. On reaching the room occupied by the twins, which I should mention was called the Blue Bed Chamber, on account of the colour of its hangings, he found the door just ajar. Wishing to make an effective entrance, he flung it wide open, when a heavy jug of water fell right down on him, wetting him to the skin, and just missing his left shoulder by a couple of inches. At the same moment he heard stifled shrieks of laughter proceeding from the four-post bed. The shock to his nervous system was so great that he fled back to his room as hard as he could go, and the next day he was laid up with a severe cold. The only thing that at all consoled him in the whole affair was the fact that he had not brought his head with him, for, had he done so, the consequences might have been very serious.

He now gave up all hope of ever frightening this rude American family, and contented himself, as a rule, with creeping about the passages in list slippers, with a thick red muffler round his throat for fear of draughts, and a small arquebuse, in case he should be attacked by the twins. The final blow he received occurred on the 19th of September. He had gone downstairs to the great entrance-hall, feeling sure that there, at any rate, he would be quite unmolested, and was amusing himself by making satirical remarks on the large Saroni photographs of the United States Minister and his wife, which had now taken the place of the Canterville family pictures. He was simply but neatly clad in a long shroud, spotted with churchyard mould, had tied up his jaw with a strip of yellow linen, and carried a small lantern and a sexton's spade. In fact, he was dressed for the character of 'Jonas the Graveless, or the Corpse-Snatcher of Chertsey Barn,' one of his most remarkable impersonations, and one which the Cantervilles had every reason to remember, as it was the real origin of their quarrel with their neighbour, Lord Rufford. It was about a quarter past two o'clock in the morning, and, as far as he could ascertain, no one was stirring. As he was strolling towards the library, however, to see if there were any traces left of the blood-stain, suddenly there leaped out on him from a dark corner two figures, who waved their arms wildly above their heads, and shrieked out 'BOO!' in his ear.

Seized with a panic, which, under the circumstances, was only natural, he rushed for the staircase, but found Washington Otis waiting for him there with the big garden-syringe; and being thus hemmed in by his enemies on every side, and driven almost to bay, he vanished into the great iron stove, which, fortunately for him, was not lit, and had to make his way home through the flues and chimneys, arriving at his own room in a terrible state of dirt, disorder, and despair.

After this he was not seen again on any nocturnal expedition. The twins lay in wait for him on several occasions, and strewed the passages with nutshells every night to the great annoyance of their parents and the servants, but it was of no avail. It was quite evident that his feelings were so wounded that he would not appear. Mr Otis consequently resumed his great work on the history of the Democratic Party, on which he had been engaged for some years; Mrs Otis organised a wonderful clam-bake, which amazed the whole county; the boys took to lacrosse, euchre, poker, and other American national games; and Virginia rode about the lanes on her pony, accompanied by the young Duke of Cheshire, who had come to spend the last week of his holidays at Canterville Chase. It was generally assumed that the ghost had gone away, and, in fact, Mr Otis wrote a letter to that effect to Lord Canterville, who, in reply, expressed his great pleasure at the news, and sent his best congratulations to the Minister's worthy wife.

The Otises, however, were deceived, for the ghost was still in the house, and though now almost an invalid, was by no means ready to let matters rest, particularly as he heard that among the guests was the young Duke of Cheshire, whose grand-uncle, Lord Francis Stilton, had once bet a hundred guineas with Colonel Carbury that he would play dice with the Canterville ghost, and was found the next morning lying on the floor of the card-room in such a helpless paralytic state, that though he lived on to a great age, he was never able to say anything again but 'Double Sixes.' The story was well known at the time, though, of course, out of respect to the feelings of the two noble families, every attempt was made to hush it up; and a full account of all the circumstances connected with it will be found in the third volume of Lord Tattle's *Recollections of the Prince Regent and his Friends*. The ghost, then, was naturally very anxious to show that he had not lost his influence over the Stiltons, with whom, indeed, he was distantly connected, his own first cousin having been married *en secondes noces* to the Sieur de Bulkeley, from whom, as every one knows, the Dukes of Cheshire are lineally descended. Accordingly, he made arrangements for appearing to Virginia's little lover in his celebrated impersonation of 'The Vampire Monk, or, the Bloodless Benedictine,' a performance so horrible that when old Lady Startup saw it, which she did on one fatal New Year's Eve, in the year 1764, she went off into the most piercing shrieks, which culminated in violent apoplexy, and died in three days, after disinheriting the Cantervilles, who were her nearest relations, and leaving all her money to her

London apothecary. At the last moment, however, his terror of the twins prevented his leaving his room, and the little Duke slept in peace under the great feathered canopy in the Royal Bedchamber, and dreamed of Virginia.

V

A few days after this, Virginia and her curly-haired cavalier went out riding on Brockley meadows, where she tore her habit so badly in getting through a hedge, that, on their return home, she made up her mind to go up by the back staircase so as not to be seen. As she was running past the Tapestry Chamber, the door of which happened to be open, she fancied she saw some one inside, and thinking it was her mother's maid, who sometimes used to bring her work there, looked in to ask her to mend her habit. To her immense surprise, however, it was the Canterville ghost himself! He was sitting by the window, watching the ruined gold of the yellowing trees fly through the air, and the red leaves dancing madly down the long avenue. His head was leaning on his hand, and his whole attitude was one of extreme depression. Indeed, so forlorn, and so much out of repair did he look, that little Virginia, whose first idea had been to run away and lock herself in her room, was filled with pity, and determined to try and comfort him. So light was her footfall, and so deep his melancholy, that he was not aware of her presence till she spoke to him.

'I am so sorry for you,' she said, 'but my brothers are going back to Eton to-morrow, and then, if you behave yourself, no one will annoy you.'

'It is absurd asking me to behave myself,' he answered, looking round in astonishment at the pretty little girl who had ventured to address him, 'quite absurd. I must rattle my chains, and groan through keyholes, and walk about at night, if that is what you mean. It is my only reason for existing.'

'It is no reason at all for existing, and you know you have been very wicked. Mrs Umney told us, the first day we arrived here, that you had killed your wife.'

'Well, I quite admit it,' said the ghost petulantly, 'but it was a purely family matter, and concerned no one else.'

'It is very wrong to kill any one,' said Virginia, who at

times had a sweet Puritan gravity, caught from some old New England ancestor.

'Oh, I hate the cheap severity of abstract ethics! My wife was very plain, never had my ruffs properly starched, and knew nothing about cookery. Why, there was a buck I had shot in Hogley Woods, a magnificent pricket, and do you know how she had it sent up to table? However, it is no matter now, for it is all over, and I don't think it was very nice of her brothers to starve me to death, though I did kill her.'

'Starve you to death? Oh, Mr Ghost, I mean Sir Simon, are you hungry? I have a sandwich in my case. Would you like it?'

'No, thank you, I never eat anything now; but it is very kind of you, all the same, and you are much nicer than the rest of your horrid, rude, vulgar, dishonest family.'

'Stop!' cried Virginia stamping her foot, 'it is you who are rude, and horrid, and vulgar, and as for dishonesty, you know you stole the paints out of my box to try and furbish up that ridiculous blood-stain in the library. First you took all my reds, including the vermilion, and I couldn't do any more sunsets, then you took the emerald-green and the chrome-yellow, and finally I had nothing left but indigo and Chinese white, and could only do moonlight scenes, which are always depressing to look at, and not at all easy to paint. I never told on you, though I was very much annoyed, and it was most ridiculous, the whole thing; for who ever heard of emerald-green blood?'

'Well, really,' said the ghost, rather meekly, 'what was I to do? It is a very difficult thing to get real blood nowadays, and, as your brother began it all with his Paragon Detergent, I certainly saw no reason why I should not have your paints. As for colour, that is always a matter of taste: the Cantervilles have blue blood, for instance, the very bluest in England; but I know you Americans don't care for things of this kind.'

'You know nothing about it, and the best thing you can do is to emigrate and improve your mind. My father will be only too happy to give you a free passage, and though there is a heavy duty on spirits of every kind, there will be no difficulty about the Custom House, as the officers are all Democrats. Once in New York, you are sure to be a great success. I know lots of people there who would give a hundred thousand dollars to have a grandfather, and much more than that to have a family ghost.'

'I don't think I should like America.'

'I suppose because we have no ruins and no curiosities,' said Virginia satirically.

'No ruins! no curiosities!' answered the ghost; 'you have your navy and your manners.'

'Good evening; I will go and ask papa to get the twins an extra week's holiday.'

'Please don't go, Miss Virginia,' he cried; 'I am so lonely and so unhappy, and I really don't know what to do. I want to go to sleep and I cannot.'

'That's quite absurd! You have merely to go to bed and blow out the candle. It is very difficult sometimes to keep awake, especially at church, but there is no difficulty at all about sleeping. Why, even babies know how to do that, and they are not very clever.'

'I have not slept for three hundred years,' he said sadly, and Virginia's beautiful blue eyes opened in wonder; 'for three hundred years I have not slept, and I am so tired.'

Virginia grew quite grave, and her little lips trembled like rose-leaves. She came towards him, and kneeling down at his side, looked up into his old withered face.

'Poor, poor Ghost,' she murmured; 'have you no place where you can sleep?'

'Far away beyond the pinewoods,' he answered, in a low dreamy voice, 'there is a little garden. There the grass grows long and deep, there are the great white stars of the hemlock flower, there the nightingale sings all night long. All night long he sings, and the cold, crystal moon looks down, and the yew-tree spreads out its giant arms over the sleepers.'

Virginia's eyes grew dim with tears, and she hid her face in her hands.

'You mean the Garden of Death,' she whispered.

'Yes, Death. Death must be so beautiful. To lie in the soft brown earth, with the grasses waving above one's head, and listen to silence. To have no yesterday, and no to-morrow. To forget time, to forgive life, to be at peace. You can help me. You can open for me the portals of Death's house, for Love is always with you, and Love is stronger than Death is.'

Virginia trembled, a cold shudder ran through her, and for

a few moments there was silence. She felt as if she was in a terrible dream.

Then the ghost spoke again, and his voice sounded like the sighing of the wind.

'Have you ever read the old prophecy on the library window?'

'Oh, often,' cried the little girl, looking up; 'I know it quite well. It is painted in curious black letters, and it is difficult to read. There are only six lines:

> *When a golden girl can win*
> *Prayer from out the lips of sin,*
> *When the barren almond bears,*
> *And a little child gives away its tears,*
> *Then shall all the house be still*
> *And peace come to Canterville.*

But I don't know what they mean.'

'They mean,' he said sadly, 'that you must weep with me for my sins, because I have no tears, and pray with me for my soul, because I have no faith, and then, if you have always been sweet, and good, and gentle, the Angel of Death will have mercy on me. You will see fearful shapes in darkness, and wicked voices will whisper in your ear, but they will not harm you, for against the purity of a little child the powers of Hell cannot prevail.'

Virginia made no answer, and the ghost wrung his hands in wild despair as he looked down at her bowed golden head. Suddenly she stood up, very pale, and with a strange light in her eyes. 'I am not afraid,' she said firmly, 'and I will ask the Angel to have mercy on you.'

He rose from his seat with a faint cry of joy, and taking her hand bent over it with old-fashioned grace and kissed it. His fingers were as cold as ice, and his lips burned like fire, but Virginia did not falter, as he led her across the dusky room. On the faded green tapestry were broidered little huntsmen. They blew their tasselled horns and with their tiny hands waved to her to go back. 'Go back! little Virginia,' they cried, 'go back!' but the ghost clutched her hand more tightly, and she shut her eyes against them. Horrible animals with lizard tails, and goggle eyes, blinked at her from the carven chimney-piece, and murmured 'Beware! little Virginia, beware! we

may never see you again,' but the ghost glided on more
swiftly, and Virginia did not listen. When they reached the
end of the room he stopped, and muttered some words she
could not understand. She opened her eyes, and saw the wall
slowly fading away like a mist, and a great black cavern in
front of her. A bitter cold wind swept round them, and she felt
something pulling at her dress. 'Quick, quick,' cried the ghost,
'or it will be too late,' and, in a moment, the wainscoting had
closed behind them, and the Tapestry Chamber was empty.

VI

About ten minutes later, the bell rang for tea, and, as Virginia
did not come down, Mrs Otis sent up one of the footmen to tell
her. After a little time he returned and said that he could not
find Miss Virginia anywhere. As she was in the habit of going
out to the garden every evening to get flowers for the dinner-
table, Mrs Otis was not at all alarmed at first, but when six
o'clock struck, and Virginia did not appear, she became really
agitated, and sent the boys out to look for her, while she
herself and Mr Otis searched every room in the house. At
half-past six the boys came back and said that they could find
no trace of their sister anywhere. They were all now in the
greatest state of excitement, and did not know what to do,
when Mr Otis suddenly remembered that, some few days
before, he had given a band of gipsies permission to camp in
the park. He accordingly at once set off for Blackfell Hollow,
where he knew they were, accompanied by his eldest son and
two of the farm-servants. The little Duke of Cheshire, who
was perfectly frantic with anxiety, begged hard to be allowed
to go too, but Mr Otis would not allow him, as he was afraid
there might be a scuffle. On arriving at the spot, however, he
found that the gipsies had gone, and it was evident that their
departure had been rather sudden, as the fire was still
burning, and some plates were lying on the grass. Having
sent off Washington and the two men to scour the district, he
ran home, and despatched telegrams to all the police inspec-
tors in the country, telling them to look out for a little girl
who had been kidnapped by tramps or gipsies. He then
ordered his horse to be brought round, and, after insisting on
his wife and the three boys sitting down to dinner, rode off
down the Ascot road with a groom. He had hardly, however,

gone a couple of miles, when he heard somebody galloping after him, and, looking round, saw the little Duke coming up on his pony, with his face very flushed and no hat. 'I'm awfully sorry, Mr Otis,' gasped out the boy, 'but I can't eat any dinner as long as Virginia is lost. Please, don't be angry with me; if you had let us be engaged last year, there would never have been all this trouble. You won't send me back, will you? I can't go! I won't go!'

The Minister could not help smiling at the handsome young scapegrace, and was a good deal touched at his devotion to Virginia, so leaning down from his horse, he patted him kindly on the shoulders, and said, 'Well, Cecil, if you won't go back I suppose you must come with me, but I must get you a hat at Ascot.'

'Oh, bother my hat! I want Virginia!' cried the little Duke, laughing, and they galloped on to the railway station. There Mr Otis inquired of the station-master if any one answering to the description of Virginia had been seen on the platform, but could get no news of her. The station-master, however, wired up and down the line, and assured him that a strict watch would be kept for her, and, after having bought a hat for the little Duke from a linen-draper, who was just putting up his shutters, Mr Otis rode off to Bexley, a village about four miles away, which he was told was a well-known haunt of the gipsies, as there was a large common next to it. Here they roused up the rural policeman, but could get no information from him, and, after riding all over the common, they turned their horses' heads homewards, and reached the Chase about eleven o'clock, dead-tired and almost heart-broken. They found Washington and the twins waiting for them at the gate-house with lanterns, as the avenue was very dark. Not the slightest trace of Virginia had been discovered. The gipsies had been caught on Brockley meadows, but she was not with them, and they had explained their sudden departure by saying that they had mistaken the date of Chorton Fair, and had gone off in a hurry for fear they might be late. Indeed, they had been quite distressed at hearing of Virginia's disappearance, as they were grateful to Mr Otis for having allowed them to camp in his park, and four of their number had stayed behind to help in the search. The carp-pond had been dragged, and the whole Chase thoroughly gone over, but without any result. It was evident that, for that night at any rate, Virginia was lost to them; and it was in a state of the deepest depression that Mr Otis and the boys walked up to the house, the groom following behind with the two horses and the pony. In the hall they found a group of frightened servants, and lying on a sofa in the library was poor Mrs Otis, almost out of her mind with terror and anxiety, and having her forehead bathed with eau-de-cologne by the old house-keeper. Mr Otis at once insisted on her having something to eat, and ordered up supper for the whole party. It was a melancholy meal, as hardly any one spoke, and even the twins were awestruck and subdued, as they were very fond of their sister. When they had finished, Mr Otis, in spite of the entreaties of the little Duke, ordered them all to bed, saying that nothing more could be done that night, and that he would telegraph in the morning to Scotland Yard for some detectives to be sent down immediately. Just as they were passing out of the dining-room, midnight began to boom from the clock tower, and when the last stroke sounded they heard a crash and a sudden shrill cry; a dreadful peal of thunder shook the house, a strain of unearthly music floated through the air, a panel at the top of the staircase flew back with a loud noise, and out on the landing, looking very pale and white, with a little casket in her hand, stepped Virginia. In a moment they had all rushed up to her. Mrs Otis clasped her passionately in her arms, the Duke smothered her with violent kisses, and the twins executed a wild war-dance round the group.

'Good heavens! child, where have you been?' said Mr Otis, rather angrily, thinking that she had been playing some foolish trick on them. 'Cecil and I have been riding all over the country looking for you, and your mother has been frightened to death. You must never play these practical jokes any more.'

'Except on the Ghost! except on the ghost!' shrieked the twins, as they capered about.

'My own darling, thank God you are found; you must never leave my side again,' murmured Mrs Otis, as she kissed the trembling child, and smoothed the tangled gold of her hair.

'Papa,' said Virginia quietly, 'I have been with the Ghost. He is dead, and you must come and see him. He had been very wicked, but he was really sorry for all that he had done, and he gave me this box of beautiful jewels before he died.'

The whole family gazed at her in mute amazement, but she

was quite grave and serious; and, turning round, she led them through the opening in the wainscoting down a narrow secret corridor, Washington following with a lighted candle, which he had caught up from the table. Finally, they came to a great oak door, studded with rusty nails. When Virginia touched it, it swung back on its heavy hinges, and they found themselves in a little low room, with a vaulted ceiling, and one tiny grated window. Imbedded in the wall was a huge iron ring, and chained to it was a gaunt skeleton, that was stretched out at full length on the stone floor, and seemed to be trying to grasp with its long fleshless fingers an old-fashioned trencher and ewer, that were placed just out of its reach. The jug had evidently been once filled with water, as it was covered inside with green mould. There was nothing on the trencher but a pile of dust. Virginia knelt down beside the skeleton, and, folding her little hands together, began to pray silently, while the rest of the party looked on in wonder at the terrible tragedy whose secret was now disclosed to them.

'Hallo!' suddenly exclaimed one of the twins, who had been looking out of the window to try and discover in what wing of the house the room was situated. 'Hallo! the old withered almond-tree has blossomed. I can see the flowers quite plainly in the moonlight.'

'God has forgiven him,' said Virginia gravely, as she rose to her feet, and a beautiful light seemed to illumine her face.

'What an angel you are!' cried the young Duke, and he put his arm round her neck, and kissed her.

VII

Four days after these curious incidents a funeral started from Canterville Chase at about eleven o'clock at night. The hearse was drawn by eight black horses, each of which carried on its head a great tuft of nodding ostrich-plumes, and the leaden coffin was covered by a rich purple pall, on which was embroidered in gold the Canterville coat-of-arms. By the side of the hearse and the coaches walked the servants with lighted torches, and the whole procession was wonderfully impressive. Lord Canterville was the chief mourner, having come up specially from Wales to attend the funeral, and sat in the first carriage along with little Virginia. Then came the United States Minister and his wife, then Washington and the three boys, and in the last carriage was Mrs Umney. It was generally felt that, as she had been frightened by the ghost for more than fifty years of her life, she had a right to see the last of him. A deep grave had been dug in the corner of the churchyard, just under the old yew-tree, and the service was read in the most impressive manner by the Rev. Augustus Dampier. When the ceremony was over, the servants, according to an old custom observed in the Canterville family, extinguished their torches, and, as the coffin was being lowered into the grave, Virginia stepped forward, and laid on it a large cross made of white and pink almond-blossoms. As she did so, the moon came out from behind a cloud, and flooded with its silent silver the little churchyard, and from a distant copse a nightingale began to sing. She thought of the ghost's description of the Garden of Death, her eyes became dim with tears, and she hardly spoke a word during the drive home.

The next morning, before Lord Canterville went up to town, Mr Otis had an interview with him on the subject of the jewels the ghost had given to Virginia. They were perfectly magnificent, especially a certain ruby necklace with old Venetian setting, which was really a superb specimen of sixteenth-century work, and their value was so great that Mr Otis felt considerable scruples about allowing his daughter to accept them.

'My lord,' he said, 'I know that in this country mortmain is held to apply to trinkets as well as to land, and it is quite clear to me that these jewels are, or should be, heirlooms in your family. I must beg you, accordingly, to take them to London with you, and to regard them simply as a portion of your property which has been restored to you under certain strange conditions. As for my daughter, she is merely a child, and has as yet, I am glad to say, but little interest in such appurtenances of idle luxury. I am also informed by Mrs Otis, who, I may say, is no mean authority upon Art – having had the privilege of spending several winters in Boston when she was a girl – that these gems are of great monetary worth, and if offered for sale would fetch a tall price. Under these circumstances, Lord Canterville, I feel sure that you will recognise how impossible it would be for me to allow them to remain in the possession of any member of my family; and, indeed, all such vain gauds and toys, however suitable or necessary to the dignity of the British aristocracy, would be completely out of place among those who have been brought up on the severe, and I believe immortal, principles of Republican simplicity. Perhaps I should mention that Virginia is very anxious that you should allow her to retain the box, as a memento of your unfortunate but misguided ancestor. As it is extremely old, and consequently a good deal out of repair, you may perhaps think fit to comply with her request. For my own part, I confess I am a good deal surprised to find a child of mine expressing sympathy with mediævalism in any form, and can only account for it by the fact that Virginia was born in one of your London suburbs shortly after Mrs Otis had returned from a trip to Athens.'

Lord Canterville listened very gravely to the worthy Minister's speech, pulling his grey moustache now and then to hide an involuntary smile, and when Mr Otis had ended, he shook him cordially by the hand, and said, 'My dear sir, your charming little daughter rendered my unlucky ancestor, Sir Simon, a very important service, and I and my family are much indebted to her for her marvellous courage and pluck. The jewels are clearly hers, and, egad, I believe that if I were heartless enough to take them from her, the wicked old fellow would be out of his grave in a fortnight, leading me the devil of a life. As for their being heirlooms, nothing is an heirloom that is not so mentioned in a will or legal document, and the existence of these jewels has been quite unknown. I assure you I have no more claim on them than your butler, and when Miss Virginia grows up I daresay she will be pleased to have pretty things to wear. Besides, you forget, Mr Otis, that you took the furniture and the ghost at a valuation, and anything that belonged to the ghost passed at once into your possession, as, whatever activity Sir Simon may have shown in the corridor at night, in point of law he was really dead, and you acquired his property by purchase.'

Mr Otis was a good deal distressed at Lord Canterville's refusal, and begged him to reconsider his decision, but the good-natured peer was quite firm, and finally induced the Minister to allow his daughter to retain the present the ghost had given her, and when, in the spring of 1890, the young Duchess of Cheshire was presented at the Queen's first drawing-room on the occasion of her marriage, her jewels were the universal theme of admiration. For Virginia received the coronet, which is the reward of all good little American girls, and was married to her boy-lover as soon as he came of age. They were both so charming, and they loved each other so much, that every one was delighted at the match, except the old Marchioness of Dumbleton, who had tried to catch the Duke for one of her seven unmarried daughters, and had given no less than three expensive dinner-parties for that purpose, and, strange to say, Mr Otis himself. Mr Otis was extremely fond of the young Duke personally, but, theoretically, he objected to titles, and, to use his own words, 'was not without apprehension lest, amid the enervating influences of a pleasure-loving aristocracy, the true principles of Republican simplicity should be forgotten.' His objections, however, were completely overruled, and I believe that when he walked up the aisle of St George's, Hanover Square, with his daughter leaning on his arm, there was not a prouder man in the whole length and breadth of England.

The Duke and Duchess, after the honeymoon was over, went down to Canterville Chase, and on the day after their arrival they walked over in the afternoon to the lonely churchyard by the pinewoods. There had been a great deal of difficulty at first about the inscription on Sir Simon's tombstone, but finally it had been decided to engrave on it simply the initials of the old gentleman's name, and the verse from the library window. The Duchess had brought with her some lovely roses, which she strewed upon the grave, and after they had stood by it for some time they strolled into the ruined chancel of the old abbey. There the Duchess sat down on a fallen pillar, while her husband lay at her feet smoking a cigarette and looking up at her beautiful eyes. Suddenly he threw his cigarette away, took hold of her hand, and said to her, 'Virginia, a wife should have no secrets from her husband.'

'Dear Cecil! I have no secrets from you.'

'Yes, you have,' he answered, smiling, 'you have never told me what happened to you when you were locked up with the ghost.'

'I have never told any one, Cecil,' said Virginia gravely.

'I know that, but you might tell me.'

'Please don't ask me, Cecil, I cannot tell you. Poor Sir Simon! I owe him a great deal. Yes, don't laugh, Cecil, I really do. He made me see what Life is, and what Death signifies, and why Love is stronger than both.'

The Duke rose and kissed his wife lovingly.

'You can have your secret as long as I have your heart,' he murmured.

'You have always had that, Cecil.'

'And you will tell our children some day, won't you?'

Virginia blushed.

Jean Rhys 1890–1979

Jean Rhys was born Ella Gwendolen Rees Williams in 1890 on the island of Dominica in the Caribbean. Her mother, Minnie Lockhart, was a white Dominican and her father, William Rees Williams, a Welsh doctor. Jean lived a lonely childhood in Dominica where whites were in the minority. She was educated at the local Catholic convent school.

When she was 16 she travelled to England with her aunt and went to school in Cambridge, then to the Academy of Dramatic Art in London. She tried a number of different jobs, including being a chorus girl in a touring theatre company, a film extra and a volunteer cook during the First World War.

In 1919 Jean Rhys married Jean Lenglet, a Dutch–French song-writer and journalist, and they had a son who died at three weeks and then a daughter. They lived in Paris and briefly in Vienna, two settings which provided Rhys with the material for her first published writing: *Vienne*, a series of sketches, and *The Left Bank and Other Stories*.

Jean Rhys used other experiences from her own life in her writing. An affair with Ford Madox Ford, who gave Rhys her pseudonym, was featured in the novel *Postures* (1928). In *Voyage in the Dark* (1934), a white West Indian becomes a chorus girl and later a kept mistress. She finds England unreal beside memories of her island: 'I always wanted to be black ... Being black is warm and gay, being white is cold and sad,' says the character, hinting at some of Rhys's feelings about her own background.

There followed a quiet time when Jean Rhys was supposed dead, but was in fact living in Devon with her third husband, Max Hamer. She came to public attention when the BBC dramatized her novel *Good Morning, Midnight* in 1949 and again in 1957.

Her most famous novel, *Wide Sargasso Sea*, was begun before the Second World War, but was not completed until 1966 when it won three awards. It takes the character of the mad woman Mrs Rochester from Charlotte Brontë's novel *Jane Eyre* and gives her a tragic past in Dominica.

The story 'I Used to Live Here Once', comes out of a return visit to Dominica by the author in the 1930s. The returning character remembers in painstaking detail all of what she sees but is bewildered by the strangely distant children.

I Used to Live Here Once

Jean Rhys

She was standing by the river looking at the stepping stones and remembering each one. There was the round unsteady stone, the pointed one, the flat one in the middle – the safe stone where you could stand and look round. The next wasn't so safe for when the river was full the water flowed over it and even when it showed dry it was slippery. But after that it was easy and soon she was standing on the other side.

The road was much wider than it used to be but the work had been done carelessly. The felled trees had not been cleared away and the bushes looked trampled. Yet it was the same road and she walked along feeling extraordinarily happy.

It was a fine day, a blue day. The only thing was that the sky had a glassy look that she didn't remember. That was the only word she could think of. Glassy. She turned the corner, saw that what had been the old pavé had been taken up, and there too the road was much wider, but it had the same unfinished look.

She came to the worn stone steps that led up to the house and her heart began to beat. The screw pine was gone, so was the mock summer house called the ajoupa, but the clove tree was still there and at the top of the steps the rough lawn stretched away, just as she remembered it. She stopped and looked towards the house that had been added to and painted white. It was strange to see a car standing in front of it.

There were two children under the big mango tree, a boy and a little girl, and she waved to them and called 'Hello' but they didn't answer her or turn their heads. Very fair children, as Europeans born in the West Indies so often are: as if the white blood is asserting itself against all odds.

The grass was yellow in the hot sunlight as she walked towards them. When she was quite close she called again, shyly: 'Hello.' Then, 'I used to live here once,' she said.

Still they didn't answer. When she said for the third time 'Hello' she was quite near them. Her arms went out instinctively with the longing to touch them.

It was the boy who turned. His grey eyes looked straight into hers. His expression didn't change. He said: 'Hasn't it gone cold all of a sudden. D'you notice? Let's go in.' 'Yes, let's,' said the girl.

Her arms fell to her sides as she watched them running across the grass to the house. That was the first time she knew.

Nathaniel Hawthorne 1804–1864

Nathaniel Hawthorne was born on 4 July 1804 in Salem, Massachusetts. His father died when he was four years old. When he was nine an injury to his foot put an end to some of his physical activities for a couple of years and helped him form the habit of reading widely.

When he was twelve, his family moved to Raymond in Maine; he enjoyed the outdoor life of the region and picked up what he later called his 'accursed habits of solitude'. He was sent back to Salem for his schooling in 1819. He studied and had a part-time job as a bookkeeper for his Uncle Robert's stage-coach line, earning a dollar a week. But this kept him from his literary pursuits: 'No man can be a Poet and a Bookkeeper at the same time' he wrote to his mother in 1820. All through his life there was a tension between his literary career and the other work he needed to do to earn his living.

From 1821 to 1825 Hawthorne attended college in Maine, supported by his uncle. Twelve years of relative solitude followed, during which Hawthorne lived in the family house at Salem with his mother and sister, writing pieces which were published anonymously or under a pseudonym. He published *Twice-Told Tales* in 1837, but described himself at this period as having the 'distinction' of having been 'for a good many years, the obscurest man of letters in America'.

He met Sophia, his future wife, in 1838 and they married four years later. In 1839 he was appointed measurer of salt and coal in the Boston custom house. He worked here for two years until he invested $1000 in a famous experimental utopian community at Brook Farm and went to live there. For three years after their marriage the Hawthornes lived in Concord; Nathaniel wrote a good deal but did not earn enough to keep them and in 1846 he took the job of Surveyor of the Salem custom house. Again, he found it difficult to write whilst in full-time work, and he felt bitter and frustrated about his career. Hawthorne was dismissed from his job at the custom house in 1849.

Hawthorne's most famous novel, *The Scarlet Letter*, was published in 1851. This book, which has become a classic of American literature, brought him literary acclaim and financial success. He travelled to Europe, acting as US Consul in

Liverpool from 1853 to 1857, developed friendships with other literary figures of the period (Herman Melville dedicated *Moby Dick* to Hawthorne), and met President Lincoln in 1862. The start of the American Civil War marked the end of Hawthorne's career; his health began to fail and he died, aged 59, in May 1864.

In 'The Hollow of the Three Hills' Hawthorne uses a supernatural setting to examine a woman's sense of guilt about the way she has lived her life.

The Hollow of the Three Hills

Nathaniel Hawthorne

In those strange old times, when fantastic dreams and mad-men's reveries were realized among the actual circumstances of life, two persons met together at an appointed hour and place. One was a lady, graceful in form and fair of feature, though pale and troubled, and smitten with an untimely blight in what should have been the fullest bloom of her years; the other was an ancient and meanly dressed woman, of ill-favored aspect, and so withered, shrunken and decrepit, that even the space since she began to decay must have exceeded the ordinary term of human existence. In the spot where they encountered, no mortal could observe them. Three little hills stood near each other, and down in the midst of them sunk a hollow basin, almost mathematically circular, two or three hundred feet in breadth, and of such depth that a stately cedar might but just be visible above the sides. Dwarf pines were numerous upon the hills, and partly fringed the outer verge of the intermediate hollow; within which there was nothing but the brown grass of October, and here and there a tree-trunk, that had fallen long ago, and lay mouldering with no green successor from its roots. One of these masses of decaying wood, formerly a majestic oak, rested close beside a pool of green and sluggish water at the bottom of the basin. Such scenes as this (so gray tradition tells) were once the resort of a Power of Evil and his plighted subjects; and here, at midnight or on the dim verge of evening, they were said to stand round the mantling pool, disturbing its putrid waters in the performance of an impious baptismal rite. The chill beauty of an autumnal sunset was now gilding the three hill-tops, whence a paler tint stole down their sides into the hollow.

'Here is our pleasant meeting come to pass,' said the aged crone, 'according as thou hast desired. Say quickly what thou wouldst have of me, for there is but a short hour that we may tarry here.'

As the old withered woman spoke, a smile glimmered on her countenance, like lamplight on the wall of a sepulchre. The lady trembled, and cast her eyes upward to the verge of the basin, as if meditating to return with her purpose unaccomplished. But it was not so ordained.

'I am stranger in this land, as you know,' said she at length. 'Whence I come it matters not; – but I have left those behind me with whom my fate was intimately bound, and from whom I am cut off forever. There is a weight in my bosom that I cannot away with, and I have come hither to inquire of their welfare.'

'And who is there by this green pool, that can bring thee news from the ends of the Earth?' cried the old woman, peering into the lady's face. 'Not from my lips mayst thou hear these tidings; yet, be thou bold, and the daylight shall not pass away from yonder hill-top, before thy wish be granted.'

'I will do your bidding though I die,' replied the lady desperately.

The old woman seated herself on the trunk of the fallen tree, threw aside the hood that shrouded her gray locks, and beckoned her companion to draw near.

'Kneel down,' she said, 'and lay your forehead on my knees.'

She hesitated a moment, but the anxiety, that had long been kindling, burned fiercely up within her. As she knelt down, the border of her garment was dipped into the pool; she laid her forehead on the old woman's knees, and the latter drew a cloak about the lady's face, so that she was in darkness. Then she heard the muttered words of a prayer, in the midst of which she started, and would have arisen.

'Let me flee, – let me flee and hide myself, that they may not look upon me!' she cried. But, with returning recollection, she hushed herself, and was still as death.

For it seemed as if other voices – familiar in infancy, and unforgotten through many wanderings, and in all the vicissitudes of her heart and fortune – were mingling with the accents of the prayer. At first the words were faint and indistinct, not rendered so by distance, but rather resembling the dim pages of a book, which we strive to read by an imperfect and gradually brightening light. In such a manner, as the prayer proceeded, did those voices strengthen upon the ear; till at length the petition ended, and the conversation of an aged man, and of a woman broken and decayed like himself, became distinctly audible to the lady as she knelt. But those strangers appeared not to stand in the hollow depth between the three hills. Their voices were encompassed and re-echoed by the walls of a chamber, the windows of which were rattling in the breeze; the regular vibration of a clock, the crackling of a fire, and the tinkling of the embers as they fell among the ashes, rendered the scene almost as vivid as if painted to the eye. By a melancholy hearth sat these two old people, the man calmly despondent, the woman querulous and tearful, and their words were all of sorrow. They spoke of a daughter, a wanderer they knew not where, bearing dishonor along with her, and leaving shame and affliction to bring their gray heads to the grave. They alluded also to other and more recent woe, but in the midst of their talk, their voices seemed to melt into the sound of the wind sweeping mournfully among the autumn leaves; and when the lady lifted her eyes, there was she kneeling in the hollow between three hills.

'A weary and lonesome time yonder old couple have of it,' remarked the old woman, smiling in the lady's face.

'And did you also hear them!' exclaimed she, a sense of intolerable humiliation triumphing over her agony and fear.

'Yea; and we have yet more to hear,' replied the old woman. 'Wherefore, cover thy face quickly.'

Again the withered hag poured forth the monotonous words of a prayer that was not meant to be acceptable in Heaven; and soon, in the pauses of her breath, strange murmurings began to thicken, gradually increasing so as to drown and overpower the charm by which they grew. Shrieks pierced through the obscurity of sound, and were succeeded by the singing of sweet female voices, which in their turn gave way to a wild roar of laughter, broken suddenly by groanings and sobs, forming altogether a ghastly confusion of terror and mourning and mirth. Chains were rattling, fierce and stern voices uttered threats, and the scourge resounded at their command. All these noises deepened and became substantial to the listener's ear, till she could distinguish every soft and dreamy accent of the love songs, that died causelessly into funeral hymns. She shuddered at the unprovoked wrath which blazed up like the spontaneous kindling of flame, and she grew faint at the fearful merriment, raging miserably around her. In the midst of this wild scene, where unbound passions jostled each other in a drunken career, there was one solemn voice of a man, and a manly and melodious voice it might once have been. He went to-and-fro continually, and his feet sounded upon the floor. In each member of that frenzied company, whose own burning thoughts had become their exclusive world, he sought an auditor for the story of his individual wrong, and interpreted their laughter and tears as his reward of scorn or pity. He spoke of woman's perfidy, of a wife who had broken her holiest vows, of a home and heart made desolate. Even as he went on, the shout, the laugh, the shriek, the sob, rose up in unison, till they changed into the hollow, fitful, and uneven sound of the wind, as it fought among the pine-trees on those three lonely hills. The lady looked up, and there was the withered woman smiling in her face.

'Couldst thou have thought there were such merry times in a Mad House?' inquired the latter.

'True, true,' said the lady to herself; 'there is mirth within its walls, but misery, misery without.'

'Wouldst thou hear more?' demanded the old woman.

'There is one other voice I would fain listen to again,' replied the lady faintly.

'Then lay down thy head speedily upon my knees, that thou may'st get thee hence before the hour be past.'

The golden skirts of day were yet lingering upon the hills, but deep shades obscured the hollow and the pool as if sombre night were rising thence to overspread the world. Again that evil woman began to weave her spell. Long did it proceed unanswered, till the knolling of a bell stole in among the intervals of her words, like a clang that had travelled far over valley and rising ground, and was just ready to die in the air. The lady shook upon her companion's knees, as she heard that boding sound. Stronger it grew and sadder, and deepened into the tone of a death-bell, knolling dolefully from some ivy-mantled tower, and bearing tidings of mortality and woe to the cottage, to the hall, and to the solitary wayfarer, that all might weep for the doom appointed in turn to them. Then came a measured tread, passing slowly, slowly on, as of mourners with a coffin, their garments trailing on the ground, so that the ear could measure the length of their melancholy array. Before them went the priest, reading the burial-service, while the leaves of his book were rustling in the breeze. And though no voice but his was heard to speak aloud, still there were revilings and anathemas, whispered but distinct, from women and from men, breathed against the daughter who had wrung the aged hearts of her parents, – the wife who had betrayed the trusting fondness of her husband, – the mother who had sinned against natural affection, and left her child to die. The sweeping sound of the funeral train faded away like a thin vapour, and the wind, that just before had seemed to shake the coffin-pall, moaned sadly round the verge of the Hollow between three Hills. But when the old woman stirred the kneeling lady, she lifted not her head.

'Here has been a sweet hour's sport!' said the withered crone, chuckling to herself.

Colette 1873–1954

Sidonie-Gabrielle Colette was born in Burgundy in France in 1873. Her mother was a widow whose second marriage was to a former captain of the infantry. Colette had an older brother and a half-brother and sister from her mother's first marriage.

In 1890, whilst Colette was living with her half-brother, she met Gauthier-Villars, son of the owner of a leading publishing house in Paris. They fell in love, married and settled in Paris in 1893. Colette's husband, who was known by his pen name 'Willy', was gaining a reputation as a journalist at this time. He and Colette became noted members of smart society. Jean Cocteau in his teens remembered seeing them at the Palais de Glace: 'At one of the rink-side tables sat Willy, Colette and her bulldog: Willy, with his walrus moustache and goatee, his heavy eyelids and flowing tie, his wide-brimmed top hat and his bishop's hands clasped on the knob of his cane; and beside him Colette . . . a thin, thin Colette, a sort of miniature fox in cycling dress . . .'

In 1900 Colette, with the help of Willy, published a best-seller called *Claudine à l'Ecole*. Three sequels followed, all published under Willy's name only: he promoted himself as Colette's creator, with her as the real-life model. In 1904 four conversation pieces between Colette's bulldog and her Angora cat were published under the name Colette Willy. Two years later Colette made her professional debut as a mime dancer in a drama called *Le Désir, l'Amour et la Chimère*. She separated from Willy, divorced him and went to live with a female friend, the ex-marquise de Belboeuf, known as 'Missy'.

Colette became a somewhat scandalous figure. In 1907 she kissed Missy on stage in a pantomime; some of the audience were outraged and further performances were banned by the police. She made a living touring as a mime artist and dancer whilst continuing to write novels, stories and autobiographical essays. She became well known for both her writing and the scandal associated with her, and when she began to write regularly for *Le Matin*, one of the leading Paris newspapers, she used the pen name Rosine because her own name was considered too notorious for a family paper.

At *Le Matin* Colette met the young editor Henri de

Jouvenel, who became her second husband. Their daughter
Colette de Jouvenel was born in 1913. When her husband
was stationed at Verdun during the First World War Colette
got through the lines and managed to join him for a couple
of weeks. She lived in Paris, writing novels, plays and stories
of backstage life at the music hall, and supporting herself by
her journalism.

In 1920 Colette wrote *Chéri*, which was dramatized and
put on the stage in 1921. In 1923 *Le Blé en Herbe*, her serial
about young love, caused another scandal: serialization had
to be stopped when it became clear that the young lovers
were about to consummate their relationship.

In 1925 Colette divorced Henri de Jouvenel. She met
Maurice Goudeket, who became her third husband and 'best
friend'. Her writings had by this time been translated into
many languages, and she toured various countries, lecturing
and performing in productions of her own work. By 1932 she
was considered chic and distinguished rather than scandalous, and she opened a beauty salon and shops in Paris and
Saint Tropez which promoted her own cosmetics. She began
working in films in 1933, writing subtitles and, later, dialogue. By 1936 she was being honoured for her contributions
to literature; she surprised the Belgian Royal Academy by
wearing open-toed sandals, revealing red lacquered
toenails, when she arrived there to receive an award.

Colette spent most of the Second World War in Paris, writing a weekly column about life in occupied France. Her husband Maurice, who was Jewish, was arrested by the Gestapo
and interned in 1941. In 1944 after the liberation of Paris, and
later in 1945 after the European war was over, Colette
became world famous as a novelist but also as an emblem of
everything that was most profoundly French. *Gigi*, serialized
during the war, was published in book form and became a
best-seller; a number of her novels were made into films and
a film was made of her life story. In her later years Colette
was bed-ridden with arthritis, but she continued to write
stories and her memoirs. She died on 3 August 1954 in Paris.
In some quarters her scandalous reputation remained, and
the Archbishop of Paris refused her family's request for the
burial service at the place of her choice.

The Colette story we have chosen is short and dramatic,
probing a murderer's conscience.

The Murderer

Colette

After he had killed her, with a blow from the little lead
weight under which she kept her wrapping paper, Louis found
himself at a loss. She lay behind the counter, one leg bent
back under her, her head turned away, and her body turned
towards him, in a ridiculous pose which put the young man in
a bad mood. He shrugged his shoulders and almost said to
her, 'Get up now, you look ridiculous!' But at that moment
the bell on the shop door rang, and Louis saw a little girl
come in.

'A card of black mending wool, please.'

'We don't have any more,' he said politely. 'We won't have
any until tomorrow.'

She left, closing the door carefully, and he realized that he
hadn't even thought that she could have walked up to the
counter, leaned over, and seen . . .

Night was falling, darkening the little stationery-notions
shop. One could still make out the rows of white boxes with
an ivory-nut button or a knot of passementerie on the side.
Louis struck a match mechanically on the sole of his shoe in
order to light the gas jet, then caught himself and put the
match out under his foot. Across the street, the wine merchant
lit up his whole ground floor all at once, and in contrast the
little stationery-notions shop grew darker in a night streaked
with yellow light.

Once again Louis leaned over the counter. To his overwhelming astonishment he saw his mistress still lying there,
her leg bent back, her neck turned to the side. And something
black besides, a thread, as thin as a wisp of hair, was trickling
down her pale cheek. He grabbed the forty-five francs in
change and dirty bills that he had so furiously refused earlier,
went out, took off the door's lever handle, put it in his pocket,
and walked away.

For two days he lived the way a child lives, amusing himself by watching the boats on the Seine and the schoolchildren in the squares. He amused himself like a child, and like a child, he grew bored with himself. He waited and could not decide whther to leave the city or to go back to street peddling like before. His room, paid for by the week, still harbored a stash of Paris monuments on stacks of postcards, mechanical jumping rabbits, and a product you squeezed from a tube to make your own fruit drinks. But Louis sold nothing for two days, while staying in another furnished room. He didn't feel afraid, and he slept well; the days flowed by smoothly, disturbed only by that pleasing impatience one feels in big port cities after booking passage on an ocean liner.

Two days after the crime he bought a newspaper, as on other days, and read: WOMAN SHOPKEEPER MURDERED IN THE RUE X. 'Aha!' he said out loud like an expert, then read the article slowly and attentively, noted that the crime, because of the victim's 'very retired' existence, was already being considered 'mysterious', and folded the paper back up. In front of him his coffee was getting cold. The waiter behind the bar was whistling as he polished the zinc, and an old couple next to him were dipping croissants in hot milk. Louis sat there for several moments, dumbstruck, with his mouth half open, and wondered why all these familiar things had suddenly ceased to be close and intelligible to him. He had the impression that, if questioned, the old couple would answer in a strange language, and that, as he whistled, the waiter was looking right through Louis's body as if it weren't even there.

He got up, threw down some money, and headed off towards a train station, where he bought a ticket for a suburb whose name reminded him of the races and afternoons spent boating. During the ride it seemed to him that the train was making very little noise and that the other passengers were speaking in subdued voices.

'Maybe I'm going deaf!'

After getting off the train, Louis bought an evening paper, and reread the same account as in the morning paper, and yawned.

'Damn, they're not getting anywhere!'

He ate in a little restaurant near the station and inquired of the owner as to the possibility of finding a job in the area. But he accomplished this formality with great repugnance,

and felt ill at ease when the man advised him to see a dentist
in a neighbouring villa who regrettably had just lost a young
man, employed until the day before to care for his motorcycle
and to sterilize his surgical instruments. Despite the late
hour, he rang the dentist's doorbell, claimed he was a maker
of mechanical toys, didn't argue about the pay – two hundred
and fifty francs – and slept that same night in a small attic
room, hung with that blue-and-gray-flowered wallpaper usually used for lining cheap trunks.

For a week he kept the job as laboratory assistant to the
American dentist, a great horse of a man, big-boned and red-
haired, who asked no questions and smoked with his feet up
on the table, as he waited for his rare clients. Clad in a white
linen lab coat and leaning against the open gate, Louis
breathed the fresh air, and the maids from the villas would
smile at his gentle, swarthy face.

He bought a paper every day. Banished from the front page,
the 'crime in rue . . .' now languished on page 2, amid colliding
trains and swindling somnambulists. Five lines, two lines
confirmed dispassionately that it remained 'a complete
mystery'.

One spring afternoon, made fragrant by a brief shower and
pierced with the cries of swallows, Louis asked the American
dentist for a little money, 'to buy himself some underwear',
took off his white lab coat, and left for Paris. And since he
was nothing but a simple little murderer, he went straight
back to the stationery-notions shop. There were children
playing in front of the lowered iron shutter and a week's
worth of splashing had left the door caked with mud. Louis
walked the hundred steps back and forth on the pavement
across the street for a long time and did not leave the street
till after nightfall.

The next day he went back again, a little later so as not to
attract attention, and the following evenings he faithfully
kept watch, after dinner, sometimes without dinner. He felt
himself filled with a strange hope resembling the anguish of
love. One evening, when he had halted to tilt his head back
towards the stars and let out a deep sigh, a hand was placed
gently on his shoulder. He closed his eyes and, without
turning around, fell limply, blissfully into the arms of the
policeman who was following him.

During the course of the interrogation, Louis confessed

that, yes, he did regret his crime, but that a moment like the one when he felt the liberating hand on his shoulder was 'worth it all' and that he could only compare it to the moment when he had, as he said, 'known love'.

[*Translated by Matthew Ward*]

Graham Greene 1904–1991

Graham Greene was born in 1904 and educated at Berkhamsted School, where his father was headteacher. Although he was academically successful, his schooling was a miserable experience. In his autobiography, *A Sort of Life*, he wrote about playing truant and finally running away: 'I endured that life for some eight terms – a hundred and four weeks of monotony, humiliation and mental pain. It is astonishing how tough a boy can be, but I was helped by my truancies, those peaceful hours hidden in the hedge.'

Greene went to university at Oxford and began a career as a journalist, working as a sub-editor on *The Times*. He had been a keen writer of poetry and fiction since his youth, and he wrote prolifically throughout his long life. In all he wrote 'some thirty novels', entertainments (his word for his thrillers and more popular fiction), children's books, travel books, autobiography, essays, criticism, film scripts and collections of plays and short stories. He worked as a film critic and as literary editor of *The Spectator* magazine.

Greene was a keen traveller who lived and worked for periods of time in Mexico, West Africa, Haiti, South America and Indochina. In 1926 he was received into the Catholic Church. His religious faith, coupled with his interest in travel, are distinguishing features of many of his books. His novels are set in a variety of countries where his characters face challenging circumstances and are often forced to make difficult moral choices which involve problems of loyalty and faith.

Greene's stories are often gripping and exciting; they contain many of the basic features of popular fiction like thrillers, adventure and spy stories. His vivid descriptions of places and people and the fast-moving pace of his plots make them well suited to the cinema, and many of his novels have been turned into successful films. Amongst his most famous books are *Brighton Rock*, *The Heart of the Matter*, *Our Man in Havana*, *The Quiet American* and *The Power and the Glory*, written as a result of a commission to visit Mexico to report on religious persecution. Graham Greene was widely honoured for his achievements in his lifetime. He died in 1991.

The story we have chosen for this volume is from a famous

collection of Greene's short stories called *21 Stories*. It is typical of his work in its pace and rather macabre twists that raise moral and ethical questions about the sanity and conscience of the main character.

A Little Place off the Edgware Road

Graham Greene

Craven came up past the Achilles statue in the thin summer rain. It was only just after lighting-up time, but already the cars were lined up all the way to the Marble Arch, and the sharp acquisitive faces peered out ready for a good time with anything possible which came along. Craven went bitterly by with the collar of his mackintosh tight round his throat: it was one of his bad days.

All the way up the Park he was reminded of passion, but you needed money for love. All that a poor man could get was lust. Love needed a good suit, a car, a flat somewhere, or a good hotel. It needed to be wrapped in cellophane. He was aware all the time of the stringy tie beneath the mackintosh, and the frayed sleeves: he carried his body about with him like something he hated. (There were moments of happiness in the British Museum reading-room, but the body called him back.) He bore, as his only sentiment, the memory of ugly deeds committed on park chairs. People talked as if the body died too soon – that wasn't the trouble, to Craven, at all. The body kept alive – and through the glittering tinselly rain, on his way to a rostrum, passed a little man in a black suit carrying a banner, 'The Body shall rise again.' He remembered a dream he had three times woken trembling from: he had been alone in the huge dark cavernous burying ground of all the world. Every grave was connected to another under the ground: the globe was honeycombed for the sake of the dead, and on each occasion of dreaming he had discovered anew the horrifying fact that the body doesn't decay. There are no worms and dissolution. Under the ground the world was littered with masses of dead flesh ready to rise again with their warts and boils and eruptions. He had lain in bed and remembered – as 'tidings of great joy' – that the body after all was corrupt.

He came up into the Edgware Road walking fast – the Guardsmen were out in couples, great languid elongated beasts – the bodies like worms in their tight trousers. He hated them, and hated his hatred because he knew what it was, envy. He was aware that every one of them had a better body than himself: indigestion creased his stomach: he felt sure that his breath was foul – but who could he ask? Sometimes he secretly touched himself here and there with scent: it was one of his ugliest secrets. Why should he be asked to believe in the resurrection of this body he wanted to forget? Sometimes he prayed at night (a hint of religious belief was lodged in his breast like a worm in a nut) that *his* body at any rate should never rise again.

He knew all the side streets round the Edgware Road only too well: when a mood was on, he simply walked until he tired, squinting at his own image in the windows of Salmon & Gluckstein and the ABCs. So he noticed at once the posters outside the disused theatre in Culpar Road. They were not unusual, for sometimes Barclays Bank Dramatic Society would hire the place for an evening – or an obscure film would be trade-shown there. The theatre had been built in 1920 by an optimist who thought the cheapness of the site would more than counter-balance its disadvantage of lying a mile outside the conventional theatre zone. But no play had ever succeeded, and it was soon left to gather rat-holes and spider-webs. The covering of the seats was never renewed, and all that ever happened to the place was the temporary false life of an amateur play or a trade show.

Craven stopped and read – there were still optimists it appeared, even in 1939, for nobody but the blindest optimist could hope to make money out of the place as 'The Home of the Silent Film'. The first season of 'primitives' was announced (a high-brow phrase): there would never be a second. Well, the seats were cheap, and it was perhaps worth a shilling to him, now that he was tired, to get in somewhere out of the rain. Craven bought a ticket and went in to the darkness of the stalls.

In the dead darkness a piano tinkled something monotonously recalling Mendelssohn: he sat down in a gangway seat, and could immediately feel the emptiness all round him. No, there would never be another season. On the screen a large woman in a kind of toga wrung her hands, then wobbled with curious jerky movements towards a couch. There she sat and stared out like a sheep-dog distractedly through her loose and black and stringy hair. Sometimes she seemed to dissolve altogether into dots and flashes and wiggly lines. A sub-title said, 'Pompilia betrayed by her beloved Augustus seeks an end to her troubles.'

Craven began at last to see – a dim waste of stalls. There were not twenty people in the place – a few couples whispering with their heads touching, and a number of lonely men like himself wearing the same uniform of the cheap mackintosh. They lay about at intervals like corpses – and again Craven's obsession returned: the tooth-ache of horror. He thought miserably – I am going mad: other people don't feel like this. Even a disused theatre reminded him of those interminable caverns where the bodies were waiting for resurrection.

'A slave to his passion Augustus calls for yet more wine.'

A gross middle-aged Teutonic actor lay on an elbow with his arm round a large woman in a shift. The Spring Song tinkled ineptly on, and the screen flickered like indigestion. Somebody felt his way through the darkness, scrabbling past Craven's knees – a small man: Craven experienced the unpleasant feeling of a large beard brushing his mouth. Then there was a long sigh as the newcomer found the next chair, and on the screen events had moved with such rapidity that Pompilia had already stabbed herself – or so Craven supposed – and lay still and buxom among her weeping slaves.

A low breathless voice sighed out close to Craven's ear: 'What's happened? Is she asleep?'

'No. Dead.'

'Murdered?' the voice asked with a keen interest.

'I don't think so. Stabbed herself.'

Nobody said 'Hush': nobody was enough interested to object to a voice: they drooped among the empty chairs in attitudes of weary inattention.

The film wasn't nearly over yet: there were children somehow to be considered: was it all going on to a second generation? But the small bearded man in the next seat seemed to be interested only in Pompilia's death. The fact that he had come in at that moment apparently fascinated him. Craven heard the word 'coincidence' twice, and he went on talking to himself about it in low out-of-breath tones. 'Absurd when you come to think of it,' and then 'no blood at all'. Craven didn't

listen: he sat with his hands clasped between his knees, facing
the fact as he had faced it so often before, that he was in
danger of going mad. He had to pull himself up, take a
holiday, see a doctor (God knew what infection moved in his
veins). He became aware that his bearded neighbour had
addressed him directly. 'What?' he asked impatiently, 'what
did you say?'

'There would be more blood than you can imagine.'

'What are you talking about?'

When the man spoke to him, he sprayed him with damp
breath. There was a little bubble in his speech like an
impediment. He said, 'When you murder a man . . .'

'This was a woman,' Craven said impatiently.

'That wouldn't make any difference.'

'And it's got nothing to do with murder anyway.'

'That doesn't signify.' They seemed to have got into an
absurd and meaningless wrangle in the dark.

'I know, you see,' the little bearded man said in a tone of
enormous conceit.

'Know what?'

'About such things,' he said with guarded ambiguity.

Craven turned and tried to see him clearly. Was he mad?
Was this a warning of what he might become – babbling
incomprehensibly to strangers in cinemas? He thought, By
God, no, trying to see: I'll be sane yet. I *will* be sane. He could
make out nothing but a small black hump of body. The man
was talking to himself again. He said, 'Talk. Such talk.
They'll say it was all for fifty pounds. But that's a lie. Reasons
and reasons. They always take the first reason. Never look
behind. Thirty years of reasons. Such simpletons,' he added
again in that tone of breathless and unbounded conceit. So
this was madness. So long as he could realize that, he must
be sane himself – relatively speaking. Not so sane perhaps as
the seekers in the park or the Guardsmen in the Edgware
Road, but saner than this. It was like a message of encouragement as the piano tinkled on.

Then again the little man turned and sprayed him. 'Killed
herself, you say? But who's to know that? It's not a mere
question of what hand holds the knife.' He laid a hand
suddenly and confidingly on Craven's: it was damp and sticky:
Craven said with horror as a possible meaning came to him:
'What are you talking about?'

'I know,' the little man said. 'A man in my position gets to know almost everything.'

'What is your position?' Craven said, feeling the sticky hand on his, trying to make up his mind whether he was being hysterical or not – after all, there were a dozen explanations – it might be treacle.

'A pretty desperate one *you'd* say.' Sometimes the voice almost died in the throat altogether. Something incomprehensible had happened on the screen – take your eyes from these early pictures for a moment and the plot had proceeded on at such a pace . . . Only the actors moved slowly and jerkily. A young woman in a nightdress seemed to be weeping in the arms of a Roman centurion: Craven hadn't seen either of them before. *'I am not afraid of death, Lucius – in your arms.'*

The little man began to titter – knowingly. He was talking to himself again. It would have been easy to ignore him altogether if it had not been for those sticky hands which he now removed: he seemed to be fumbling at the seat in front of him. His head had a habit of lolling suddenly sideways – like an idiot child's. He said distinctly and irrelevantly: 'Bayswater Tragedy.'

'What was that?' Craven said sharply. He had seen those words on a poster before he entered the park.

'What?'

'About the tragedy.'

'To think they call Cullen Mews Bayswater.' Suddenly the little man began to cough – turning his face towards Craven and coughing right at him: it was like vindictiveness. The voice said brokenly, 'Let me see. My umbrella.' He was getting up.

'You didn't have an umbrella.'

'My umbrella,' he repeated. 'My – ' and seemed to lose the word altogether. He went scrabbling out past Craven's knees.

Craven let him go, but before he had reached the billowy dusty curtains of the Exit the screen went blank and bright – the film had broken, and somebody immediately turned up one dirt-choked chandelier above the circle. It shone down just enough for Craven to see the smear on his hands. This wasn't hysteria: this was a fact. He wasn't mad: he had sat next a madman who in some mews – what was the name, Colon, Collin . . . Craven jumped up and made his own way out: the black curtain flapped in his mouth. But he was too late: the man had gone and there were three turnings to choose from. He chose instead a telephone-box and dialled with an odd sense for him of sanity and decision 999.

It didn't take two minutes to get the right department. They were interested and very kind. Yes, there had been a murder in a mews – Cullen Mews. A man's neck had been cut from ear to ear with a bread knife – a horrid crime. He began to tell them how he had sat next the murderer in a cinema: it couldn't be anyone else: there was blood on his hands – and he remembered with repulsion as he spoke the damp beard. There must have been a terrible lot of blood. But the voice from the Yard interrupted him. 'Oh no,' it was saying, 'we have the murderer – no doubt of it at all. It's the body that's disappeared.'

Craven put down the receiver. He said to himself aloud, 'Why should this happen to *me*? Why to *me*?' He was back in the horror of his dream – the squalid darkening street outside was only one of the innumerable tunnels connecting grave to grave where the imperishable bodies lay. He said, 'It was a dream, a dream,' and leaning forward he saw in the mirror above the telephone his own face sprinkled by tiny drops of blood like dew from a scent-spray. He began to scream, 'I won't go mad. I won't go mad. I'm sane. I won't go mad.' Presently a little crowd began to collect, and soon a policeman came.

1939

James Joyce 1882–1940

James Joyce was born in Dublin, the eldest of ten children. He attended schools run by the Jesuits and did well academically. The family's financial fortunes were declining during his youth because of Joyce's father's spending and drinking habits.

Joyce lost his Catholic faith as a young man. He attended University College, Dublin, and graduated in 1902 with a degree in modern languages. He was a skilled linguist and had good beginnings in Italian, French, German, literary Norwegian and Latin. After university he left for Paris to study medicine, although his literary interests were clearly established and he was already publishing reviews and poems.

In 1903 he returned to Dublin, where his mother, who he was very close to, was dying of cancer. The following year he met Nora Barnacle, who was to become his wife and lifelong companion. They travelled together until their son Giorgio was born in 1905, when they settled in Trieste, where Joyce taught at a language school. Their daughter Lucia was born in 1907.

Joyce made his last trip to Ireland in 1912, but continued to draw upon his early life there in all of his writing. *Dubliners*, a collection of short stories, and his autobiographical novel *A Portrait of the Artist as a Young Man* were published in 1914. Joyce received some income to support his writing from patrons, but his personal life was not easy: he suffered from glaucoma and other diseases of the eyes, and the mental state of his daughter Lucia became increasingly unstable. The family moved between Zurich, Paris and London. By 1920 Lucia was diagnosed as having schizophrenia and her breakdowns and periods in hospital dominated much of the family's life in future years.

In 1922 Joyce's novel *Ulysses* was published in Paris. In this novel, which is about one day in Dublin in 1904, Joyce experiments with language, using a stream of consciousness technique to take the reader inside the characters' minds to reveal the flow of their thoughts and emotions. The purest form of this experiment comes at the end of *Ulysses* in Molly Bloom's soliloquy, when her drifting mental processes while she lies half asleep are written in unpunctuated prose that moves from one apparently disconnected thought to another. *Ulysses* caused a scandal; it was not allowed publication in America until 1934 after it had been officially judged not to be pornographic by the United States court.

In 1939 Joyce published *Finnegan's Wake* which contains his most ingenious linguistic innovation. He coins new words and language formations, and plays with words, allusions and symbols in a manner which makes the novel very rich but difficult for many readers. Joyce died in Zurich in 1940. He is widely held to be one of the most innovative and important writers of the twentieth century.

The story 'Eveline' is an earlier work from *Dubliners*, written in a realistic style. It illustrates Joyce's concern with the frustrations in the lives of ordinary people facing up to important decisions.

Eveline

James Joyce

She sat at the window watching the evening invade the avenue. Her head was leaned against the window curtains, and in her nostrils was the odour of dusty cretonne. She was tired.

Few people passed. The man out of the last house passed on his way home; she heard his footsteps clacking along the concrete pavement and afterwards crunching on the cinder path before the new red houses. One time there used to be a field there in which they used to play every evening with other people's children. Then a man from Belfast bought the field and built houses in it – not like their little brown houses, but bright brick houses with shining roofs. The children of the avenue used to play together in that field – the Devines, the Waters, the Dunns, little Keogh the cripple, she and her brothers and sisters. Ernest, however, never played: he was too grown up. Her father used often to hunt them in out of the field with his blackthorn stick; but usually little Keogh used to keep *nix* and call out when he saw her father coming. Still they seemed to have been rather happy then. Her father was not so bad then; and besides, her mother was alive. That was a long time ago; she and her brothers and sisters were all grown up; her mother was dead. Tizzie Dunn was dead, too, and the Waters had gone back to England. Everything changes. Now she was going to go away like the others, to leave her home.

Home! She looked round the room, reviewing all its familiar objects which she had dusted once a week for so many years, wondering where on earth all the dust came from. Perhaps she would never see again those familiar objects from which she had never dreamed of being divided. And yet during all those years she had never found out the name of the priest whose yellowing photograph hung on the wall above the broken harmonium beside the coloured print of the promises made to Blessed Margaret Mary Alacoque. He had been a school friend of her father. Whenever he showed the photograph to a visitor her father used to pass it with a casual word:

'He is in Melbourne now.'

She had consented to go away, to leave her home. Was that wise? She tried to weigh each side of the question. In her home anyway she had shelter and food; she had those whom she had known all her life about her. Of course she had to work hard, both in the house and at business. What would they say of her in the Stores when they found out that she had run away with a fellow? Say she was a fool, perhaps; and her place would be filled up by advertisement. Miss Gavan would be glad. She had always had an edge on her, especially whenever there were people listening.

'Miss Hill, don't you see these ladies are waiting?'

'Look lively, Miss Hill, please.'

She would not cry many tears at leaving the Stores.

But in her new home, in a distant unknown country, it would not be like that. Then she would be married – she, Eveline. People would treat her with respect then. She would not be treated as her mother had been. Even now, though she was over nineteen, she sometimes felt herself in danger of her father's violence. She knew it was that that had given her the palpitations. When they were growing up he had never gone for her, like he used to go for Harry and Ernest, because she was a girl; but latterly he had begun to threaten her and say what he would do to her only for her dead mother's sake. And now she had nobody to protect her, Ernest was dead and Harry, who was in the church decorating business, was nearly always down somewhere in the country. Besides, the invariable squabble for money on Saturday nights had begun to weary her unspeakably. She always gave her entire wages – seven shillings – and Harry always sent up what he could, but the trouble was to get any money from her father. He said she used to squander the money, that she had no head, that he wasn't going to give her his hard-earned money to throw about the streets, and much more, for he was usually fairly bad on Saturday night. In the end he would give her the money and ask her had she any intention of buying Sunday's dinner. Then she had to rush out as quickly as she could and do her marketing, holding her black leather purse tightly in her hand as she elbowed her way through the crowds and returning home late under her load of provisions. She had hard work to keep the house together and to see that the two young children who had been left to her charge went to school regularly and got their meals regularly. It was hard work – a hard life – but now that she was about to leave it she did not find it a wholly undesirable life.

She was about to explore another life with Frank. Frank was very kind, manly, open-hearted. She was to go away with him by the night-boat to be his wife and to live with him in Buenos Ayres, where he had a home waiting for her. How well she remembered the first time she had seen him; he was lodging in a house on the main road where she used to visit. It seemed a few weeks ago. He was standing at the gate, his peaked cap pushed back on his head and his hair tumbled forward over a face of bronze. Then they had come to know each other. He used to meet her outside the Stores every evening and see her home. He took her to see *The Bohemian Girl* and she felt elated as she sat in an unaccustomed part of the theatre with him. He was awfully fond of music and sang a little. People knew that they were courting, and, when he sang about the lass that loves a sailor, she always felt pleasantly confused. He used to call her Poppens out of fun. First of all it had been an excitement for her to have a fellow and then she had begun to like him. He had tales of distant countries. He had started as a deck boy at a pound a month on a ship of the Allan Line going out to Canada. He told her the names of the ships he had been on and the names of the different services. He had sailed through the Straits of Magellan and he told her stories of the terrible Patagonians. He had fallen on his feet in Buenos Ayres, he said, and had come over to the old country just for a holiday. Of course, her father had found out the affair and had forbidden her to have anything to say to him.

'I know these sailor chaps,' he said.

One day he had quarrelled with Frank, and after that she had to meet her lover secretly.

The evening deepened in the avenue. The white of two letters in her lap grew indistinct. One was to Harry; the other was to her father. Ernest had been her favourite, but she liked Harry too. Her father was becoming old lately, she noticed; he would miss her. Sometimes he could be very nice. Not long before, when she had been laid up for a day, he had read her out a ghost story and made toast for her at the fire. Another day, when their mother was alive, they had all gone for a picnic to the Hill of Howth. She remembered her father putting on her mother's bonnet to make the children laugh.

Her time was running out, but she continued to sit by the window, leaning her head against the window curtain, inhaling the odour of dusty cretonne. Down far in the avenue she could hear a street organ playing. She knew the air. Strange that it should come that very night to remind her of the promise to her mother, her promise to keep the home together as long as she could. She remembered the last night of her mother's illness; she was again in the close, dark room at the other side of the hall and outside she heard a melancholy air of Italy. The organ-player had been ordered to go away and given sixpence. She remembered her father strutting back into the sick-room saying:

'Damned Italians! coming over here!'

As she mused the pitiful vision of her mother's life laid its spell on the very quick of her being – that life of commonplace sacrifices closing in final craziness. She trembled as she heard again her mother's voice saying constantly with foolish insistence:

'Derevaun Seraun! Derevaun Seraun!'

She stood up in a sudden impulse of terror. Escape! She must escape! Frank would save her. He would give her life, perhaps love, too. But she wanted to live. Why should she be unhappy? She had a right to happiness. Frank would take her in his arms, fold her in his arms. He would save her.

She stood among the swaying crowd in the station at the North Wall. He held her hand and she knew that he was speaking to her, saying something about the passage over and over again. The station was full of soldiers with brown baggages. Through the wide doors of the sheds she caught a glimpse of the black mass of the boat, lying in beside the quay wall, with illumined portholes. She answered nothing. She felt her cheek pale and cold and, out of a maze of distress, she prayed to God to direct her, to show her what was her duty. The boat blew a long mournful whistle into the mist. If she went, tomorrow she would be on the sea with Frank, steaming towards Buenos Ayres. Their passage had been booked. Could she still draw back after all he had done for her? Her distress awoke a nausea in her body and she kept moving her lips in silent fervent prayer.

A bell clanged upon her heart. She felt him seize her hand:

'Come!'

All the seas of the world tumbled about her heart. He was drawing her into them: he would drown her. She gripped with both hands at the iron railing.

'Come!'

No! No! No! It was impossible. Her hands clutched the iron in frenzy. Amid the seas she sent a cry of anguish.

'Eveline! Evvy!'

He rushed beyond the barrier and called to her to follow. He was shouted at to go on, but he still called to her. She set her white face to him, passive, like a helpless animal. Her eyes gave him no sign of love or farewell or recognition.

Janet Frame 1924–

Janet Frame was born in Dunedin in New Zealand. She is the third of five children; two of her sisters were tragically drowned in separate accidents during their adolescence. Janet was the first child of the family to reach high school, and in 1943 she went on to Dunedin Teachers College and attended university courses in English, French and psychology. She did not take to teaching, and in her first year walked out of the classroom never to return.

In Frame's family 'writing was an accepted pastime'; her mother, particularly, wrote poems, songs and stories. Frame's first published stories appeared in 1951. She has established a considerable body of work since that time, including twelve novels, three collections of short stories and sketches, a volume of poetry and a book for children.

Janet Frame's own mental health has been fragile over the years, and she has spent a good deal of time in hospital. In 1947 she voluntarily entered Seacliff Psychiatric Hospital, and remained in psychiatric hospitals for the next eight years. In 1957 she left New Zealand and travelled to Ibiza and then to London on a State Literary Fund grant. In London doctors confirmed that she was not in fact schizophrenic. In 1961 she published the novel *Faces in the Water*, in which she explored some of her experiences in hospital.

Janet Frame's personal story of loneliness, despair and later success and recognition as a writer is charted in her three-part autobiography: *To the Is-land*, published in 1983; *An Angel at My Table*, published in 1984, and the third volume, *The Envoy from the Mirror City*, published in 1985. This autobiographical work has formed the basis for a highly acclaimed film, which has also been shown on television.

'Snap-dragons' is from Frame's first collection of stories, called *The Lagoon*. Writing from her own experiences, Janet Frame uses this story to examine some of the confusions, tension and pain in saying goodbye. The delicacy of the writing, with its carefully woven imagery, allows the reader to track the shifts in Ruth's emotions as her insecurity about leaving the hospital mounts.

Snap-dragons
Janet Frame

How fat the bees were. Some seemed to have got caught in the thin red throats of the snap-dragons, which now rocked up and down in the wind. Inside, the bees mumbled and knocked and Ruth, sitting on the verandah steps in the sun, watched them. How fat the bees were, and how thin the snap-dragons. If you squeezed the throats of the flowers their red jaws would pop open in a gasp and the bees come zooming blindly out, colliding with the sunlight, and then of course they would get their bearings and plan their course, and fly away. Perhaps. Ruth smiled to herself. If you were free did you always fly away?

But oh for a sweet red prison instead of this one, this where Ruth was. Some called it asylum, others mental hospital, in slang terms it was a loony-bin, but whatever its name it was still a prison and not a soft dark one where only bees pounded on the walls, let me out let me out. Ruth smiled to herself again, she could permit a smile because she was going home today, her mother was inside now talking to the nurse. Perhaps I am a bee, ready to collide with the sunlight, she thought. And then fly away home. She had had letters from home. Dear Ruth we hope you are keeping well and are able to come home soon. Had they changed at home? Would they stare at her because of where she had been? Would they watch her and say where are you going, whenever she went outside the door? Would they be frightened of her, and anxious? She heard her mother's high voice talking inside to the nurse, as if she were trying to be heard above a storm. Her mother always talked like that, as if the world were in great danger, she had talked like that when they were little and the rains came, inside kiddies, a storm, forked lightning, hide the scissors and cover up the machine.

Was there a storm now? In spite of the bees and sun and

snap-dragons? Ruth listened. She didn't smile any more then
because she knew there was really no sun shining and no bees
only in the wards there were people saying, let me out, such a
storm of people beating the air with their cries, and that was
why her mother raised her voice. Thank you, she was saying
to the nurse, thank you for looking after her, thank you,
thank you. She said it over and over again, like a warning.

And now she was coming out on to the verandah. She had
her new fluffy brown coat on, and her blue dress with the
white collar, and her black shoes with pointy toes, like the
shoes of a witch or a pixie. Her face was flushed. She held her
kid gloves in one hand, and Ruth could see that her skin was
wrinkled and rough and her hands were hard from housework. Ruth had a sudden vision of a fat woman far far away
from the world, scrubbing a stone step of her little red house
until the step shone as white as daylight.

– Have you said goodbye to your friends? asked the fat
woman. She wasn't scrubbing now. She was standing at the
door of her house shaking a little red mat up and down in the
wind.

– Yes, said Ruth, I've said goodbye.

She was far far away from her mother, the little red mat
waved up and down like the tiniest of handkerchiefs and her
mother's voice came blowing thin and strange, like paper.

– Yes, I've said goodbye, a merry Christmas.

She had gone over to the Nurses' Home where many of her
fellow patients worked. They had been having morning tea.
They each had fat floury scones in their hands, and seeing her
they had stopped eating to stare. She had felt alone and
strange in her best coat and good shoes and her going home
look. They knew she was going home.

– I suppose you've come on your rounds, Mrs James had
said.

Mrs James was one of the saddest people. She was thin and
small with black hair and dark-rimmed glasses. In the morning she used to lie in bed, with just her eyes and nose and
glasses showing over the top of the bedclothes, and then she
looked like a wasp.

– Yes, I've got some cigarettes for you. I hope you have a
happy Christmas. Goodbye, Leda, goodbye, Marion, goodbye,
Miss Clark.

How easy it was to say goodbye if you said it quickly and

firmly and then hurried away, and even if you were shaking
inside with sadness, nobody would know but yourself.

– Goodbye, Mrs James.

Mrs James had come forward.

You're in a hurry, she said. I suppose you are glad to get rid
of us.

And then she had put her arms around Ruth's neck and
kissed her.

– Goodbye, Ruth, you lucky pig.

If you were free did you always fly away? Or were you ever
free? Were you not always blundering into some prison whose
door shut fast behind you so that you cried, let me out, like
the bee knocking in the snap-dragon, or the people beating
their hands on the walls of their ward?

For a moment Ruth had wanted to stay there being friends
with Leda and Marion and Miss Clark and Mrs James.

They were so unhappy and lost and kind.

– Goodbye, they said. They were caught in a war. The fat
floury scones clutched in their hands seemed like peace
offerings then.

– Goodbye . . .

Standing there by the verandah, near the sun and the bees
and the snap-dragons, Ruth spoke aloud.

– Goodbye.

Her mother glanced anxiously at her. What was she seeing?
Who was she talking to?

– Goodbye, Ruth said again.

Her mother spread her hands over her stomach. She patted
her hands. They seemed crinkled and webbed like a fowl.

– We'll catch the slow train, Ruth. And then home.

Home. If only her mother would come near. If only she
would be very close and fat and friendly. She was a fat far
away woman, oh so far away, Ruth felt she would have liked
to stretch out her arms over dark hills to reach her. The tiny
red mat seemed still to be in her hand, she was shaking it up
and down, standing on the white stone steps, and looking out
over the curled up hills. Her face was flushed, and seeing the
flushed face from so far away, Ruth's face flushed too. What if
they stopped her from going home? What if it wasn't real? If
only the little fat woman would come near her and tell her it
was real about going home, if only she would put her arms
round her neck and kiss her, and say, you lucky pig, Ruth.

Dad would be waiting at home, and Fred and Tiny. Would they be frightened of her? Dad and Fred and Tiny and the dog and the cats. I've put the dahlias in, Dad would say. But would he be frightened? Would he? she had been a long time away from home.

– It'll be nice to have you home again, said the little fat woman. I feel so sorry for the poor people who are not allowed out.

Would she never come closer? Her little red house seemed such a long way over the hills. When the wind passed it seemed to rock and swing, it looked like a snap-dragon.

ALSO IN

**HEINEMANN·
NEW WINDMILLS**

Founding Editors: Anne and Ian Serraillier

Chinua Achebe Things Fall Apart
Douglas Adams The Hitchhiker's Guide to the Galaxy
Vivien Alcock The Cuckoo Sister; The Monster Garden; The Trial of Anna Cotman; A Kind of Thief
Margaret Atwood The Handmaid's Tale
J G Ballard Empire of the Sun
Nina Bawden The Witch's Daughter; A Handful of Thieves; Carrie's War; The Robbers; Devil by the Sea; Kept in the Dark; The Finding; Keeping Henry; Humbug
E R Braithwaite To Sir, With Love
John Branfield The Day I Shot My Dad
F Hodgson Burnett The Secret Garden
Ray Bradbury The Golden Apples of the Sun; The Illustrated Man
Betsy Byars The Midnight Fox; Goodbye, Chicken Little; The Pinballs
Victor Canning The Runaways; Flight of the Grey Goose
Ann Coburn Welcome to the Real World
Hannah Cole Bring in the Spring
Jane Leslie Conly Racso and the Rats of NIMH
Robert Cormier We All Fall Down
Roald Dahl Danny, The Champion of the World; The Wonderful Story of Henry Sugar; George's Marvellous Medicine; The BFG; The Witches; Boy; Going Solo; Charlie and the Chocolate Factory; Matilda
Anita Desai The Village by the Sea
Charles Dickens A Christmas Carol; Great Expectations
Peter Dickinson The Gift; Annerton Pit; Healer
Berlie Doherty Granny was a Buffer Girl
Gerald Durrell My Family and Other Animals
J M Falkner Moonfleet
Anne Fine The Granny Project
Anne Frank The Diary of Anne Frank
Leon Garfield Six Apprentices
Jamila Gavin The Wheel of Surya
Adele Geras Snapshots of Paradise

Graham Greene The Third Man and The Fallen Idol; Brighton Rock

Thomas Hardy The Withered Arm and Other Wessex Tales

Rosemary Harris Zed

L P Hartley The Go-Between

Ernest Hemingway The Old Man and the Sea; A Farewell to Arms

Nat Hentoff Does this School have Capital Punishment?

Nigel Hinton Getting Free; Buddy; Buddy's Song

Minfong Ho Rice Without Rain

Anne Holm I Am David

Janni Howker Badger on the Barge; Isaac Campion

Linda Hoy Your Friend Rebecca

Barbara Ireson (Editor) In a Class of Their Own

Jennifer Johnston Shadows on Our Skin

Toeckey Jones Go Well, Stay Well

James Joyce A Portrait of the Artist as a Young Man

Geraldine Kaye Comfort Herself; A Breath of Fresh Air

Clive King Me and My Million

Dick King-Smith The Sheep-Pig

Daniel Keyes Flowers for Algernon

Elizabeth Laird Red Sky in the Morning; Kiss the Dust

D H Lawrence The Fox and The Virgin and the Gypsy; Selected Tales

Harper Lee To Kill a Mockingbird

Julius Lester Basketball Game

Ursula Le Guin A Wizard of Earthsea

C Day Lewis The Otterbury Incident

David Line Run for Your Life; Screaming High

Joan Lingard Across the Barricades; Into Exile; The Clearance; The File on Fraulein Berg

Penelope Lively The Ghost of Thomas Kempe

Jack London The Call of the Wild; White Fang

Bernard Mac Laverty Cal; The Best of Bernard Mac Laverty

Margaret Mahy The Haunting; The Catalogue of The Universe

Jan Mark Do You Read Me? Eight Short Stories

James Vance Marshall Walkabout

Somerset Maugham The Kite and Other Stories

Michael Morpurgo Waiting for Anya; My Friend Walter; The War of Jenkins' Ear

How many have you read?